To Karen,
Blessings
Life filled w
Love + Joy!
Rie Anders

Hunter's Moon

a novel

Rie Anders

www.rieanders.com

First Edition

ISBN: 9798643830481

Other Books by Rie Anders:

Island Series

Pavey Boulevard

On Island

Hunter's Moon

Island Romance Short Stories

Snug Harbor

Meadow Rising

True Blue – *Coming March 2021*

Cabin Christmas Romances

Snow & Mistletoe

Dear Santa, Define Good

Naughty & Nice – *Coming December 2020*

Crown Family Series

Chrysalis – *Coming April 2021*

Solara – *To Be Announced*

Phoenix – *To Be Announced*

The Promise of Hunter's Moon

At some point we're all coming back as birds.
We'll begin in the muck, unrecognizable, stinking,
Until creatures with hands or tools for hands
Scoop us up and start squeezing and pulling.
Suddenly there we are, unmistakably beaked,
Straining against thin leather thongs that someone
Had the good sense to tie around rocks and our twiggy legs.
It's a good thing, this confinement, because free
We'd rip and tear apart anything we could reach.
The things with hands, or tools like hands, feed us
A mixture of water and the blood of the beheaded,
And with this inside of us we develop fast,
Looking more like giant birds you'd recognize
By the minute. Our feathers grow black and glossy,
And the thicker they become the meaner we feel.
When they just can't grow anymore, they fall out.
Our featherless bodies are disgusting to touch,
Hideous to behold. Where once we were murderous,
We grow timid under the mirror-hot sun. Then
More feathers appear, small at first, white feathers,
Beautiful, snowy plumes that dazzle under a Hunter's Moon.
When we're ready She comes. Out of the sea and sky,
Out of the barren ground She comes. Astonishing
Is her loveliness, perfected is Her power. She rises and walks
Among us as we bow, obedient, peaceful, and so in love.

Robert McDowell

1

My best friend, Evie Reid, was getting married.

Her fiancé, Ethan, had an incredibly large family and they had all arrived a few days prior, swarming in like a huge hug, embracing Evie and everyone around them.

I'll admit, I was a little jealous of her new extended family, feeling momentarily displaced, and a little lonely.

Growing up an only child, the Reids were the closest I had to siblings. It was difficult to let Evie go.

The day before Evie's wedding, my plan was to spend most of my time at the vineyard making sure everything was ready. Since the event was taking place at my venue, I'd become the unofficial wedding coordinator, deciding on flowers, and caterers, and landscaping.

Waking with the sun, I slipped out of bed and made a pot of strong coffee.

As it brewed, I dressed for the day in my old baggy jeans and a t-shirt. I pulled my blonde, bobbed hair back into a short ponytail and wrapped a bandana around my head, intending to shower and dress later for the rehearsal dinner.

Pouring a large mug of black coffee, I curled up in the window seat and opened the bay windows, letting in the cool morning air. Sipping my coffee, I closed my eyes and felt the soothing rush of caffeine kickstart my system, giving me the energy I would need to get through the day.

I inhaled deeply and smelled the fresh, mossy fragrance of the earth and the bold scent of my coffee.

A low morning fog had settled over the acres of vineyards, damping the sounds and creating a ghostly environment. On mornings like this I loved to relax and enjoy the quiet, undisturbed and reflective.

In the distance, I heard a ferry horn deliver a long, single blast, indicating it was leaving the dock from the landing at the northern tip of the island. The ferry horn was a consistent reminder of the isolation of the island, which was accessible only by boat or plane.

The unique rumble of a diesel engine truck interrupted my thoughts before I saw it coming down the main drive. My morning of serenity had come to a swift end.

The familiar, mud splattered, allegedly black, Ford 350 appeared through the fog. I slid off the bench seat, closed the window, and poured two cups of coffee in steel to-go mugs.

Making my way down the narrow steps that led into the wood-paneled tasting room, I used my elbow to switch on the heater to take the chill out of the still-cold room.

Transferring one of the mugs to my left arm and holding it close against my side, I opened the front door and stepped out to the wooden deck, under the slanted roof. The rattle of the diesel engine stopped in front of the building. The driver stepped from the cab, bypassing the running boards by jumping straight to the ground.

"Morning, Juliette."

"Morning, *Bob the Builder.*"

"Har-har. You ready to go?"

A flatbed truck, carrying the trellis and tents for the party, rumbled down the drive, and we both turned at the sound.

The driver pulled up alongside us and manually rolled down his window. "Where do you want us, Riley?"

Turning slowly back to me, one eyebrow raised and a smile on his face, he said, "Just waiting on the boss."

I handed him his coffee and side-eyed him as I walked, almost ostentatiously, around the front of his truck, stepping up into the cab, smirking as I teased. "And don't you forget that."

Riley laughed at my attempt to convey a haughty tone and stepped back into the truck. We drove up to the ceremony site, where he'd already laid a concrete foundation in the area we'd chosen for the vows. When, and if, I received funding for the resort, this would be the focal point in the center of the grassy area.

I stared out the windows at the rows and rows of vines. The dirt road we were on would be paved in a few months, and lined with Italian Cypress trees – pending funding, of course.

As my parents' only child, I'd lived a charmed, albeit somewhat sheltered, life. It also meant I was the sole heir to Hunter's Moon – our two vineyards and winery.

My parents planned on staying on-island through Evie's wedding, and then they would promptly retire to our property in eastern Washington. They'd turn the vineyard over to me to run and manage as I saw fit.

I'd always known this would happen one day, and as the day had loomed closer, I saw fit to expand.

About a year ago, I'd started floating my idea to Nick and Ethan, getting their input and legal advice. When I'd felt like it could really happen, we'd started developing the business plan.

Since Ethan is a property attorney, he'd worked on a number of development properties over the years in the San Juan Islands. Both he and Nick were helping me with the future plans.

Ethan had helped me with finding an architect to create formal drawings of my vision. He'd also helped me gather the information for an environmental impact statement. When we'd felt we had all the requirements of the business plan ready to show to investors, Ethan had reached out to his contacts, sending them a preliminary teaser about the resort.

As Riley and I drove, I commented that we hadn't planned the timing very well.

"It'll all come together. It may not be perfect for tomorrow, but Evie knows that. And you know her – she'll love it no matter what."

"I know she will. I just wish the main building didn't look so po-dunky."

He laughed a very masculine laugh and reached for my hand, squeezing it in consolation. "Hey! It's beautiful and rustic, and it worked for over thirty years. You'll have your resort, and then you'll look back and want the simplicity of before. Enjoy it today."

Glancing down at his hand holding mine, I felt a warmth seep into me, comforting and unexpected.

Riley had built Ethan's – and now Evie's – house. He was also the architect Ethan had recommended. He lived in Friday Harbor, on San Juan Island, another island a short ferry ride from here. From what I understood from Nick and Ethan, his craftsmanship and individualized architectural designs had won him many awards. I trusted both Ethan and Nick to build a team that would deliver a world-class resort for me, and they had recommended Riley.

My time alone with him had been limited, but always friendly – although, I sensed he was restraining himself from getting too close to any of us. He was polite, professional, and had a little bit of swagger that I always found kind of sexy. Jason had had it. Maybe that's why I steered clear of Riley.

Riley and I'd met for the first time last summer, then again on Friday Harbor when Evie and I had gone dress shopping. His truck was a frequent fixture on both islands as his reputation was growing as the 'builder to hire' in the islands.

I didn't have time to analyze the zing that ran through me at his friendly overture, so I gently pulled my hand from his and focused on the road ahead.

As we crested the hill, Riley pulled into a makeshift parking lot and waved out the window to the flatbed to pull up in front of him. In a few months, this is where the main house and dining area would be, looking down towards the vineyard, and out towards the Strait of Juan de Fuca, and the Pacific Ocean. Tomorrow it would be the location for the two-hundred-person tent that would shelter Evie and Ethan's wedding reception.

I stared wistfully out at the ceremony site and lost myself in the imaginings of a fairy tale. A fairy tale Evie deserved. A fairy tale I'd lost.

"The landscaping looks great!" Riley said as he stepped out of the truck, interrupting my reflective thoughts. Turning to me from outside the cab, he held on to the door frame and asked, "You coming?"

"Right. Yes." I mumbled as I stepped out of the truck, then we strode down to the location of the trellis together.

"The landscaping looks fantastic, Julie. Did you design it?"

"I did. I wasn't sure all the trees and plants would survive, but they seem to be doing well."

"Has Evie seen it?" He'd stopped on some wood-look porcelain pavers. They led around the grassy area intended for the folding chairs to the main area built for the nuptials. Cornflower blue Agapanthus were planted along the walkway, their frivolous sprays sparkling in the morning sun.

"No. She wanted to wait until you'd installed the trellis. She wants to see it for the first time when it's finished."

A feeling of jealousy snuck over me, and I pushed it away. Riley and Evie were good friends. He'd asked her out once, but to me they'd always seemed more like brother and sister. He was still very protective of her.

"Well, let's get this thing built then." He waved high above his head at the crew by the trucks, put his fingers in his mouth, whistled loudly, and waved the crew down.

Then he turned to me and said more quietly, "C'mon, builder girl, you can help."

Two of the men from the construction crew carried the beams and bolts down to the site, while the other two started laying out the tent.

A bricklaying crew had come earlier in the week and built two-foot casings for the posts. The main arch trellis was six feet across, with beams and lattice extending out twenty feet in both directions. I intended to plant vines and roses. Once they wrapped themselves around the lattice, this would be a stunning garden.

As they worked, another crew arrived with tables and chairs, and quiet generators to power the dimmed lights and chandelier Evie had requested.

Later in the day, I ran into town to get sandwiches and water for all the men. When I returned, Riley had just finished connecting the final pieces to the main arch.

I extended a bottle to him. "Water?"

He reached for the hem of his dirt smudged T-shirt, lifted it and wiped the sweat from his brow. "Thanks."

My eyes darted to the sprinkling of blond hairs on his belly, and I felt myself flush.

He took the bottle from me, unscrewed the cap, and took a big long drink, causing the plastic to cave in on itself.

I might have mumbled, "You're welcome." I wasn't sure, though, since my mouth seemed to have gone dry.

Completely oblivious to my discomfort, he reached for my hand, his now-cold fingers gripping my suddenly warm ones, and told me to come take a look.

Bunches of grapes had been intricately carved into the main arch, giving the illusion of vines. I reached out and delicately touched them, running my fingertips over the bumps and grooves, marveling at the craftsmanship.

I sighed with awe. "Riley. They're exquisite." I looked at him over my shoulder. "I don't know what to say."

He pulled me to the other side. "Here, look at this one."

At the top of the arch was a full moon, complete with shadows. A goddess, with a bow and arrow and her arm pulled back aiming for the moon, was carved on the other side.

My gut clenched and I turned watery eyes to him. "Why?"

He looked caught off guard. "What do you mean?"

"Why did you go to so much effort?"

"Evie thought you would like it. It's Diana, the Huntress, and the Hunter's Moon. She said your middle name is Diana, and it's your vineyard now, so…" He shrugged.

My heart was stuck in my throat. "It's lovely. Thank you."

His smile was broad, his slightly crooked tooth making him appear devilishly sexy. "You're welcome."

Feeling somewhat uncomfortable, I looked at the time on my phone, and then back at him. "I need to start getting ready for the rehearsal dinner. So, I guess I'll see you tomorrow? At the wedding?"

I turned to walk away, and he caught up next to me. "Let me give you a ride back."

"No. It's okay, I need to walk. I'm okay. Thanks though." He stopped in his tracks, and I continued to walk. "See you tomorrow."

I heard him playfully shout from behind me. "See you tomorrow, Juliette."

2

I WAS COMPLETELY overwhelmed by the size of Ethan's family. They just kept showing up to the rehearsal dinner, and I couldn't keep them straight. I'd also never experienced so much testosterone in one location.

It was like a sugar-rush, with so many delicious men! They were all gorgeous. *Thank you, Ethan, for bringing me toys to play with!*

On the dockside of the Islander restaurant was a small party room with an attached deck that looked out towards the marina.

The Islander was the summer resort; boaters, families, and weekenders were frequent visitors. Sailboats and larger powerboats were anchored in the large bay, leaving just enough room for the daily float planes to take off and land from the water.

I waited at the front door entrance to the lobby of the resort and greeted everyone as they arrived, directing them to the party room.

Ethan's brothers Lane and Galen looked exactly like him – same chestnut-colored hair and sherry eyes, albeit a little taller. But his brother Ames looked like their mom: dark hair, lean, a little lost and tired looking.

Morgan, one of his twin sisters, was the spitting image of Ethan – the girl version, of course. Skylar, the other twin, had yet to arrive.

The one thing that stood out to me was their love for one another, and for Evie. I could hear the squeals and laughter through the main lobby as each of them greeted Ethan and Evie, weaving a web tighter around her… and pushing me out.

Shaye and Nick arrived with Nick and Evie's parents. Shaye hugged me tightly, always keeping me close now, and asked me to watch for the float plane.

"Ethan's sister Skylar is arriving shortly, and I want to greet her when she lands."

"Do you want me to go down and get her?"

Shaye looked at me in surprise. "Would you?"

"Sure. That way you can visit with the rest of the family."

Her face softened and she reached for my hands, clasping them with hers. "Thank you, Julie." She leaned in to kiss me, and then Nick gently pulled her towards the rest of the guests.

Nick's mom Martha came in next, trying to corral both Noah, Ethan's little boy, and JT, Nick and Shaye's boy, who was about the same age.

Noah's mom, Ethan's former fiancé, had died in a helicopter crash, and Noah had been given to Ethan to care for. Ethan hadn't even known Noah existed until about a year ago. While the demands of being a dad were daunting at first, he'd adjusted quite quickly, and he and Evie had made a cute little family.

Taking JT from Martha and lifting him in my arms, I nuzzled on his neck, and he squirmed playfully.

Basking in the little-boy-giggles, I playfully swung side to side, and asked Martha, "Where are Ellie and May?" Ellie was Nick and Shaye's first little girl, and May was their newborn baby girl.

"Kira is watching them. They're all too much for me to handle at one time." Kira was a high school student who worked in Evie's bakery, as well as being a part-time nanny.

I laughed at her exasperated expression and turned, once again, to nuzzle JT's neck. He giggled and squirmed until I put him back down. "Yeah, he's a little hellion for sure."

Noah was standing stoically at Martha's side, and I greeted him cautiously. "Hi, Noah. Are you excited for the wedding?"

He shrugged and stepped back behind Martha's leg. When he glanced back up at Martha, she leaned down to pick him up. "He's a little overwhelmed, I think, with all his new family. Aren't you, little guy?"

She turned back to me and said, "I think I'll take him to his Grandma Bonnie. He's very attached to her."

I nodded and smiled in understanding. "Okay. I think everyone is here now, except Skylar. I'll head down to the dock and wait for the plane."

Martha reached up to pat my cheek. "You're a good girl, Julie. Don't you forget that." She added, "A little crazy, but we love you anyway."

I chuckled and tried not to get choked up. In my mind, she was supposed to have been my mother-in-law. My eyes welled up, and I simply nodded. She was as close to me as my own mother – maybe even more so, since she was more in tune with my loss.

Out the front windows, I saw the float plane approaching the bay. Flying low over the trees, I watched as he maneuvered over the water, careful not to hit any of the boats moored in the bay. The pontoons skimmed down to touch the water, slowing the speed of the plane.

I went out the back door and down the dock to meet Skylar.

The tide was low, exposing the muddy bottom of the bay and intensifying the saltwater scent. Seaweed, murky green and brown, lay like frosting over the rocks, and created a tide-line.

I reached the plane just as the dock-worker tied it to the dock cleats, and the pilot opened the door for the movie-star-sister, Skylar Archer.

She was stunning in her burgundy halter dress and heels. In person, her skin was even more flawless than camera makeup could ever achieve. Deep, rich auburn hair with expensive highlights fell over one shoulder. I thought my jaw would hit the dock.

"Shaye?" I heard her speak; I might have mumbled my own name in response.

"Oh, Evie's best friend. I'm so glad to meet you, Julie. Evie talks about you all the time. She said we would be fast friends."

I was just thinking I'd have to kick her ass for being prettier than me, when she reached out to hug me.

When she pulled back from me, her eyes roved over my face. "You're gorgeous! You look just like Bebe Rexha. Has anyone ever told you that?"

"Once or twice, yes. And thank you!"

The pilot handed me a very expensive suitcase and I took it from him, setting it on the ground.

I looked to the dock worker and asked him to please take it up to Shaye's office and lock it. "I'll let her know it's there, and we'll take care of it later."

Turning to Skylar, I directed her up the dock, making small talk along the way. She was here only for the wedding, and then would leave almost immediately after the ceremony. She'd chartered a plane to take her to Vancouver, British Columbia, where she was filming her next action movie.

Intrigued, I asked her if she did her own stunts.

"Oh, Lord no! For one thing, I'm afraid of heights, so that certainly wouldn't work."

As we approached the resort and deck, I saw Evie waving enthusiastically at us. Then she ran around to the walkway and down to greet us.

"Skylar! I'm so glad you could make it!" She hugged her tight, and I felt another pang of jealousy.

"I wouldn't miss my brother's wedding! And especially since he's marrying such a beautiful girl."

"C'mon, we're ready to start."

Evie linked elbows with Skylar and I followed behind, my stomach in knots. My chest was constricting with almost unbearable jealousy.

Skylar received the same level of enthusiasm from Evie as all her greetings, while I sought out the pastor that Evie and Ethan had chosen to officiate their wedding.

Now that everyone had arrived, I gathered them all together, and we talked through the ceremony as a group.

Shaye, Morgan, and I were Evie's bridesmaids, and Ethan's brothers would stand up for him. Nick and a friend of Ethan's from college would be the ushers.

Evie was glowing, looking lovely in a mint green dress that hung so beautifully on her slender frame.

I zoned out a little as the pastor droned on about the vows and who would say what and when. While Ethan's brothers were nice to look at, I didn't feel anything towards them. I wanted to. For once, I actually wanted to be the cute, party girl everyone assumed I was, but I couldn't even gather the energy to flirt.

The planning of the resort had been consuming so much of my time, I couldn't even remember the last time I'd had sex. I tried to run through the last few guys I'd dated, and they all seemed faceless now – blurs. I know I hadn't been interested in going to bed with any of them.

I was standing in the maid of honor position when a brown construction jacket caught my attention. I glanced to my left to see Riley walking down the ramp towards the boats docked in the slips.

He had such a sexy walk, and I found myself staring at the way his jeans hugged his back-side. He was everywhere lately, and if I received my funding, he would be around me every day. Evie's pet. It almost didn't seem fair.

"Julie?" Evie's concerned voice interrupted my thoughts.

"I'm sorry, what?"

"Are you okay?"

Oh my God! I'd groaned *out loud.* "I'm so sorry. I was thinking about something else." All eyes were on me, and I flushed. "I have a lot going on right now."

Evie laughed, "Uhm, yeah, so do I."

Everyone laughed at the implication, and I refocused my attention on the rehearsal.

"Please continue."

The rest of the rehearsal passed easily, and afterwards we all sat down to dinner. Evie had seated me with her parents, Bonnie, Morgan, Skylar, Galen, and Ames.

Martha was a little nervous around Skylar, and commented how fun it was to meet a movie star in person.

"Please, Mrs. Reid, my mother says I'm a country girl at heart and doesn't pay any attention to my career. I do the dishes and clean the stables just like my brothers when I'm home."

Galen jumped in and teased, "Which is probably why you never come home."

She swatted him with her napkin and said, "You're one to talk. It was years before you finally came home to help instead of playing cowboy." She turned her attention back to the table, "Galen was off traipsing around the world for years as a bull rider with the PRCA."

We all stilled and I saw the shock register on Martha's face. Even Galen looked sheepish.

Skylar continued enthusiastically. "Oh, I'm sorry, you probably don't know what the PRCA is. It's the Professional Rodeo Cowboys Association. Galen traveled for years competing, and he *always* brought home trophies."

Martha looked down at her napkin, while Marcus excused himself from the table, heading in the direction of the bar.

I cleared my throat and said, "Evie's brother, Jason, was a cutter."

It took her a second before she realized what she'd said. She glanced at Galen and he pulled his lips together, raising his eyebrows at her as if to say, 'Yeah, remember, I told you.'

She put her hand to her mouth. "I am so sorry. I must have forgotten. I'm so sorry."

Martha, the ever-steady mother, reached across the table and squeezed her hand. "It's okay. He loved the circuit. It's okay."

Skylar looked so distraught. I felt horrible for her and tried to lessen the tension by asking Galen, "Did you know Jason very well?"

He looked back and forth between Martha and myself, gauging how to respond. "I didn't. I knew of him and saw him frequently, but we ran with different people, so our interactions were few. I know everyone talked about his blue eyes. And he was quite the ladies' man, always had a cute girl on his arm."

Oh, this was just getting worse and worse. I'm sure he was just trying to make Martha feel better, but ended up slighting me in the process.

Martha dropped her head again, shaking it side to side and laughed, "Oh dear. Yes, he was quite the looker. Takes after his dad." She paused and then said quietly, "Took after his dad."

Ames rocked back on the heels of his chair, and quipped, "How about that stock market?"

I shot him a look that clearly said humor was not a welcome addition to the conversation. Marcus returned with a gin and tonic, and we all resumed eating, quietly making small talk about the weather.

When Marcus rose to make the rounds of the room, I excused myself from the table and headed to the bar.

Jumping up on a barstool, I crossed my legs, adjusted the hem of my dress, and knocked on the bar, to get the bartender's attention. "Eric, I need a Jack and coke please. Make it a double."

"It can't be that bad already, can it?" He asked, as he placed the drink in front of me.

"Worse." I rolled my eyes.

Shaye said from behind me, "Can I join you?"

I turned and saw her worried expression, extended my hand to the seat next to me, and said, "Please."

Eric asked, "Can I get you anything Shaye?"

"Just water please."

"You got it."

I looked at her belly and asked, "Lord, Shaye. What are you, pregnant again?"

She raised her eyebrows at me.

"Seriously?"

"No, I was just teasing. I'm breastfeeding, so I'm not drinking."

"Well, I'll drink your share. Cheers to a high probability that I will be drunk by the end of this weekend."

I raised my glass and took a hefty drink of my cocktail.

"What's going on with you?"

Sighing heavily, I dropped my shoulders. "I don't know. I'm being a shit, aren't I? I'm happy for Evie, I really am, but I feel like we're falling apart. You have Nick, and a million kids, and I feel like things are shifting."

Shaye took my hand. "They are, but it doesn't change our friendship. And Evie loves you so much. If she didn't, we certainly wouldn't be friends, would we?"

I laughed at her. "So, you've forgiven me?"

"I forgave you a long time ago, Julie. I know you were hurting. We were all hurting. If you were meant to be with Nick, you would've been."

I hated that I'd had a brief affair with Nick after she'd left the island all those years ago. I hated that I had been so desperate for love, I'd tried to replace Jason with Nick. He was in pain too, so it worked for a bit. Until it didn't.

"He wasn't very good, you know?" I joked, a smile on my face.

"You can try and deflect with humor, but I know he doesn't mean anything to you. Not in the way that matters." She paused. "And you matter to me, Julie. You don't have to pretend to be strong with me."

My eyes watered, and I rubbed my fist against my chest. I looked out at the marina, taking a deep breath and exhaling loudly. "I miss Jason so much lately. I don't know why. It's been years since he's been gone, but the feelings seem so strong. My heart just hurts. Like it's anchored to his and I can't get free."

I glanced back at Shaye and she was looking at me sadly.

"Don't pity me."

"I don't pity you. You said to me once, 'I always had the impression you were made of stronger stuff than this.' Now I will say it back to you. You aren't alone, Julie. This is just one day, and you'll get through it."

"It's actually a weekend."

"Whatever." She smiled at my attempt to argue. "Are you excited about the resort?"

"I am. Riley brought the trellis out today and had the tent put up. I really hope I get the funding for the building. I have such big dreams for the vineyard. I know I can make it exceptional."

"Have you met Dax yet?"

Dax Bentley was a prominent Seattle property investor, and the man Ethan and Nick had been courting these past few months as a potential investor.

"No. Apparently he was invited to the wedding, though, so I'll meet him tomorrow."

Shaye grinned mischievously at me. "I heard he's a looker. Swoon-worthy."

"Oh, please. You've been watching too much Disney."

She laughed, "No, seriously, have you seen him?" She pulled out her phone and searched for Dax Bentley. "Here, look. He's gorgeous!"

"Huh, let me see that." I took her phone from her and swiped through a few pictures. "He certainly is, but I was told to be on my best behavior."

"No flirting, no sex?"

"I think Nick's exact words were, 'Don't fuck this up Julie. We can't do this without him.'"

She cringed. "I'm sorry. That was kind of harsh of him."

I shrugged. "He's right, though. I've learned a lot from him and Ethan over the past few years about business, but this is big time, and I can't sleep my way to a deal."

We were both silent, lost in our own thoughts, until Shaye quietly interrupted mine. "You know, you've never really told me what happened with you and Jason. Do you want to? Maybe that will help."

"Oh look, the party is breaking up. We should go, I'm Evie's ride home."

Shaye groaned, "Julie."

"I will, Shaye, I promise. But not tonight. And not this weekend. This weekend is for Evie."

"Okay, but we really need you to..." She started to say, but I was already leaving the bar.

3

Evie had asked – no, insisted – that Shaye and I stay the night with her in one of the cottages on her parent's property.

While I balked a little at Evie's request for us to be together on her last night of being single, I was secretly happy about it.

"It'll be the last time. I want the three of us to be together," she'd begged in her endearing, lovely, almost manipulative way, even though she didn't have a mean-spirited bone in her body.

Her wedding day dawned in almost a magical way. The morning sun was peeking through the shades covering the bedroom window, a prelude to a perfect summer wedding day.

It was a day that Evie had dreamt of forever, and neither Shaye nor I would deny her anything. We would never deny her anything. Our pasts had connected the three of us in a way not many people would ever understand. We were bonded.

The three of us had fallen asleep in the king size bed that used to be Evie's, giggling and teasing each other about shenanigans from the past.

Shaye nudged me early in the morning, whispering that she needed to get back to her house to check on the babies. "I'll be back in about an hour with breakfast."

Sleeping in the middle, I rolled to my side, grabbing her hands between mine, whispering back, "This is going to be such a long day."

"Don't wake her yet. Let her sleep."

"I can't believe Ethan tried to convince her to come home with him. What a lame-o."

She giggled quietly and said, "You were so funny, tugging on her arm so she wouldn't go."

"She was going over my dead body."

"And Ames trying to toss her over his shoulder."

"Ethan has some hottie brothers, that's for sure."

Wiggling out of bed, she waved her hand at me. "Come outside."

I slipped out of bed, put Evie's slippers on my feet, and quietly followed her out the front door of the cottage, shutting the door carefully so it wouldn't creak.

The morning air was crisp, the earth damp from the humidity. I inhaled deeply of the fresh, salty air, and watched as Shaye zipped up her jacket, tucking her chin into the neck.

I laughed at her. "That is the weirdest habit you have."

"What?"

"You always tuck your chin into your coats."

She scoffed at me. "It keeps me warm."

"Silly." I wrapped my arms around myself and asked her what time the hair and makeup girls were going to be at the cottage.

"They're scheduled for eleven. That gives us time to have breakfast and get organized. Morgan will be here a little after noon, then we can all help Evie get dressed. Nick will be here at three to pick us up."

"Okay. I need to call Amy and make sure she has all the catering ready. And the flowers. Oh, crap! I just remembered, I need to call the florist and make sure they have flowers for the archway."

"How did it look? I saw Riley a few days ago at the grocery store and he said he was almost finished with it."

"Oh, Shaye. It's beautiful. He carved grapes and vines into the wood and it is exquisite."

She smiled slyly at me. "He's very talented. What did you think of the Hunter?"

"You knew?" I was a little stunned.

"I was at Evie's picking up JT when he was there designing it. He wanted something that you would want forever, not just for Evie's wedding. I saw the sketch. I can't wait to see it today."

I felt her watching me intently, so I shooed her away. "Hurry back with breakfast, I'm already hungry."

She pointed her finger at me. "Don't wake her yet."

"I won't. Go!"

I watched her walk towards the path that led through the wooded forest to her home. I closed my eyes briefly, calming myself and thinking about the day.

In the distance, I heard the rumbling of a familiar diesel engine, and I turned just in time to see Riley's truck coming down the driveway.

I ran as fast as I could to stop him. When he saw me, I put up my hand, and he stopped abruptly, eyes wide.

He put the truck in park, killed the engine and jumped from the cab. Glancing down at my feet he commented, "Cute."

"What are you doing here so early?"

"If I'd known you'd look so adorable in your jammies, I would have come sooner."

He towered above me. Without my shoes on, I was a foot shorter than him, and his morning voice was doing something to my insides – something I didn't want to examine.

I drew my brows together and tried to sound offended. "'Jammies' is a stupid word. Seriously, Evie is still sleeping, and this beast of a truck is really loud."

"Well, my dear Juliette, I'm not here for Evie. I'm here for Ames. We're playing golf this morning."

It was then that I noticed he wasn't wearing his usual jeans and work boots. Instead, he looked like a frat boy. "Ethan is getting married today, and you guys are playing golf?"

"What else would we do? You girls do your thing, and we do ours."

I pointed my finger up and down the length of him. "I don't like this look on you."

His eyes twinkled. "Want me to take it off?"

Behind me, I heard the door to the second cottage shut. Ames appeared, dressed similarly to Riley, and with a pair of golf shoes in his hands. "Hey, Jules. Cute slippers."

"They're Evie's."

Riley was still looking at me, but addressed Ames. "You ready?"

Ames opened the door to the truck, responded yes, and said he would see me later.

Riley stepped really close, leaned down, and whispered, "I don't like this look on you either."

"Clever. Are you going to follow up with something trite like, 'It would look better on my bedroom floor?'"

His eyes scanned me from head to toe. "Is that an offer?"

I rolled my eyes. "Please. You're not my type."

"From what I've seen, you aren't that discriminating."

I inhaled sharply. I saw red and I almost slapped him, but then something in his expression shifted. He almost looked surprised at my reaction, like he didn't expect me to be hurt by his flippant remark. He took a step towards me and started to reach for my hand. He was so close; I could smell the mint from his toothpaste.

My head was spinning with a whiplash of conflicting emotions. I couldn't determine whether the look in his eyes was more apology or pity, but either way, I felt the need to deflect whatever action he was about to take. He was too close, either for comfort or comprehension, I wasn't sure which. But it didn't matter. His body in my personal space was beginning to feel like an intrusion, and I couldn't sort out my feelings fast enough to tell if it was a welcome one or not. That indecision was making me even more testy, and I hadn't had enough coffee yet, this early in the morning, to be able to deal with such an avalanche of feelings. Right now, confusion was giving way to renewed anger, and I needed to get him away from me as quickly as possible. So, I chose the words I thought would be the most effective in getting him to back off. Doing my best to keep my dignity, I said, as evenly as I could, "Evie's scraps don't interest me."

His nostrils flared, his eyebrows popping up – and then suddenly he backed up, grinning broadly. "Fair enough, Juliette. I withdraw the remark, as Ethan and Nick would say."

He turned towards his truck and I shouted after him, "Would you please stop calling me that? You're annoying me."

When he shut the truck door, he turned on the ignition and gunned the engine.

Under my breath I said, "You are so pissing me off."

He waved as he backed down the driveway, until he rounded a corner and I could no longer see him.

Huffing back to Evie's cottage, I tried to shut the door quietly. If the engine hadn't woken her, I certainly didn't want to. But as the door clicked shut, I heard Evie call from her bedroom, her voice gravelly from lack of use, "Did I hear Riley's truck?"

I looked heavenward. Too late.

I went to her, crawling in behind her and snuggling up. I closed my eyes and rested my head on her pillow. "Yes. He was here to pick up Ames. Apparently, they are going golfing on our rinky-dink course."

She sleepily said, "They'll probably just smoke cigars and drink G and T's. It won't matter to them what the course looks like."

"Hmmm. I guess."

We lay quietly together for a bit, and then I asked her why Riley was going with them.

"I asked Ethan to include him. Also, they're friends."

She rolled over so she could see me, and I scooted back on the mattress a little to let her adjust. "Do you not like him?"

"He's okay, I guess. I don't know him very well."

She laughed a little. "That's a weird thing to say. You've been with us a lot."

"As a group, yes. But I've never spent much time talking to him."

"He said you're funny."

I leaned up on my right elbow, adjusting myself so I could see her better. "You talk about me?"

"No, we don't talk about you. I asked him how the trellis looked, and he said it looked great and that you did a beautiful job on the landscaping. He also said you called him Bob." She smiled her angelic smile at me.

"Well, I did. You know, like Bob the Builder? It just came out."

She laughed. "See? Funny."

I lay back down on my side, cheek on my arm stretched out above me. "Shaye went to take care of the babies. Said she'd bring back breakfast. Do you want some coffee?"

Evie looked at me, tears in her eyes. "I'm getting married today, Julie."

My heart squeezed and my eyes stung. She'd waited so long for the right guy. She loved Ethan intensely, and he loved her.

"I know, sweetie." I reached out and brushed her hair off her face. "He's a keeper."

"I couldn't do this without you, Julie. You are my sister. You know that, right?"

I swallowed past the lump in my throat and said softly, "I know."

"Maybe one of Ethan's friends will be good for you."

I jumped out of bed. "I am not having this conversation." I went into the kitchen to make a pot of coffee. "Why are both you and Shaye trying to hook me up with these people? I can find my own dates."

She'd followed me in and was waiting for the coffee to brew. "You do kind of pick the shitty ones."

My eyes bugged out of my head. "Wow! So little faith in me from everyone these days."

"I just want you to be happy."

"And a guy will make me happy?"

"You know what I mean." Her sad eyes met mine. "You did kind of have a melt-down earlier this year over Jason."

A few months before, I'd been cleaning out storage and came across a box of clothes that had belonged to Jason: a pair of old ripped jeans and a hoodie. I'd put them on and proceeded to get drunk.

Ethan had been out of town, and Evie had texted me to meet her for a drink. I'd ended up crying my eyes out and had spent the night with her.

I shrugged and looked down at my feet. "I was having a moment of weakness."

Softly she said, "It's okay to have those, but you have to let him go. You've been holding on to a vision of what could have been, and you're missing out on what could be. He's been gone for a long time.

He loved you Julie, but you know he wasn't ever going to commit like you wanted him too."

The coffee beeped. "Lord, Evie, you are starting to depress me. And this is your wedding day. Let's not talk about Jason or setting me up with anyone. This is your day. Here, drink your coffee."

I handed her a mug, and then poured one for myself. "Let's sit outside and enjoy this beautiful morning while we wait for Shaye to feed us."

I didn't wait for a response. Instead, I left the cottage and sat at the bistro set on the tiny patio that looked out towards the water.

Evie followed me out and sat timidly next to me. Quietly she asked, "Are you still my Maid of Honor?"

I couldn't help but laugh. "Yes, but I don't think most people think I have any honor."

We talked about the flowers and the catering until Shaye showed up with bacon-and-egg bagels.

"Oh yum! Give me one of those." She handed me the sandwich and I bit into it, moaning at how delicious it was. "You do know this is seriously the worst thing we could eat this morning."

"You need your protein. And Evie won't be eating at all tonight, I'm sure, so, eat up." She handed Evie a sandwich, and we all ate heartily, washing them down with the orange juice Evie brought out from her kitchen.

The morning passed by way too fast. The three of us took a walk on the beach, throwing rocks into the ocean and simply breathing in the fresh sea air, calming our souls.

By the time we returned to the cottage, it was almost eleven and the hair and makeup artists arrived. They'd brought a trunk of high-end, long-lasting products, and expensive hair tools, putting my personal arsenal to shame.

Shaye went first, and by the time she was finished, Morgan had arrived.

The cottage became a whirlwind of giggling girls, champagne pops, and teasing innuendos about how sexy Ethan was.

If Evie had told me when we were little girls that I would be wearing a dusty blue, strapless, floor length tulle dress as her bridesmaid, I would have ended our friendship right then and there. But her choice was exquisite – soft and flowy, simple and flattering. The layering of tulle was so pretty, I actually felt like a princess myself.

While Evie had her hair styled, I helped Shaye get into her dress. It was a little too tight, and she had to suck in her stomach, while I wrangled the zipper in the back.

"I hope you don't pass out. It's going to be a long day," I said as I gripped the zipper and tried to pull the sides of the dress together.

"My saving grace is that I can't drink, so I won't bloat."

"Your boobs might fall out of the top, you know?" I teased her. She was still breastfeeding, and I was quite certain she'd ordered a smaller size with higher expectations of fitting in it.

She inhaled and said, still holding her breath, "Just zip it up! I can't hold my breath forever."

Zipping it up as fast as I could, I hooked the top closure and told her to relax.

She put her hand to her belly, gasping for a breath. "Oh, good Lord. How did women ever wear corsets?"

"Don't worry, you'll be back in your leggings and sports bras before you know it."

Evie's mom arrived a short while later with Evie's dress. We all waited expectantly in the living area of the cottage while she helped her put it on.

While we were all chatting, Morgan told us she was a librarian, and that she was working on her first novel.

"Oh, what do you write about?" I asked as I filled her champagne glass.

She took a small sip and muttered, "Romance."

"Huh, that's interesting. Historical, or what?" Her pretty skin turned a shade of pink, and I was intrigued. "Aha, naughty romance. Even better."

I whispered back, "Do you have a pen name? I would be happy to read it for you."

We were interrupted by Evie stepping out of her room and twirling in front of us. "Well?"

My heart skipped a beat and I took a few stuttering breaths so I wouldn't cry. In my mind, she immediately became six years old – the memories of us as girls planning this day with childlike innocence: happy-ever-afters, beautiful dresses, and true love.

I now understood the phrase 'you took my breath away.' In Evie's case, the saying was woefully inept. "Oh, Evie."

Shaye went to her and took her hands. "You look gorgeous. Ethan is going to cry like a baby."

Evie stepped out from Shaye's embrace. "Julie?"

Evie stood before me as the most beautiful creature I'd ever seen. She'd always been pretty, in a girl next door kind of way. Now, with makeup accentuating her arctic blue eyes and elegantly contouring her delicate features, she was otherworldly.

Her shiny black hair had been styled in a voluminous updo – soft and loose, with tendrils framing her face. A tiny halo of flowers and pearls wrapped around her hair, held loosely at the back in a low chignon.

The exaggerated sweetheart neckline on the ivory silk ballgown highlighted her tiny waist. Layers of raw silk handiwork softened the look. When she moved, she seemed to float rather than walk.

She looked dreamy, and everything Evie.

"Evie." I sighed. I couldn't even speak. "I can't even…" I felt my eyes burning, and I blew out my breath slowly. "You look beautiful."

I heard sniffles behind me and I turned to see her mom already pulling tissues out of her bag. I teasingly scolded her to help keep my own emotions under control. "Martha! You need to keep it together or none of us will get through this day. And our makeup will be ruined."

She blew her nose. "I know. I just can't believe my baby girl is getting married."

Someone had to take control before we all dissolved into a puddle of tears. "She won't be getting married if we don't get her there. Where are Nick and Marcus?" I looked back and forth between Shaye and Martha.

"I just texted Nick. He's on his way," Shaye said. Just then, Evie's dad pulled up in his SUV to take Martha, Evie, and myself to the vineyard.

"Do you want us to wait?" I asked Shaye.

"No, go ahead. Morgan and I will be right behind you." Shaye was putting Evie's cosmetics in a bag to take with us.

I looked to Evie: my best friend, my most cherished person. "You ready?"

She nodded, conserving her emotions, too afraid to speak.

I smiled lovingly at her, held her hand, and led her to the door. "Then let's do this."

4

IT SEEMED STRANGE to be driving to my vineyard, instead of waking up there.

Tomorrow, it would be all mine. My parents had spent the past few months cleaning out the house I grew up in, preparing it for me to move into.

It was a small Victorian that my father had also grown up in, remodeled for modern times. The master bedroom and bath were on the second floor, with a smaller bedroom, bathroom, kitchen and living area on the first. In the back of the house was a small laundry room and greenhouse.

The covered front porch looked out in the same direction as the tasting room, winery, and wine cellar, across the vineyards.

Making small talk with Evie as we drove along the bay road, I asked her if she thought I should move out of the studio apartment above the tasting room and into the house.

"It would certainly give you more room." She responded

absent-mindedly, and her mother looked back at us from the front seat, smiling serenely.

Evie and I were in the back seat of her Dad's SUV. I stared out the window as we passed by the marina and the Islander resort. I mumbled, almost to myself, "I don't really need more room. And I really like the small, quiet space I have. I guess I can think about it tomorrow."

"Maybe you should talk to Riley. Get his input."

The tone of our conversation up to that point had been flat, only filling the time as we drove to the vineyard. But now I almost felt defensive. "Why would I talk to Riley?"

"He's your builder, he might have an idea what to do with it. Maybe it could be the office, or a rental." She fiddled with her dress and I realized that she was getting nervous. She had been oblivious to my outburst.

I reached for her hand. "Hey, are you okay?"

She nodded quickly. "Yes, just nerves."

"Evie, Ethan loves you to the moon and back. And little Noah is just the cutest little man on this planet. He adores you too."

I reached down into my bag and pulled out a tiny bottle of prosecco I'd grabbed from her refrigerator before I left, and whispered, "Do you want me to open this?"

She giggled and whispered back, pointing to the front seat, "I think they would hear it pop."

"Oh well. When we get to the tent then." I shrugged. The mood once again lightened, at least.

A few minutes later, we pulled into the vineyard and followed the road past the tasting room and private party patio. We slowly drove along the gravel road, careful not to raise dust, past the house and wine cellar, eventually turning onto the dirt road Riley and I'd taken yesterday.

A hundred or more cars lined the drive and sat in the lot that had been razed just for today. Her dad brought the SUV to a stop at the back of the tent. He stepped from the driver's seat to come around and open her door.

I followed and stood to the side to help gather her dress.

Her dad smiled lovingly at her and asked, "Ready, darlin'?"

He held out his hand to her while I held up her train to keep it out of the dirt.

Her smile lit up the day and my heart squeezed with love. Nick and Shaye pulled up a moment later, and we all went into the tent together.

Nick went directly to the end of the tent and peeked out towards the ceremony site. "Looks like everyone is here, Evie. When you're ready I'll go let Ethan and the pastor know. Riley will be up in a minute to get Mom. Do you need anything? Xanax? Whiskey?"

"Seriously, Nick?" Shaye asked him.

"Just trying to lighten the mood. She looks a little pale."

Shaye, Morgan, and I stood close to her, calming her nerves and rubbing her back. "You're okay, sweetie. You're good."

She simply nodded.

Sharply, I said, "Okay, this is ridiculous. Nick, open that bottle of champagne. Evie needs a drink." I turned my attention back to Evie. "You need to calm down – you do look like you are going to pass out."

Riley came through the tent flap at the back, a big grin on his face. "Hey, guys, it's such a beautiful day isn't it?"

We all turned towards him, our eyes trying to convey that Evie was kind of freaking out. When he made eye contact with me, I widened my eyes and tilted my head towards Evie.

He immediately saw that she was a bit skittish and went to calm her. "Hey, hey, what's going on here?"

His presence had a calming effect on her. Her body visibly relaxed, and she let out a breath.

When he saw her shoulders lower, he laughed. "It's Ethan remember? He's your guy, okay?"

"Right. Okay."

Riley looked at me, smiling, his eyes roving my face and down my body. "You sure look pretty. How are you?"

I instantly felt angry. I didn't know why, but it felt like I was an afterthought, that Evie was first, and I was an obligation. Tersely, I responded that I was fine. Instantly I regretted my harsh response. His smile dropped a bit, a flash of confusion in his eyes.

I couldn't bear the look on his face, so I turned away, smiling and announced to Morgan and Shaye that we should get ready.

Behind me, I heard Riley ask Evie's mom if she was ready. Glancing covertly over my shoulder, I saw him hold his elbow out to her, placing his other hand over hers in a gentle, comforting way.

I watched through the tent flap as Riley kindly escorted Martha down to her seat, waiting until she was settled, and waited for him to look up at me.

When he smiled up at me, I was momentarily disoriented. I felt a pull towards him and started walking out of the tent, almost in a dream state.

Shaye gripped my elbow and pulled me back. Laughing, she asked, "What are you doing?"

I focused my attention on her and Morgan, and then Evie. A little confused myself, I said quietly, "I have no idea."

"Wait until the music starts. Morgan goes first, then me, and then you, remember?"

"Right." I shook my head to clear it and grabbed my bouquet from the banquet table.

"Put this around the stems, you might need it."

I looked down at Shaye's extended hand. She was holding out a lavender handkerchief, initialed with SRR.

"Thank you."

Her eyes were kind, and knowing. She knew I was almost on the verge of tears, and took charge as soon as the music started. For all my earlier show of strength, she knew today was equally difficult and emotional for me.

Directing Morgan to start the wedding procession down the floral edged path, Shaye held the tent curtain open for her. After waiting for Morgan to get a few feet's head start, she then turned to me. "Guess I'm up." And she disappeared out of the party tent, the flap closing behind her.

With one glance back to Evie, I saw she was more relaxed than she'd been on the drive here. Her dad held her tightly to his side, and I smiled sweetly at her. "See you down there."

Her eyes shone with love. She was ready. After years spent imagining this day, it was finally unfolding right in front of us. We used to pretend Jason and I were getting married, and Evie was our minister. We'd named all ten of our combined children and married them off to each other, thinking we could stay family. At that young age, we hadn't known it was illegal.

I chuckled briefly at our childish innocence. The fantasies of young girls could never compare to the soul-consuming love of being an adult.

"I love you, Evie."

"I love you, Julie."

I turned to leave the tent, descending the path through the trees and plants, and up the center aisle to the archway, where I saw Ethan and his groomsmen waiting.

The four of them were like runway models, cowboys, and a candy store, all packaged deliciously in heather gray tuxedos.

And I felt…nothing. That thought stumped me, and I guess I must have paused at the altar, because Shaye raised her eyebrows, eyes wide.

When I pulled myself together, I finished my walk and turned to face the guests.

There were so many people, and I felt a moment of panic for Evie. If she was nervous before, this would make her hyperventilate. I waited for the music, watching the tent, praying she would be okay.

Ethan and Evie had chosen "The Glasgow Love Theme" from the movie *Love Actually*. As soon as it started, Evie and her dad emerged from the tent.

Any worries I had about Evie being alright vanished when I saw her look at Ethan.

The music played, and the two of them, eyes locked, couldn't have been less aware that there were other people present. We were simply witnessing this extraordinary love.

She was floating. The only things missing were deer and bluebirds, otherwise I would have thought I was in a dream.

Handing me her bouquet, she reached out and wiped a tear from my eye. I hadn't even realized I was crying.

Words were spoken, vows exchanged, and before I knew it, they were announced as husband and wife.

I had enlisted the help of our friend Amy, who owned the local pizza restaurant, to coordinate the catering and photographer, and keep everyone on track for the wedding.

It was a blur after the ceremony, being pulled from one picture to the next. My face was starting to hurt from smiling, and I really needed a drink.

Shaye kept getting distracted by Nick and JT. The boy wanted his mom, and he kept pulling on her dress to be picked up.

I heard her say as she bent down to him, "I'll come give you kisses soon. Right now, Mommy needs to take pictures with Auntie Evie and Uncle Ethan."

He threw himself on the grass, and Nick had to pick a wiggling JT up off the ground. "I'll have Kira take him home for a nap."

I watched as Noah started to cry when he realized his friend was leaving, and the picture taking turned into a farce.

And then I saw him. Standing at the top of the path, just outside the party tent, watching us take photos. Gorgeous. Sleek. And oh, so pretty. In person, he was even more attractive.

He obviously knew who I was because he raised his glass in a salute, smiling down at me.

If this moment had been in a movie, it would have been shot in slow-motion. If it were a Disney movie, birds and stars would have been dancing around his head, illuminated by a golden glow. If it had been a romantic comedy, the wind would have been blowing around him, but his perfect hair would have stayed in place.

But it was none of those things. It was my life, and he was my investor. Potential investor. Dax was city-slick and polished. The suit he was wearing was a mid-weight wool, and it was cut perfectly for his lean body, almost as if the suit was just an extension of his good breeding and social status.

The photographer was lining us up for a bridesmaid photo, and I whispered to Shaye, tilting my head slightly in the direction of the tent, "Dax is here."

She adjusted her skirt, and I saw her glance his direction. She tried not to giggle. "Oh my. He looks like sin in a suit."

I turned to her and laughed. I'd never actually heard her talk about any other guy, other than Nick. And she would *never* say Nick was that.

"Okay, married woman. That was a little too much."

"Hey, just because I can't buy anything, doesn't mean I can't window shop."

I burst out laughing. "Oh my God! Are you serious right now?"

She sighed. "Maybe I just need some sleep. Or sex."

I covered my ears. "Lalala. I can't hear anymore." I removed my hands and asked Evie, "Are we almost done here?"

Smiling her beautiful bridal smile, she said that yes, we were finished and it was time to start the reception.

We made our way to the tent. The DJ announced the wedding party, introducing Evie and Ethan last.

"Let us welcome, for the very first time as husband and wife, Ethan and Evie Archer! Please give them your heartfelt applause!"

The DJ put on "Levels" by Avicii, and Ethan and Evie came dancing through the entrance to the tent, grinning ear to ear like they had been given the gift of eternal life. Ethan had never done anything for me physically, but even I had to admit that he was a super sexy guy, and could most definitely dance.

When he picked Evie up and carried her, twirling her around the dance floor, everyone cheered.

Over my shoulder, I heard, "I should probably introduce myself."

Turning to my left, I smiled coquettishly at the man next to me. "No need." I put out my hand. "Julie Hunter. It's nice to meet you Mr. Bentley."

"Dax." He shook my hand.

I nodded approvingly. "Dax it is."

"When Ethan invited me to the wedding, I was surprised. But then, when he explained it would be a good time for us to meet, in a more relaxing environment, how could I resist?"

Oh, he was smooth, and very well spoken. I sat on the fence between flirting and keeping things professional, and decided to stay there until I knew him better.

"Indeed. It was a beautiful ceremony, don't you agree?"

He teased me and replied, "Indeed."

We smiled at each other for a moment, each sizing the other up. He wasn't very tall. At least, not compared to Ethan and Nick, and even Riley.

With my heels on, I almost looked him in the eye, which would have made him a few inches under six feet tall. His hair was jet black, his nose aristocratic, but his eyes were sparkling, and I felt he was most likely a good person.

Nick and Ethan were very smart; I knew they wouldn't surround themselves with less than ethical people.

I asked Dax what he thought of the vineyard so far.

He grabbed my elbow and steered me outside. "Walk with me for a minute?"

"Of course."

The afternoon sun was starting to drop low in the sky, casting a golden glow over the vineyard. I prayed he could envision the dream I had.

Making small talk, I asked him where he was staying.

"I'm actually not. I'm taking the last boat off the island tonight."

We meandered through the vines, me telling him about our brands and the harvest cycle, he asking impressive and inquisitive questions.

He commented on the flowers, and the landscaping I'd planted. "You've done a really nice job, Julie. Tell me more about your vision."

I felt a brief moment of panic, as if I'd been ambushed. Then I realized that I lived and breathed this place, the soil and the grapes were part of who I was, how I was beginning to define myself. If it wasn't what he wanted, then his investment wouldn't be what I wanted.

Taking a moment to collect my thoughts, I took a deep breath and stared out towards the grapes.

"I grew up here. My mother is from Chêne Bleu, a vineyard near Marseille. I remember being there as a child in the summertime, the feel of the dirt on my bare feet, the sweet-yet-bitter taste of the grapes, the endless summer evenings."

"My family would invite the workers and the neighbors over, what seemed like all the time, but I know it wasn't. As a child the parties just seemed magical, mystical and never-ending. The wine, the food… My mother would pour me small glasses of wine and then add water." I turned to him laughingly. "My father told me it was sacrilegious to dilute the wine, but she didn't stop."

By now we had walked all the way down into the vineyard. "My parents met when my dad was backpacking through Europe after he graduated from the University of San Francisco. He's from here, and, like me, was born into this business. He fell in love with her instantly. Or so he said. He said, 'Ta mère dansait joyeusement dans les vignes avec un vieil homme. Ses cheveux étaient en feu par les rayons du soleil, sa silhouette de Madone visible à travers le tissu transparent de sa robe, et j'étais captivée.'"

I held the grapes lovingly, and turned to him to continue. His look stopped me. "What?"

He chuckled. "I have no idea what you just said."

"Oh no. Did I just slip into French?" I blushed. "I am so sorry. I speak French to my mom, and I must have just dropped into it." I shrugged. "He said he was captivated the first time he saw her dancing in the vineyards. It was love at first sight."

"That is a lovely story."

"We have more grapes in eastern Washington, and a few years ago they started building a retirement home. I've known for a while they would be leaving, and I also knew I could never leave here. The closer it got to them leaving, the more I started feeling alone. I started running my idea by Nick and then Ethan, and then it just started blowing up. And here we are."

"But why?"

"Why what?"

"Why do you need a resort?"

I heard Ethan's voice in my mind, 'He wants more than just another investment property.'

Turning to face him, my feet in the dirt, the sun at my back, I said, "I want a place where people feel at home. Where the parties, and the food, and the wine never end. Where stories are told, and memories are made." I felt myself choking up. "I want a family. I want a home."

His grin grew wide and he grabbed my hand, nodding his head back to the party. "I believe, Ms. Hunter, we have some business to conduct."

5

The party was in full swing when we returned to the tent. We made a beeline to Nick.

Dax put his hand on Nick's shoulder. It made for an interesting picture, given that Nick was almost a half head taller than him. "Nick, I need to catch a ferry, but consider me in. I'll be back in a few weeks and we can sign all the necessary agreements."

He turned kind eyes to me. "I'm impressed with Ms. Hunter and her vision. It will be my pleasure to provide the capital you need to get started."

Nick did his hand shaking and grinning. "Good to know, Dax. This is shaping up to be a great day all around. I'll let Ethan and Riley know."

"I'll say my good-byes to the bride and groom. Ms. Hunter, I'll call you this week to arrange the meeting."

"Thank you for coming all this way. I am thrilled to get started. Thank you so much. Thank you."

Nick and I watched as Dax made his way across the crowded dance floor, seeking out Ethan and Evie.

Nick shoved a stuffed mushroom in his mouth and mumbled, "Guess you didn't say anything stupid."

"Why are you still so mean to me? Why do you doubt me so much?"

He actually looked a little apologetic. "I think it's a habit. I'm sorry."

"Well, stop, okay? I'm not going to do anything dumb. I've been on my best behavior, and you and Ethan have taught me a lot. Stop doubting me. I thought we were friends."

He wiped his mouth and took a drink of his wine. "I think…," he paused, and swallowed, "You haven't had the best reputation the past few years."

"That's a shitty thing to say. And you were part of my shitstorm, Nick, so don't be a hypocrite."

"That was a long time ago. I mean, c'mon Julie, you can't honestly say you've been a pillar of the community."

"How can you say that to me? We host the Halloween party for the island every year, and I do the orphan Thanksgiving. This island is my home just as much as it's yours." I had to pause to take a breath and calm myself down. "I don't want to argue with you. You have sufficiently made me feel like crap. I'll be on my best behavior with Dax. Not for you, but for me. Because this is my home, this is my vineyard, and you work for me. As my attorney and counselor. So, don't lecture me on the mores of society."

His eyes went wide, and then he started to laugh. And laugh. Clapping, he said, "Brava, Julie, brava. I think you just became a grown-up."

I turned on my heel in defiance and left him standing at the buffet table. A waiter passed me with a tray of champagne flutes. I quickly grabbed one, making my way to the edge of the tent.

The atmosphere was crackling with joy and laughter. Evie and Ethan were making their way around the tent, greeting their guests, hugging and kissing friends and family.

Shaye, her mom, and her mom's boyfriend, Tom, were tucked away in a back table with the new baby. Love shone from their faces.

Nick had been pulled into a conversation with a group of his law school buddies. I saw one of them give him a big hug. Jason had died the summer Nick graduated, and it had taken awhile for him to reconnect with his friends.

The heavy, anchored feeling in my stomach took hold again. The sadness of being alone pulled at me. I was so tired of misconceptions and pretending they didn't bother me.

Tossing back what was left of my champagne, the carbonation burning through my thoughts and tickling my nose, I placed the empty glass on a side table and exited the tent.

Solar tiki torches lined the path that led to the wine cellar. I lifted the hem of my skirt as I walked, careful not to trip.

I loved that my parents had placed the wine cellar so close to the house. Growing up, it had doubled as a playground.

When it rained, which was often here in the islands, Jason and I would play house. We would pretend to pour wine into the hand-blown wine glasses from the local glass blower.

When we got older, we would actually open the bottles. Between the two of us, we would drink an entire bottle. If my parents ever knew, they never said anything. But it did get more and more difficult to hide the empty bottles.

Opening the heavy carved-wood door, I flipped on the low lighting and perused my wine choices. I trailed my fingers over the bottles as I walked. Cabernet. Merlot. Malbec. Sangiovese.

The wine cellar was quiet and cold. I felt at peace here, and only briefly wondered if I was being missed at the wedding.

I pulled a bottle of cabernet from the shelves, a wine glass and wine key from the bar, and hopped up on a barrel.

Carefully uncorking the bottle, I poured a small amount into my glass, inhaled the bold, fruity scent, and took a heavy drink. Exhaling forcefully, I allowed myself to relax and let the wine seep into my body.

I leaned back against the cold tongue and groove decorative paneling that covered the thick insulation. My thoughts wandered to the party. I knew I should get back, but the happiness in the room had become more than I could endure.

Evie had been swept up in the thrill of it all, and quite honestly, I didn't think she would even realize I was missing.

My thoughts turned again to Jason and how much I missed him. It was sad to me that so much time had passed and I still mourned the loss of him. I think that had my grief been acknowledged, I would have healed sooner. But since Shaye had been dating him when he died, and he and I'd had such a tumultuous break-up, no one considered that my loss had struck so deep.

The people on the island wrapped their comfort around the Reid family, and Shaye, and my relationship with him was forgotten. What had pissed me off the most was that Shaye was already sneaking around with Nick. That had been the cause of the argument that had driven Jason to drive off in anger.

Years later, when I'd had the affair with Nick, I'd wanted to say it just happened; but deep down I knew I was trying to punish her, to take back what I thought she'd stolen from me.

I couldn't imagine my life without her now. She had become just as important to me as Evie. But I was starting to feel I had nothing.

My heart was cold, and all the guys I'd slept with over the years just made it colder. What I'd said to Dax was true: I wanted a family and a home. But I didn't even know where to start.

The thought brought tears to my eyes, and when they started to fall, I couldn't stop them. I doubled over, wrapping my arms around my middle, and cried.

When the tears started to slow, I sat back, eyes closed, and just let the soft whimpers wear themselves down. Taking slow, steadying breaths, I started to relax when I heard a concerned voice from the doorway. "Julie?"

I opened my eyes to see Riley coming towards me cautiously, as if approaching a skittish colt.

I didn't want anyone to see me like this and I lashed out. "What are you doing here? Mourning the loss of your little girlfriend? Sad you couldn't steal her from Ethan?"

"Whoa, whoa, whoa. I came to see if you were okay." His brows came together. "You looked sad when you left the tent and I thought you might want someone to talk to."

"Well, I don't. You can go back to your puppy-dogging." I felt tears starting to rise again and steeled myself to them.

"I'm not your enemy. You don't need to act that way with me. I'm just here to be a friend. How you act in public is none of my business, but in private, you don't need to act."

He wouldn't leave. Instead, he stood calmly a few feet in front of me. Close enough that I could see sadness in his eyes. Far enough away that I could have jumped off the barrel and left the cellar if I wanted to.

"Do you want to talk about it?" He tilted his head, slanting it so he could catch my eyes.

I looked up at him and wiped the tears from underneath them. "Not really."

My melancholy was hard to hide, and he chuckled at my attempt. Nodding at the bottle, he asked, "Drinking away your sorrows?"

I glanced down at the bottle and then back at him. "A proven technique to wash away malaise."

Taking a few steps closer, we simply stared at each other. I didn't like the pity I saw in his eyes and I told him so.

"I don't pity you. I like you. And you seem upset."

I dropped my eyes to my lap. "I'll be fine. I'm just having a moment. This day came and went so fast. It seems like it took the past ten years with it." I raised my eyes to him and felt the tears coming again. I couldn't stop them and I choked out, "I feel like…I feel as if I just lost everyone I cared about in one fell swoop." My words broke on a sob, and then I couldn't stop.

Riley stepped forward and pulled my cheek to his chest, his hands on my head and back. "Shhhh, you're okay. You're okay." He just kept repeating it over and over, like a mantra, until my tears turned to shuddering breaths again, and I calmed down.

I tucked my fingers into the waistband of his slacks and turned so my forehead was resting on his chest. I mumbled, "I'm sorry."

Lifting my chin with his finger he said, "You don't need to apologize. It's been a long day, and weddings make people emotional, in nice and not so nice ways." He cradled my face in his palms, wiping away the tears with his thumbs. "Please don't be embarrassed. And certainly don't think I'm holding a candle for Evie."

He wasn't flirting. His tone was friendly and consoling. But something shifted in me. His touch was gentle, but his hands were calloused. They felt rough, but tender. My breath caught in my throat, and I looked to his mouth.

His lips parted. When I looked up, I saw confusion in his eyes. My fingers pulled him closer, and I felt his hands slide to the back of my head, under my hair, caressing me. We watched each other warily; his eyes darted between my eyes and my mouth.

With painstaking slowness, almost like he knew we would never come back from this, he lowered his mouth, gently pressing his lips to mine, gauging my reaction. The softness of his lips surprised me. When I inhaled, we exploded, opening to each other, frantic to get closer.

Our kiss was rough and urgent, shocking both of us with its intensity. My hands went around him, pulling him closer, and I felt his palm up under my dress, pushing aside the tulle, and gripping my thighs.

I was small compared to him, but I was curvy. When he palmed my naked bottom, he pulled back as if in shock. I hadn't put any underwear on this morning.

He muttered, "Oh, fuck!"

Panting, desire clouding my eyes, I looked at him, almost desperate. He pushed up the rest of my dress, gripped my hips, and pulled me towards him. His mouth was hot against my skin as he worked to kiss every inch of my neck and exposed chest.

Our kissing was crazy, fast, and so intense I thought I would pass out.

We fought for each other's mouths, but couldn't keep them together, we were so desperate to get close to each other.

I hadn't felt like this for anyone. Not since Jason, and even then, it wasn't this desperate.

Suddenly he stopped. We both paused, our breaths mingling together. Slowly, he started to release me, gently lowering me back to the ground, each of us trying to catch our breath.

The silence around us emphasized our heavy breathing. We stood quietly, holding onto each other, shocked and not quite sure how that had just happened.

With great care, he gripped me under the shoulders and lifted me back onto the barrel. When he stepped back from me, he tilted his head, questioning. I raised my eyebrows to him and lifted my palms out.

He said, "Uh, are we gonna talk about this?"

"That's a girl question." I jumped off the barrel and started to leave the cellar.

"Julie!" He barked my name. "You're just gonna leave?"

Haughtily I responded. "It kind of looks like it."

He started to laugh. "Are you kidding me?"

I didn't know how to respond. He was so attractive right now, with his hair mussed from my hands, that I didn't really trust myself to talk.

With kindness in his eyes, he walked back towards me, and I crossed my arms in front of me.

He stopped. "Don't be like this."

I tipped my chin up in defiance. "Like what?"

"Don't shut me out. I don't know what happened here, but it's not like I do this kind of thing every day."

Words wouldn't come to me. This was so unexpected. I felt as if Dax had planted a seed of romantic possibility, and here I was making out with Riley.

I said the most neutral thing I could possibly think of. "I like your haircut."

He laughed again. A short, low, sexy, laugh. "That's your olive branch? Okay. I can wait."

Making his way to the cellar door, he told me he was headed back to Friday Harbor in the morning. "I'll be back in a few weeks. A surveyor will be out this week to stake the land, and one of my crew will bring a trailer as the construction office. Assuming your funding gets transferred, we have the excavation and concrete crews on retainer to start right away."

My head spun at how fast he had shifted into work mode. "Uhm, okay. How did we pay them?"

He turned to face me, waited a beat and then said quietly, "I have a lot at stake in this project too, Juliette."

I thought he might be implying he had invested his own money into this project. I didn't want to like him anymore than I was already starting to, so I didn't ask.

"My parents' house will be empty. Will it save money if we use it as the construction office?"

He smiled – his sexy smile, with the crooked tooth that made him look both approachable and dangerous. "Are you sure about that?"

"Sure. Why not? It'll be empty, and it's fully functional. A kitchen and bathroom." His smile made me feel defensive, so I added, "I mean, it just makes sense."

He nodded slowly and put his hands at his hips. "I'll tell the construction manager tomorrow to cancel the trailer and start bringing everything over."

"You act as if we're getting the funding."

"You'll get the funding, Juliette. You'll get the funding."

His absolute confidence shook me. The last time I was told things would be fine I was asking Jason to wait for me.

As I leaned against the wine barrel, I thought back to high school, reminiscing about my last night with Jason before I left for my family's vineyard overseas.

"Wait for me Jason," I'd said. "I'll be back in a year, and then I'll go with you." I'd picked the hay out of my shorts so I could put them back on. They'd been buried under the piles and drifts of straw that covered the floor of the barn loft, where we had just finished making love.

"They want me as soon as I graduate. They're already pressuring me to drop out and join the rodeo circuit now." Jason leaned back against a hay bale, one elbow resting behind him, a sprig of hay in his teeth. He was naked. With one knee bent, he unabashedly watched me while I continued to dress. I pulled my bra on around my back and snapped it in front.

"Then I'll come to you as soon as I can." I pushed his leg down and sat down on his lap, straddling his legs. He wrapped his arms around me, pulling me close.

I sighed and dropped my head to the crook of his neck. "I wish my parents weren't sending me to my relatives."

His chest rumbled underneath me as he laughed. "You're such a snob. Do you know how many people would love to be in your place? Who gets to live on a vineyard for a year? For *free*!"

"I know I sound ungrateful, but I'll miss you so much." I started to cry. Caressing his chest, I played with the sprinkling of hairs that were just starting to grow. "I love you, Jason."

His hand gently stroked my back and I felt soft kisses on my head as he whispered. "Everything'll be fine Julie. It'll all work out. You'll see. We'll be fine."

The words came back to haunt me, and a shiver ran up my spine. I stared after Riley.

I whispered goodnight, but he'd already left.

6

THE DAY FINALLY arrived when I would sign my partnership agreement with Dax, and I was incredibly nervous.

I'd had difficulty concentrating all day long, anticipating the dinner meeting Nick had arranged.

Evie had asked me to come help her at the bakery, but after thirty minutes of taking orders and not being able to keep up, she sent me home.

Finally, I'd resigned myself to cleaning my apartment, and looking online at linens for the resort.

When I'd run out of hours in the day, I spent my time getting ready and making myself as presentable as possible – in a business way. It pissed me off that Nick was a voice in my head, but he'd been doing this way longer than I had, so I swallowed my pride, and did as he said.

When I arrived at the restaurant, Nick and Ethan were already there, seated at a round table for five.

The dimly lit restaurant, with its romantic candlelight, was Lopez Island's most elegant eatery. Elegant by Island standards, but also by any other. With no more than twelve tables, each had been strategically placed to allow for intimate, yet inclusive dinners. In the summer, the wait list for dinner was usually several days.

Low, gothic style chandeliers hung from the ceiling, adding to the romantic environment. Exposed wood beam ceilings and white, painted, tongue-and-groove paneling provided contrast to the upscale elegance, giving it a shabby-chic vibe.

Out the rear windows, I could see the bay stretching out towards the marina and the Islander Resort.

For the last few weeks, we'd been preparing the final pitch to persuade Dax to fund my idea to build the low-key, yet sophisticated, resort and get-away on my property.

I wanted the exact opposite of the local, long-time marina and resort. I wanted peace and quiet, solitude and relaxation – good food, good wine, and rest. I wanted my guests to feel rejuvenated.

In the mornings, I wanted them to be able to sit on their private decks and smell the floral, fruity scent of the grapes, and the musty, earthy smell of the vineyard. In the evening, I wanted them to dress elegantly for dinner and enjoy evening receptions in a great room, on the mezzanine.

Tonight was when I'd know for certain if I could make my dreams come true.

The jangling of the bell above the door when it opened matched my nerves, and they didn't get much better when I turned and saw Dax.

As Dax approached the table, we all stood and greeted him. Ethan buttoned his suit jacket when he stood, and gripped both of Dax's hands in his.

"Good to see you Dax. Glad you could make it up this way again to meet with us."

"You too, Ethan." He shook his hand in return and then turned to Nick. "Nick. Thanks for the invitation."

"Of course. We all want what's best for the vineyard, and according to Ethan, that would be you."

They all laughed that ridiculous man-laugh they do when conducting business, and then Dax turned his attention to me.

"Julie, a pleasure to see you again. You look lovely." He took my hand and kissed the back of it. As he bowed his head, the fresh scent of him wafted up to me. He even smelled expensive.

"Dax. It's good to see you again. I hope you enjoyed your time here for Ethan and Evie's wedding?"

"I had a wonderful time. Thank you."

I'd been looking forward to this partnership with even greater enthusiasm ever since Evie's wedding.

Ethan had told me that Dax was a hands-off kind of investor. He looked for properties that he would want to visit as a guest. He didn't want to run them or manage them; he just wanted to visit them.

A solid business plan and a committed heart was what he was looking for, and we were ready to deliver.

As Ethan and Nick sat back down, Dax graciously held out my seat for me and gently pushed it back in before seating himself.

"I hope you got settled comfortably at the resort. Was your plane on time?" I reached for my water and took a small sip, waiting for him to answer.

"It was. And yes, Shaye met me at the dock and made sure that the resort staff took very good care of me. Didn't she just have a baby? My apologies if it's not my place, she just seemed really energetic."

Nick laughed at Dax's apparent disbelief. "Yes. Two months ago. Shaye loves her job. Especially the float planes. She's finally working on getting her pilot's license after all these years. I was able to convince her to stay home for the first month after baby May was born, but I have a hard time keeping her away from the planes. She only works a few days now and takes the little one to work with her. The other two stay with my mom."

I looked teasingly at Ethan and added, "Or Evie."

Turning back to Dax, I said, "JT, Nick's oldest, and Noah, Ethan's little boy, have become fast friends."

Bringing Nick and Ethan back into the conversation, I said, "I feel sorry for all of you with the trouble those two are going to get into one day."

Defending his son, Nick shared that he was at least grateful Eleanor would have two boys to protect her.

I rolled my eyes and laughed at the formal use of her name. "*Ellie* will most definitely not appreciate it, if JT is anything like you were with Evie."

To Dax, I said, "Nick was so overbearing when it came to Evie. Poor Ethan was skulking around for weeks, trying to avoid Evie, afraid Nick would fire him."

Nick guffawed and waved the waitress over at the same time. "Poor Ethan, my ass. He would have taken her away from us if I didn't approve. I never had any powers of persuasion over Evie once she set her mind to him."

The waitress appeared, and he pointed to a wine on the menu, continuing to talk. "Regardless, Dax isn't here to talk about our love lives. He's here to learn more about your vision for the vineyard."

Dax smiled his perfectly white smile. "It's alright Nick, I like hearing about your families. I have a large family myself, three brothers and two sisters. I know how it is with siblings. And love is the answer to everything, isn't it?" He glanced my way and added, "Or so say the poets."

His flirtation warmed me, and I felt myself blush. Nick and Ethan both laughed, as if to brush it off, but I knew they were both hopeless romantics. Ethan had recited Lord Byron to Evie the night he proposed. He was the biggest romantic of us all, I think.

I heard Dax asking, "Would you agree, Julie?"

Dax looked so hopeful, waxing poetic, that I didn't want to bring the kind of maudlin I was experiencing lately into the conversation. So, I just smiled serenely and said, "It certainly is."

The waitress brought the wine to the table, interrupting our conversation, poured a small amount for Nick to sample, and waited patiently for his approval. He gave her an approving nod and she proceeded to fill our glasses.

Ethan brought us back to the business of the evening by asking if we wanted to review the contract one more time.

I looked agreeably to Dax. "I'm happy with the terms, unless either Nick or Ethan have any changes to make."

Nick turned to each of us, making eye contact and stating that he thought it was pretty fair and reasonable. "I don't have any concerns about it." He turned to me and said proudly, "I know you have plans ready to go and are anxious to get started. Once the funding is in place, you have everyone scheduled to start. You've done well, Julie. I'm really proud of you. And I know the island is certainly excited to see what you build."

Ethan jumped in and added, "And I'm glad you took our recommendation on the architect and builder. You'll be pleased with his work."

At his mention of the builder, I gritted my teeth. Not so much that anyone would notice, but enough that I felt the pressure on the sides of my temples.

I also found it somewhat strange that Ethan was talking about him as if they weren't friends. I briefly wondered if all business dinners were conducted in this bizarre manner.

Months ago, I'd been thrilled at their recommendation. Since the wedding? Not so much.

The waitress took that moment to approach us and ask if we were ready to order.

Nick looked to the three of us. "I think we need a few more minutes to look at the menu, and we're waiting for our last guest."

She nodded, a still smile on her face, and left us to review the menu.

The expression on Nick's face changed a moment later, from business to acceptance, as I heard the bells jangle over the restaurant door. A thrill of awareness ran up my spine. I didn't need to turn and look to know our fifth guest had arrived.

He reached our table in a whirlwind of energy, his masculinity sucking the air right out of me.

"Hi. Sorry I'm late. Had a concrete pour today and wanted to get cleaned up."

After shaking hands with Nick, Ethan and Dax, he sat in the chair next to me, laid his arm across the back of mine, and smiled his bad-boy-smile. "Juliette."

I turned my most pleasant glare to him and smiled, tight-lipped, crinkling my eyes. Riley had arrived, and I was less than thrilled.

7

Sitting next to him in the restaurant was disturbing. His energy was practically crackling.

The fresh smell of soap on his skin tickled my nose, causing me to want to lean into him.

We hadn't seen each other since the wedding. A few texts and a handful of emails asking for documents and contacts. Otherwise, nothing personal. And for some reason, that had bugged me.

The construction office had been set up in the empty house, complete with printers and copy machines, project schedules on the wall, hard hats and steel-toed boots for visitors. A couple of desks, a few worn couches, and a card table with folding chairs completed the sparse furnishings.

My head was buzzing, trying to keep up with the conversation. But Riley wouldn't remove his arm from the back of my chair. He was leaning in to me as he talked with Dax.

Doing my best to re-engage in the conversation, I asked Dax about his philanthropic work with Seattle Children's Hospital.

"It's an organization my family is deeply committed to. My youngest sister died of childhood leukemia, and my parents have made a point of supporting the hospital ever since."

I put my hand over my mouth. I hadn't thought that through very well, and I was embarrassed I'd asked the question. "I'm so sorry."

He put his hand over mine. "Don't be. It was a long time ago."

I saw Riley pull back from me, and I felt like I could breathe again.

Addressing Riley, Dax asked, "Your family's company is a Children's Miracle Network Hospital Partner, aren't they, Riley?"

I turned my head to Riley, eyes wide. "They are?"

"We try to support." He took a long drink of the water in front of him, avoiding eye contact with me.

Noticing that our last guest had appeared, the waitress approached us, full of smiles and enthusiasm for the nightly specials.

I absent-mindedly ordered the fresh Alaskan halibut with sweet and sour blueberry sauce. While the rest of the table ordered, I waited patiently to continue the conversation about the Children's Hospital.

I was disappointed when Riley turned the talk to expectations for construction, and the extent to which Dax would be here to oversee the project.

"I'll be here next week for the pouring of the foundation, and after that, I'll be around for the inspections, but I don't have a lot of time for the day to day. I expect you have a construction manager for that work?"

"Actually, I was planning on managing this one. My sister will be in Friday Harbor to wrap up our current projects, and my dad has a golf resort project in Eastern Washington. It's the best place for me right now."

I interrupted the conversation to ask where he was going to be staying.

"I have my boat at the marina. I brought it over for the wedding. It has a small cabin and shower."

Nick interrupted and offered up one of his parents' cottages.

"Thanks Nick, but I'm good on the boat. Most of my time will be spent on-site, so I really don't need the comforts of a home right now."

"Well, what about the bedroom in Julie's house? Since you guys turned it into the construction office, you could stay upstairs. Unless, you planned on moving in, Julie?"

I choked on my water. My eyes watered, and I had to beat on my chest for a second.

"Excuse me, I'm sorry. Give me a minute." I said between coughs, and then gently wiped my mouth with my napkin.

Riley chuckled, and everyone turned to stare at me.

Ethan added, "It's actually a really good idea. You have a pretty aggressive construction schedule. It would be beneficial to have him on-site. Dax, what do you think?"

For the first time tonight, I sensed a competitiveness in Dax. "I think that if Riley wants to stay on his boat he shouldn't be pressured to stay at the vineyard."

Leaning back in his chair, Riley said, "Actually Ethan, you have a point. But I'll defer to Julie, since it's her home."

Butterflies fluttered in my stomach. "It does make sense. If you don't mind the lack of furniture, I don't have a problem with it. I like living above the tasting room, and hadn't given much thought to the house. It's up to you." I shrugged, feeling as if I'd said too much.

Dinner arrived and Nick said enthusiastically, "It's settled then. Riley, let us know if you need anything."

He glanced at me and said, a little wickedly, "I think a mattress should be sufficient."

I smiled the most authentic smile I could muster, lifting my wine glass. "Cheers to a successful endeavor."

Cheers went around the table, and for the rest of dinner, I turned my attention to Dax.

Dax had said we had his full support, but until the contracts were signed and the funding was in the bank, I wasn't going to start writing checks.

As dinner was wrapping up, I was anxious to get everything signed. I excused myself to use the restroom, and while I was there, I texted Nick. *I'm nervous, how does this work?*

His response came quickly. *Breathe*

Out loud to myself, I said "Breathe? What's that supposed to mean?"

When I returned to the table, they all rose and then sat again after Dax tucked in my chair.

The waitress had cleared the plates, and coffee had been delivered.

Nick cleared his throat. "Dax, I think this might be a good time for us to get your input on our partnership. Julie has done a lot of research, and I feel confident she has a solid business plan that shows clear profitability in the next three years." He made eye contact with me, demonstrating he was clearly on my side. "Ethan and I have worked with her, side by side, this past year, and both of us stand behind her vision. I think your investment in her, and the resort, is a sound one. You've read the contract and we've negotiated the changes you requested. Is there anything else that would prevent you from signing and getting this project started?"

Dax was nodding. He appeared very relaxed, suit jacket unbuttoned, a small smile on his face.

I felt Riley's leg pressed against mine. He was nervous too. I reached under the table to squeeze his knee and I saw, out of the corner of my eye, that he visibly relaxed.

Taking his napkin off his lap, Dax made eye contact with each of us as he spoke. "I have invested in many projects that cater to an elite group of people – golf resorts, high-end spas, luxury high-rise buildings that most people can never afford. I've been looking for a project that speaks to me, that feels like a home. A place that would welcome all kinds of people, but maintain its roots in a peaceful lifestyle. A place to build stories and memories."

Turning to me, he reached for my hand. "Julie, when I asked you about your vision, your words resonated with me in a way that I hadn't been able to articulate until that moment."

With a quick glance at Nick and Ethan, he said quickly, "Don't get me wrong, your business plan is solid."

He then spoke directly to me. "But you, Julie. You are the one that is going to bring it to life, and I would be happy to give you the capital you need to get started."

I squealed and jumped out of my chair to hug him.

"Yes!" I heard them all laugh. "Oh, I'm sorry, that was a tad inappropriate. I'm just…I'm just so excited. Thank you! Thank you!"

They all continued to chuckle at me, with Riley saying a quiet congratulations.

Nick pulled us all back to the moment, suggesting a time to meet at his office in the morning to sign the contracts.

"Does 8:00 a.m. work for you, Julie?"

If I could've kicked him, I would have. Tomorrow was Sunday. If he wanted me in my pajamas, 8:00 a.m. would be perfect. "Absolutely!"

"Great! Then it's settled. I'll call Suzi and make sure she has everything set up and ready to go."

I almost laughed out loud. I would be surprised if Nick's ears weren't bleeding by the time he got home. Suzi had worked for his father as his Administrative Assistant, and now for Nick and Ethan. She was *not* going to be happy at being called in on a Sunday morning.

We all stood and casually made our way to the door. Nick held the door for all of us, quietly congratulating me as I passed by.

Addressing Dax, he asked, "Can I give you a ride back to the resort? I'm headed home that way, and I'm happy to give you a lift."

"That'd be great Nick, thank you. If I could get a word with Julie first before we go?"

"No problem. We'll wait."

Ethan said his goodbyes, and Riley engaged Nick in a quiet conversation.

Steering me towards a more private space, Dax smiled at me, and stared in a way that made me a little uncomfortable.

I asked, "Is everything okay?"

"Yes. I wanted a moment with you before tomorrow." Dax walked me towards a bench at the top of a set of stairs that went down to the beach below. It was dark now, and the only lights on the water were from the reflection of the boats moored in the bay. He gallantly gestured for me to sit.

I watched as he unbuttoned his suit jacket and sat perched on the bench, angled towards me. The tide was out and the salty seaweed scent drifted through the cool evening air. "I'm really looking forward to working with you. I meant what I said when I said I was inspired by your vision."

"Thank you. I'm looking forward to working with you too."

He smiled and shifted a little on the bench. I tilted my head towards him questioningly.

Continuing, he said, "I'd like to invite you to a gala for the children's hospital in a few weeks. It would be a great opportunity for you to meet a lot of potential future guests, and many of my friends and business partners."

"Oh! Well, I would love to, but isn't that something you would want Nick or Ethan to attend with you?"

He chuckled and I blushed. "Oh, Julie, you really are quite a stunning woman. I know it probably isn't good business practice, but, well, I like you Julie. I'll be perfectly honest. I'd like this to be a date, of sorts."

I opened my mouth to speak and only a squeak came out. "Uh, that sounds…" Oh goodness, Nick was going to kill me. I took a breath. "That sounds lovely. Thank you. I would love to join you."

"Excellent!" He stood and held out his hand to me. "I will email you later this week with all the details. I'd like to keep this separate from the resort business, if that's okay with you."

Phew! That would make things easy for me. "Of course!'

I stood and we casually walked back towards the restaurant, where Nick and Riley were waiting for us.

When Nick and Dax drove away, I waited until I could no longer see their tail-lights before I turned back to Riley.

He was leaning against my truck, arms and ankles crossed, a knowing smirk on his face.

"This is a nice truck. International Scout?"

"Thank you, yes. It has holes in the floorboards and the heat is spotty at best. But it serves a purpose."

"It suits you."

"Reliable *and* fickle?"

"Dependable and classic."

He stood from the truck and put his hands in his pockets. "What did Dax want?"

I looked over my shoulder and then through the windows of the restaurant. Anywhere to avoid looking at him. Shrugging, I said, "Just that he was looking forward to working with me. Small talk, you know."

With a knowing laugh, he said, "You're such a bad liar."

"Fine. He invited me to the Children's Hospital Gala in a few weeks."

His smile dropped. "Why would he do that?"

I crossed my arms in front of me and snapped, "Because he likes me, Riley. Why else?"

I stepped around him to get to my truck.

Gently, he reached for my arm as I passed. "Julie, wait. I did want to talk to you."

His voice was so calm and soothing. I had a fleeting image of him stroking a little girl's head and whispering that everything in the world would be okay, and she would believe him. I felt myself relax and stepped in closer to him.

"I wanted to talk with you about moving into your parents' house. It was kind of thrown at you and I don't want to make you uncomfortable. If it doesn't work for you, then Nick and Ethan don't need to know that I never moved in. It's not a big deal."

His magnanimous gesture was endearing. "Actually, it's not a bad idea. I don't know what you do on the weekends, or if you have other projects, but there's no point in you being cramped on your boat. And if you stay on your boat, or at the cottages, then *they* might think something was wrong, and there's nothing wrong. I mean, that's not the point, but…" I paused. "It's probably a good idea."

He laughed at my rambling. "You okay?"

"Yes." I was afraid of saying much more than that.

"You seem flustered."

"I'm not flustered. I mean, kind of, after what happened."

"What happened?"

I had to force myself to keep my mouth shut. We both stared at each other. He, on the verge of laughter. Me, on the verge of stomping my heel.

I can play this game too.

Stepping towards my truck, I said, "I seem to have drawn a blank. Guess it wasn't memorable."

At that, he did laugh and then reached for my door handle. "Here, let me help you."

He waited until I'd tucked my dress underneath me and fastened my seat belt.

"Feel free to come by anytime tomorrow. I'll be doing inventory after we sign the contracts. You can find me in the cellar."

He teased, "I know where that is."

I scoffed, and he whispered as he shut my door, "I'll see you tomorrow."

8

"I SAW THEM, Jason. How can you possibly think I wouldn't see them? You have a hundred thousand followers."

"I don't remember it, Julie, I promise. Girls are everywhere, all the time."

"How stupid do you think I am? These weren't taken at the rodeo; they were in your trailer, and you were half dressed!"

My teeth started to fall out and I tried to pick them up off the ground.

"Look, I don't want to argue with you half a world away. When are you coming to visit?"

A vision of Jason on a mountain, trying to climb to the top. Water started rushing all around him.

"I'm not. I'm going home. You said you would wait, that we would do this together. Why are you trying to get away from me? Come home."

"Julie, you were a good time, but I think we're over." Horns popped from his head, and I was pushed into a pool of water.

I fell in and started to sink. I came out of the bottom of the pool and I was standing in my vineyard.

Jason was staring at the grapes. "They're dying Julie."

"No, we can save them." I tried to grab his hand but another girl stepped in and took it instead.

I couldn't see her face, but then there was another one and another one. They all started chanting. "Juliette, Juliette, Juliette."

"Juliette! Juliette."

I groggily woke from my dream, disoriented and confused; my pillow wet from my tears.

Slowly, my brain cleared, and the fog-shrouded words morphed into reality. Listening quietly, I realized it was coming from outside my window. The gruff voice was getting more insistent. "Juliette!"

Tentatively touching my teeth, I closed my eyes and sighed with relief that they were still there. What a bizarre dream.

I swiftly swung my bare legs out from under the downy covers and padded to the window, flinging it open and staring down at the bothersome man standing below.

Crossing my arms in front of me to ward off the morning chill, I responded as Shakespeare's famous teenage heroine. "Aye, me."

Riley grinned up at me. "She speaks."

"You do know that relationship didn't end very well."

He jerked his head back, eyes opening in surprise and chuckled. "Are we in a relationship?"

"You wish."

"Good morning, Riley. It's so nice to see you. You look very sexy in your construction boots. Oh, thank you Julie, you look pretty darn cute in your bunny pajamas, yourself. Is that coffee you brought me? It is. I thought I would help get your day started with a Mocha latte, extra shot as per the barista. You're the best Riley, I'll be right down."

I could not stop laughing. "Do you even need me for this conversation?"

"Conversation? No." He waggled his eyebrows and squinted his eyes at me seductively. "I like you better when you aren't talking."

I did my best to frown at him and said, as I shut the window, "I'll be right down."

Quickly brushing my teeth and washing the sleep from my eyes, I did a passable job of making myself look presentable. I dressed in my standard work attire, grabbed my fleece jacket, and headed outside to meet Riley.

He was waiting patiently for me on the covered porch, leaning against the railing. He handed me a coffee after I pulled the door shut behind me.

"Good morning," I said as I greedily reached for it.

His proximity to me made me nervous. He took up so much space with his height and broad shoulders, especially in his sherpa-lined construction jacket.

It was still cold and damp this early in the morning, and I could see the breath coming from our mouths as we talked.

"Good morning."

I took a tentative sip to test the heat. Then I took a bigger drink and sighed. "Mmmmm. Thank you."

He nodded, and I continued. "What are you doing here so early?"

"You have 25 cement trucks arriving in…" He looked at his watch, "approximately 17 minutes. Aren't you excited?"

The reminder that the cement trucks were arriving today, and that they were, at this moment, on a ferry boat headed my way, caused a stir of excitement. I grinned teasingly at him and drawled, "Maybe."

The Sunday morning after our business dinner, Nick, Ethan, and I had met with Dax. We'd reviewed the contract, agreeing and signing where necessary. It had seemed to go by so fast, but in reality, we were there for over five hours.

Dax had flown out on the 3:00 p.m. float plane, and the next morning, when I checked my bank balance, I had over half of the necessary funding. I'd had to blink a few times to make sure all those zeros were real. I'd felt my heart squeeze and I'd blinked back tears, immediately texting Evie and calling Riley. I think I might have squealed when he answered the phone. He'd told me he would get his crew out right away to excavate and prep for the foundation.

The past week, I'd seen him and his crew working tirelessly to get the property ready, coming and going all day, every day, long into the evenings.

We hadn't talked much other than me giving instructions to him on moving into the house, and briefly when we ran into each other on the construction site.

And now, here he was, smiling at me as if he did it every day.

"Do you want to walk up to the site with me? Wait for the trucks?" His tone was casual and friendly, as if taking a walk every morning was just something we did. We'd yet to talk about the kiss at Evie's wedding, and I was kind of curious why he never brought it up.

"Can't we just take the golf cart?" I looked over my shoulder at the cherry red electric golf cart plugged into the side of the tasting room.

He turned his body towards the direction of the vineyard instead of following the road and jerked his head for me to follow. "Come on, it's a nice walk. It'll calm you."

I followed behind him, accelerating my steps to keep up with his long stride. "I just woke up. I am calm."

By the time I caught up to him, I was mildly winded. I reached for his arm and tugged gently. "Wait. Slow down. Let me catch my breath."

He looked down at my delicate hand on his arm then back up to my flushed face. My hand slid off when he looked up to face me, and I inhaled deeply, giving my heart a chance to slow down.

I closed my eyes and inhaled again, relishing in the earthy smell of the dirt, letting it seep into my senses. "I love it here so much."

His chuckle forced me to open my eyes. "I thought all you island people were always trying to escape."

"I guess so, when we're younger. But, not now."

He extended his hand to me. I stared at it, startled.

"Come on," he said, "I'll slow down."

Tentatively, I reached out to take his hand and he held it as we walked through the vines, careful to keep a good distance from each other, but not letting go. When we came across a dip, he squeezed a little tighter and stiffened his arm so I wouldn't lose my balance. "Careful."

Quiet with our own thoughts, I followed him as we wound through the vines and back up the hill towards the wedding venue. Cresting the top, I saw a swing had been attached to the wedding archway. Dropping his hand, I handed him my coffee and ran to the swing.

"Riley! It's gorgeous!" I couldn't keep the joy off my face as I lovingly ran my fingers over the scrolls cut into the western red cedar.

It was finished with a wood stain that would protect it from the rain, and hung from four chains attached to the top of the arch. Inscribed in the center of the back of the chair were the words *Hunter's Moon*, complementing the Diana carved into the arch.

"I can't even… I don't even know what to say. It's gorgeous." It was hard to stop the tears that had formed in my eyes. I just shrugged and threw my hands in the air.

Taking a seat on the swing, he patted the space next to him. I sat down, pulling one leg up onto the padded bench, dangling the other over the side. "How did you do all this?"

"I've done projects like this before, Julie. You think you want it to change, but when it does, the quaintness of your tiny vineyard will be gone. Evie and I wanted you to have someplace special, someplace Zen, if you will, where you could look out to your land and not see the resort. Everything is behind you from this place."

He looked over his shoulder at the building site, and I turned to see the scarred land that had been framed for concrete, pipes and sewer lines popping up from the ground waiting to be connected. When I looked back, he was already looking back out towards the grapes, the peace and serenity of the moment recaptured.

"She loves you so much. You know that, don't you?" His voice was soft and quiet.

"I know." I lowered my head. "Her brother, Jason, and Evie and I were the three musketeers. I don't remember any life events that don't include them. Well, when I was younger anyway."

With what sounded like empathy, he said, "I never met him."

"No, you wouldn't have. He died before we ever met you."

Leaning back, he stretched his arm across the back of the chair. "Do you remember the first time we met?"

I laughed out loud. "How could I ever forget that day? That was when Ethan got socked in the face by the kayak guy, Joe, or whatever his name is. I never liked him anyway, but Evie was always so smitten. He does have a hot bod, I'll give him that, but he was such an ass."

Now it was Riley's turn to laugh. "Yeah, I was kind of surprised by that."

"By his hot bod?"

He rolled his eyes at me as if to say, 'Seriously?'

I giggled quietly and looked back out towards the vineyard. We sat in silence for another few moments, sipping our coffee and enjoying the warming of the day.

Speaking quietly, Riley interrupted my thoughts. "Evie's an

interesting person. She pulls you in with her kindness, but she is obtuse when someone really cares for her. It's fascinating."

I couldn't decide if I felt angry about his comment or intrigued. "How so?"

He still wasn't looking at me, just staring out towards the vineyard. He cleared his throat. "Well, when I met her, I thought she was striking, of course. The more I talked with her, the more obvious her sweetness and purity. I wanted to feel something more. But, setting aside the fact that Ethan was already in her heart and she didn't even know it, all I felt towards her was friendship. Like she was my sister."

"Oh, poor Riley, nobody loves you." I teased him, but when he turned his eyes to me, his brow was furrowed in annoyance.

"Why do you always tease? You did it that first day too."

I jerked my head back in surprise. "I did?"

"Yes, you cooed at me like I was a piece of meat, and congratulated Evie on a job well done." The annoyance had left his voice, and was replaced with curiosity. "You're more than a flirt. Why do you do that?"

I covered my mouth with my hand to stifle the giggle that was bubbling up. "I don't know. Because it's easy? No one ever takes me seriously, and for the most part, I feel like everyone ignores it. I guess it's become a habit."

He leaned forward, and I could feel his breath on my face. "You're smart Julie. Not just anyone could have pulled off what you are about to embark on. Don't treat men like toys or dogs. One of these days, one will bite back."

I inhaled sharply and glanced quickly at his mouth. I felt a rush of weakness as I leaned into him, desperately needing to kiss him. His strength and confidence in challenging my unacceptable behavior drew me in. I wanted to savor the taste of his lips – lips that I remembered were so soft and gentle, yet insistent and greedy. If I was being honest, I hadn't stopped thinking about them.

The ground shook beneath me, and I heard the rumblings of cement trucks, breaking the tenuous moment that had been unfurling between us.

As much as I was a flirt, I would never – and I mean never – overstep a boundary with someone that Evie liked or had dated. Riley didn't fit into either of those categories. Still, I kept him in that friend, but moderately easy to tease, category. The more time I spent talking to him, and especially after that kiss, the more I felt a little off balance around him.

The cement trucks came into view, giving visible proof to the reason for earth shaking. I turned to see a convoy driving onto the property, followed by a very shiny, very sleek, very expensive black sports car.

I jumped up off the bench and turned a jubilant smile back to Riley. "Are you ready?"

As he stood, he mumbled under his breath sardonically, "Mr. Moneybags is here."

I tried to scold him, but I was so excited it came out on a laugh. "Do not mock. You and I both know we couldn't do this without him." I reached for his hand and pulled him along as I skipped up to the road. "Come on! It's a big day for us!"

The trucks rolled onto the property, and when the first one stopped in front of us, the stout driver jumped from the cab, shaking hands with Riley and slapping him hard on the back. "Early mornin' today, Riley, early mornin'."

He smiled his cheeky grin, his sexy crooked tooth showing, easily slipping into that country boy talk that helped him fit in so easily with the island workers. "We got a lot of concrete to pour today. Need to get these trucks to work."

The trucks all came to a stop, lined up one by one, their concrete mixers turning, engines running. A sense of anticipation was bubbling up inside me, my heart squeezing with excitement, the smile on my face almost hurting.

It wasn't hard to deduce that Dax was the driver of the shiny car. As he approached us, I watched as his grin grew the closer he got to me. As inappropriate as it might have been, I couldn't resist running to hug him. "Dax!"

He harrumphed when I slammed into him, reaching my arms around his neck. His laughter tickled in my ear and I gripped his arms, his grin matching mine. Teasing me, he said, "Maybe I should spend more time here."

A blush crept up my cheeks. "I'm so sorry. I'm just so excited for today."

He set me back from him and went to greet Riley. "Morning, Riley. We ready?"

I watched their interaction and was struck by the contrast between the two of them. They were both fit, though Riley was much taller. Dax had the clean lines of doing cardio in a gym, long legs and close-cropped hair. Riley had the bulk of someone used to carrying lumber and swinging tools. His hair had recently been cut, so it was somewhat on the neat side. Before that, though, it had been messy and unruly, touching the top of his jacket collar.

Where Dax was dark and sleek, like his car, Riley was rough and calloused. If I hadn't kissed him, or talked with him, I might assume he wasn't that smart, but that was far from true – degreed, and esteemed in the construction world. I felt a surge of resentment towards him. It was odd that I found myself angry at him for being something more than I expected.

I hadn't realized I was scowling until Riley shouted to where Dax had left me standing. "Why the frowny face?"

Blinking a few times, I shook my head and put the smile back in place. "Sorry, I don't know where I went."

Laughing at me, he waved for me to follow him. "C'mon, Juliette, concrete can't pour itself."

9

I'd never been so tired in my entire life.

I was sprawled out across the couch in the construction office, which used to be my parents' house. Shoes on the floor, top button of my jeans undone, a sweatshirt thrown across my face. This was exactly how Evie found me when she abruptly barged through the front door.

"Julie! The concrete looks amazing. And it's bigger than I thought it was going to be."

I felt her lift my feet and place them in her lap as she sat down on the couch.

"How can concrete look amazing?"

She *tsked.* "You know what I mean. It looks like progress."

Mumbling from under the sweatshirt, I said, "I think I have concrete in every crack and crevice of my body. Kill me now."

She reached for the sweatshirt and pulled it from my face. When she saw me, she laughed. "Oh dear. You do look a little haggard. You didn't actually *do* anything today, did you?"

I simply glared at her and tried to lift myself up on my elbows. "Actually, I did. I had the brilliant idea that I wanted to help. Never again."

"Kudos to you for trying. What exactly did you do?"

"The list is long." I groaned again and flopped back down on the cushions.

She rubbed her hand up my calf and started squeezing my aching muscles. "Do you want me to make you dinner?"

I groaned in pleasure. "Oh my God! Can you just keep doing that please? I think I might cry."

"You need a bath and a massage, a glass of wine and a good dinner."

"And then I'll sleep for a week."

She chuckled softly and continued kneading my calves.

With my eyes closed, I said, "I'm so glad my best friend makes bread."

A few minutes later, as I was blissfully relaxing from Evie's leg massage, Riley and Dax came through the front door, bringing the smell of the outdoors and wet mud with them.

"This is cozy," Riley commented as he made his way to the kitchen to wash his hands.

Dax took a seat in one of the folding chairs across from us, and I rolled my head to the side to look at him.

"How do you look so fresh, while I feel like something the cat spit up?"

All he did was chuckle. "You up for dinner tonight? I was going to head back to the resort and clean up. I could come back and get you, or you could meet me there."

I didn't intend to groan, but when his face fell, I realized it was out loud. "Oh, Dax, I'm so sorry. All I want is a shower and my bed." I didn't want to tell him that Evie had already offered.

"No worries. How about breakfast tomorrow morning? The concrete will need time to cure before we can start framing, so I'll be heading out on the noon ferry."

"That sounds lovely! Yes. Text me in the morning?"

Riley came back into the room as Dax stood to leave. "Riley, see you in a few weeks."

He nodded and responded. "Thanks for showing up today, Dax. It means a lot that you were here."

The two of them seemed awkward around each other, and I felt Evie's hand tense on my leg.

"Ow."

"Oh, sorry," she mumbled.

I tried to roll myself to a sitting position, grunting with the effort. "I'll walk you out Dax."

As Riley turned to head upstairs to the master bedroom, where he was currently making his home, he said to Evie, "I'm going to get cleaned up. Give me ten minutes."

I shut the front door behind me, following Dax down the front steps to his car.

"I didn't know construction work was so hard."

"You really shouldn't be working. You're supposed to be enjoying the process, not participating in it."

"I guess so. But I always help with the harvest of the grapes, so it seemed like I should at least be present."

"This is a much bigger project than harvesting grapes."

I laughed at him because he clearly had no idea what was involved. "Oh yeah? Maybe you should come help this year. I'd like to see you do manual labor."

His eyes twinkled at me, his small smile softening his face. "I'd like that."

Feeling myself blush, I was grateful we were standing in the twilight shadows. Changing the topic, I asked, "What time should I meet you in the morning?"

"At 8:00 a.m.?"

"Oh my God! I will never sleep in again."

His laughter warmed me. "Ok. How about 9:00?"

"That works. I'll see you then."

He reached for my hands and leaned in to kiss me tenderly on the cheek. I closed my eyes, allowing the moment to wash over me. It was soft and sweet, lingering a second longer than a friendly good-bye.

He whispered, "Goodnight, Julie."

"Goodnight, Dax."

I floated back into the house, savoring the tingling on my cheek.

Evie was gathering up her purse and heading out the door. "Julie, Ethan just called. He's not making it back tonight, so I need to get Noah from Shaye's house."

I blinked a couple of times in surprise.

"I'll call you tomorrow." She paused long enough to catch my eye. "Sorry I can't make you dinner."

"No worries. Thanks for the calf massage. I'll see you this week?"

"Yes, come by the bakery. I'll feed you."

She hugged me again, and then I shut the door behind her, a little confused as to what I should now do with myself.

Behind me, I heard Riley bounding down the stairs. Dressed in clean jeans and a T-shirt, he looked refreshed and ready to go out.

"Evie leave?"

"She did. Ethan was delayed, so she needed to get Noah."

He paused, placing his hands on his hips, scowling at me thoughtfully. "What should we do about dinner?"

"I need to shower. I can't sit in these clothes one more minute."

"Okay. Why don't you head upstairs, take a hot shower, and I'll make some pasta?" He wandered into the kitchen and opened the refrigerator door. "I think I can find some chicken and vegetables to toss in."

"I live a half a mile away. I'll be back in thirty minutes."

"You won't come back. You'll lie down with a towel wrapped around your wet hair, and you'll pass out. Go on. It's your house anyway. Grab some sweats and a T-shirt off the chair up there. They're clean, I just haven't put them away. I'll make us dinner."

"You sure?"

"Go!"

"Okay. I'll be back down in a few minutes."

"Take your time."

I lugged my aching body up the stairs and into what used to be my parent's bedroom. It was sparse now. The only remaining proof that my parents had been here were the curtains: dark green blackout curtains, with a lace overlay decorated in butterflies and flowers.

As a child, they always seemed the perfect complement to the masculine, dark cherrywood furniture my parents had. Now, there was simply a mattress with plaid flannel sheets, which clashed with the feminine curtains, and a heavy down comforter. A white, prefabricated dresser stood against one wall, and a stack of clothes sat on a loveseat sofa near the window. The whole room screamed *bachelor*.

I riffled through the clothes, found a pair of gray joggers and a dark V-neck T-shirt, and made my way to the bathroom across the hall.

The bathroom was just as sparse, and all male now. It seemed that Riley had a thing for big fluffy towels. The rich chocolate color matched the area rug and patterned shower curtain. I giggled, imagining him in a Target, or Bed, Bath & Beyond. I was certain a young clerk was more than happy to help him.

That thought of Riley flirting with someone sent a jolt to my system. He was really sexy, but other than, well, our kiss, and some friendly flirting, he didn't seem that into me.

Reaching behind the curtain, I turned the water on and let it run until it was steaming. Peeling off my dirty work clothes, I piled them neatly on the floor and stepped into the shower, letting the hot water wash over my aching muscles. I moaned out loud and felt so glad I hadn't walked home. I used Riley's soap to wash and scrub my skin until it turned pink.

When I finally felt I'd removed all the caked-on cement particles, I stepped out of the shower, dried myself off, and brushed my hair back into a low ponytail.

Riley's clothes drowned me, and I had to roll the bottoms up four times so I wouldn't trip. I looked like a little kid in their parent's nightshirt.

Picking my dirty clothes up off the floor, I went back downstairs. I could hear the fan whirring above the stove where the pasta was boiling.

"Almost ready? I'm starved."

Riley turned from where he was cutting up red and yellow peppers. I saw him try and hide his smile.

"I saw that."

He chuckled, and I asked him for a bag for my clothes.

Pointing with his knife, he said, "Above the toaster."

Dropping my clothes in the bag, I went back out into the front room and set it by the door.

Our project plan was on a large whiteboard behind the folding table. I read through everything in order: framing, plumbing, insulation, drywall, fixtures. It was all so perfectly planned. And accelerated. I'd proposed an opening day to coincide with the harvest in October. This put us five months out. Manageable, but stressful.

"You hungry?"

I turned at Riley's voice and saw him standing with two bowls in his hands, a dishtowel hanging from his waistband.

"Starved."

Placing the bowls on the table, he asked if I wanted anything to drink.

"Just water. My skin feels like a snake."

He talked as he walked back into the kitchen. "That's the concrete, it dries out your skin. Put a lot of lotion on and drink a ton of water. You'll be okay."

When he returned with a glass of water for me and a beer for him, he toasted me. "To your very first day on the job."

I raised my water glass. "And my last."

Chuckling, he took a large drink. Then he visibly relaxed, inhaling and exhaling deeply. "Ah, better."

We both greedily dug into our pasta. I was so hungry; I don't remember eating half of it.

"This is so good!"

"No, you're just hungry."

"Was it really just this morning you were bringing me coffee?" I shook my head in disbelief.

"At least we have a break from construction until the concrete cures. But we do need to confirm your lighting fixtures. The chandelier you wanted for the entry was on backorder, so you might need to get something else." He shrugged like this happens all the time.

"Do you have the catalogs? I really want the firework one. Remember? The one with the twenty bursts? It will look so beautiful against the wrought iron railing."

"I'll check with them in the morning."

Now that my stomach was full, I was starting to feel sleepy, and I yawned as I leaned back in my chair.

Riley took a break from his eating and said, "Evie said you spent some time in France after high school? That your mother's family lives there?"

"You have really got to stop talking to Evie about me. Or vice versa. Ask *me* whatever you want to know. Or tell her to stop. Better yet, I'll tell her to stop."

"Tell me about Jason."

"Anything but that." I slurped up a mouthful of pasta that I didn't really want, and didn't even care that I wasn't being ladylike.

"France it is then." He didn't seem bothered or fazed that I wouldn't talk about Jason.

It wasn't that I wouldn't tell him eventually. Maybe. I just didn't want to talk about anything too depressing or emotional tonight.

"France it is." I pushed my bowl towards the middle of the card table, and crossed my arms in front of me, resting them on the table. "I'm an only child, and I always knew I would take over the vineyard. But my mom wanted me to experience it the way she did growing up. We'd spent time there, in the summers and a few Christmases, but she wanted me there for an entire season. She wanted me to learn about the regions and the grapes. 'Juliette, you will fall in love with the soil. You will turn your face to the sun and feel it caress you. A soft breeze to cool you, and good wine to comfort you. You will return no more a child, but a woman who knows the value of her home.' But she said it in French, and, well, she was wrong, kind of. I was already in love. I did feel the sun on my face, but sadly, I came home and was a bit more of a mess than when I left."

He was leaning back from the table, twirling his beer between his fingers. His voice was soft, a small smile on his face when he said, "You seem to have turned out okay."

"The day of Evie's wedding, you said I wasn't very discriminating when it came to men." I held my breath, not breaking eye contact with him, waiting to hear what he would say.

He leaned forward and reached out for my fingers, pulling my hand out from under my arm. "I apologize. That was a thoughtless thing to say, and I really didn't intend to upset you. Sometimes I get a kick out of the way we tease each other. That day I took it too far. I crossed a line. Forgive me?"

My fingers were tingling. "I forgive you."

He released my hand and put his to his heart. "Under love's heavy burden do I sink."

I threw my napkin at him and laughed. "Knock it off!"

He caught it and laughed. "But it really is so easy."

"Tell me about your family."

"One of my sisters is in Friday Harbor, the other sister is in Seattle."

"What are they like?" I crossed my arms on the table and put my cheek down to rest on my forearm.

"Maggie is feisty and outgoing. A lot like you. She is just figuring out how to handle herself on a construction project and..."

His voice was soothing, almost humming. I found myself drifting off, his words fading into the background of a dream. In my imagination, he was cradling my head in his lap, smoothing back the wisps from my forehead and slipping his fingers through my hair. I heard him whisper, "and my other sister is a Sasquatch, and escaped from her crib at a young age. We haven't seen her in twenty years."

My eyes popped wide open. "What?"

Riley laughed and stood from his chair. "I'm just kidding. You fell asleep. I know my life is kind of boring, but I don't think I've ever had a girl fall asleep on me." He reached for my hand. "C'mon, rest on the couch. I'll make you some coffee."

I felt like I weighed five hundred pounds. Every muscle ached, and my feet felt like lead weights.

"Okay. I'll just rest for a minute and then you can take me home."

Curling up on my side, I tucked my hands under my cheek and mumbled, “Just for a minute.” Then a heavy knit blanket was placed over me, tucked under my chin, and I was asleep.

10

"WE SHOULD THINK about getting a couple of real desks. These card tables aren't very sturdy for all this paperwork we have."

Riley's voice broke through my dream state and I rolled my head over to see him trying to organize invoices and catalogs into neat piles.

Blinking my eyes a few times, I sat up and reached my hands high above my head to stretch. "Did I fall asleep here last night?"

In a leisurely way, he came towards the couch and said that I had. "You looked so peaceful; I didn't have the heart to wake you. Do you want some coffee?"

My mind was still a bit fuzzy and my arms ached from working yesterday. "Coffee?"

"Yes, you know, crushed up beans with hot water poured over?"

Abruptly, I tossed off the blanket and stood, heading towards the kitchen to check the time.

"I know what coffee is. What time is it?" Before he could answer I saw that it was 8:45, and I shouted at him. "Riley! Why didn't you wake me? I'm late."

He looked perplexed. "Late for what?"

"I'm having breakfast with Dax. Give me the keys to your truck!" I held out my hands and watched as he laughed sarcastically at me, somewhat amused.

"No."

Walking towards him, I begged. "Please. I'm already late. You can walk down later and get it."

Reaching into his pockets with the pace of a sloth, he pulled them out slowly. "What do I get in return?"

He held them high and I jumped up to grab them. Running towards the front door, I shouted behind me, "You get to keep your job."

I jumped in his truck, struggling to move the seat forward and adjust the seat belt, cursing myself the entire drive back to the tasting room and my studio apartment. "Stupid, stupid girl."

Screeching to a halt, I jumped out, leaving Riley's keys in the ignition. I ran up the front porch and pushed through the door to the tasting room, up the stairs to my apartment, flinging off Riley's clothes as I ran.

I felt like I was doing cardio, running to the bathroom to brush my teeth and hair, and then back out to find something to wear.

I hated that I didn't have time to do my hair. All I could do was brush it out and pin it in a French twist with a couple of bobby pins. At least it was better than the ratty ponytail I'd had when I woke up.

"Breakfast, breakfast, breakfast, what to wear to breakfast." I muttered to myself as I flung dresses off the hanging rack onto my bed.

Settling on a paisley print handkerchief dress, I slipped my feet into silver wedges, grabbed my bag, ran down the stairs and back out the door.

I would be ten minutes late, but that was okay, right?

My Scout was parked around the side of the building where I'd left it two days prior. I shut the rickety door, turned the key, and... nothing.

"What? No, no, no. C'mon baby, start." I said out loud.

Jumping back out, I ran back to Riley's truck and took it instead. I would send him a text when I got to the resort.

The drive to the resort took less than ten minutes. I took that time to take a few calming breaths. My fingers were gripping the steering wheel and I had to flex them to relax.

This island was still densely covered in fir and pine trees. I was grateful that the summer people who built their homes here had the decency not to completely clear and raze their land.

The irony of the fact that I'd completely deforested my land to build the resort did not escape me.

When I wasn't rushed, I usually enjoyed the ride into town and around the bay to the Islander resort. Today, it felt like forever.

What felt like an eternity later, I pulled in front of the Islander Resort and Marina, parking next to Dax's shiny sports car.

My phone was at the bottom of my bag, and I pulled it out to text Riley. *My Scout wouldn't start. I have your truck at the Islander. Sorry, be back in about an hour.*

I slowly stepped from the truck, putting my phone back in my bag and straightening my dress.

When I entered the lobby, I saw Dax sitting by the window of the restaurant, staring out the window towards the marina.

With confidence, I walked to him, smiling brightly as if being late was no big deal. "Dax! Good morning."

At my voice, he turned and smiled broadly at me. "Don't you look fresh as spring!"

He reached for my hands and leaned in to kiss both my cheeks.

"Aren't you kind. Thank you."

Holding out my chair, he helped me get settled, and I felt my phone vibrate in my bag.

I ignored it, placing my napkin on my lap and smiling broadly at Dax. He looked fresh and shiny this morning in casual clothes.

He raised his finger for the waitress. When she approached the table, Dax asked me if I wanted coffee.

"Yes, please. With cream."

"I know how you take your coffee, Julie." She said disdainfully and walked off.

Dax looked a little surprised at her contempt, and I had to explain that I had dated her ex-boyfriend. I didn't add that he had still been her boyfriend at the time. "The island is small. People are slow to forgive, and they certainly don't forget. And you know what they say, 'You don't lose your boyfriend, you just lose your turn.'"

He snorted in laughter. "No, I've never heard that before."

I shrugged awkwardly. I really needed to apologize to her. "It was a long time ago. Tell me what your plans are for the day."

He started talking and I listened half-heartedly. I wanted to be interested in what he was saying, but my phone kept vibrating and it distracted me.

I finally caught up to the conversation when I heard him say, "I was thinking that you might want to fly down to Seattle and I can pick you up at the float plane dock. I'll get a hotel for you, and maybe we can spend the weekend together. If that's something that would interest you."

Oh crap. Was he talking about the gala? I was hoping he was, and I responded, "That sounds wonderful! Thank you, yes!"

"It's black tie. Do you have something to wear?"

A feeling of being unworthy surfaced. Did he think I was just some country floozy? I didn't own a gown, but it's not as if I didn't know what black tie meant. And over the past few years, I'd made an effort to purchase clothes that were fashionable and stylish.

My image and reputation on the island had taken a turn down a slippery slope after Jason died, and at first, I acted like I didn't care. For the most part I really didn't, but keeping up the pretense was getting exhausting.

The winery was successful. We'd won numerous awards and had been featured in magazines up and down the west coast. Those features had required that, as the face of the winery, I be polished and sophisticated.

I forgave him the judgement. He had only seen me dressed up once during our business dinner, and yesterday I'd looked like hired help. But it still stung a little, like maybe he thought I didn't belong in his silver-spoon world.

Briefly, I thought about Nick and Jason and Evie – Island royalty. They had trust funds from their family, certainly not as much money as Dax, but they'd never acted entitled or belittling of others.

I had to give Dax the benefit of the doubt. I tried to anyway. He wasn't island born and bred, but manners were manners wherever you went.

Brushing aside the feeling of inadequacy, I lied and said I did. "Is there a theme? It will help me decide which one I should wear."

He raised his eyebrows in surprise. "Actually, there is. It's called 'Sapphire Stars, shining light on the Children of Seattle.'"

"That sounds lovely." I was genuinely impressed, and gave myself a mental pat on the back for being somewhat knowledgeable about these things.

Looking at his watch, he commented that he had a ferry to catch and he stood to leave, throwing down a couple of twenties onto the table. "Walk me out?"

"Of course." I stood from my seat, and felt my phone vibrating again.

"What do you have planned for the next couple of days?" He asked as we walked.

"I need to thin the crops. We call it a green harvest. I need to make sure the grapes that have potential will get as full as possible. It will increase the quality, and we can get a higher price."

We had reached his car, and he turned to me before getting in, reaching up to cup my cheek in his hand. He whispered, "Fascinating."

He leaned in to kiss me sweetly on the lips. My eyes closed, and I felt the soft, wet fullness of his mouth as he gently sucked on my bottom lip and then released me.

Brushing his thumb over my cheekbone, he quietly asked, "I hope that was alright?"

I was a little speechless and a lot surprised. Nodding and smiling at him, I said, "Mmhmm."

Backing up from me, he laughed as he stepped down into his car. "Good. I'll call you later this week. The lumber should be delivered in the next week or two so we can start the framing. It's going to be great, Julie!"

I watched as he started his car and backed out of the parking lot, waving at him as he drove away towards the ferry.

When his car was out of sight, I ran back inside and quickly pulled out my phone.

Juliette?

Juliette, I tried your Scout, your battery is dead.

I need a ride

Where are you?

You're starting to piss me off

I hit the return call button and after a few rings it went to voicemail.

I'll be there in 15 minutes, I texted back.

I saw Shaye pull in at the end of the parking lot and I ran to meet her. "Shaye, just the person I need."

"Hey Julie, what's up?"

"I need your help with a dress."

She looked at me dubiously, and I watched her grab a bag out of the back seat of her SUV. She told me I had to walk and talk. "I have a flight, and need to get down to the dock."

She had a long stride and I had to walk quickly to keep pace with her. We rounded the corner of the building and cut across the grass down to the dock. All of the boat slips were full this time of year. All except one long extension where the float planes came in.

"Ok, well, I'm going to a gala with Dax in a few weeks, and it's black tie."

"That sounds fancy. How fun!"

"Right? Well, here's the thing… I told him I had a dress but I don't. I was wondering if you wanted to go dress shopping with me. You've been to lots of things with Nick and with your parents, I assume."

"Julie," she cautioned me, "you shouldn't have lied to him. I'm sure he wasn't judging. He doesn't know you very well but he seems to like you. Be honest from now on."

"Fine. Starting now. In the meantime, can you help me?"

"When is it?"

I told her the date and she said she was going to be in Seattle that weekend. "You can fly down with me and we can shop in the city."

"He said he would get me a hotel."

We paused on the small dock and waited for the plane to arrive.

She tilted her head, and looked at me speculatively. "Do you want to do that?"

"Honestly?"

"No, lie to me Julie. It always works out so well for you."

"Don't shame me, Shaye."

"I was going to say that you could stay with me at my Mom's if you want to. I'm bringing May for a visit."

Her invitation intrigued me, and I felt a little calmer about the whole weekend idea. "I think I like that idea better. I really like Dax, but I want to be careful about overstepping personal and professional boundaries."

"Look at you, being all respectable."

"I don't know who I dislike more, you or Nick."

She laughed. "What did Nick say?"

"At Evie's wedding he congratulated me on being a grown-up."

At that she laughed even harder. "You already are a grown-up Julie. You were a long time ago. If I haven't told you yet, I'm really proud of you. I know the past few years haven't been easy, but you should know I love you like a sister."

I hugged her, squeezing her hard, making fun of her. "Oh, look at you, loving me."

The seaplane had landed and was taxiing to the dock. "Let me go, so I can pull him in."

I released her and watched as she expertly grabbed the rope hanging from the wing and assisted the plane in gently docking the pontoons alongside the wooden dock.

When the engine spooled down, the pilot stepped out and greeted us.

"Hi, Tom. Where you guys going today?"

"Just around the islands. Shaye is going to be practicing landings today."

I turned to her in shock, my eyes wide with surprise. "You really are learning to fly?"

She giggled. A real giggle. "I am. I've spent almost my entire adult life around these planes. It's just a formality, really. You know I could fly these things anywhere."

"Shaye," I said in awe, "now it's my turn to be really proud of you."

"And Nick said he would buy us a plane, so there's that."

I laughed. "Of course he did."

Shaye looked over my shoulder and waved at someone on the dock.

I turned and saw Riley. "Oh, crap. He looks mad."

"Why would he be mad?"

"Long story. I gotta go. Have fun flying, and let's talk later this week about the gala weekend, okay?"

She looked really confused. "Uhm, okay."

I turned to run up the dock as best I could in my wedges, trying to catch Riley before he made it to us.

Fortunately, Shaye had already stepped up into the plane, so I avoided a scene in front of her. Riley had a backpack over his shoulder, and a scowl on his face.

"Riley, I am so sorry."

He was pissed and continued to trudge past me. "I know you had a *really* important breakfast with your investor this morning, but at least answer your fucking phone."

"I felt bad because I was already late. I thought it would be rude to interrupt our conversation." I said from behind him, and I was almost jogging to keep up with him.

Hitching his backpack higher up on his shoulder, he turned, stopping abruptly and glared at me. I almost ran into the front of him.

He ran his eyes down my body, resting on my feet and my blue painted toes.

When he brought his eyes back to mine, he said, "It was rude to take my truck and leave me stranded."

His voice had softened, and I felt my insides warm. "I…I didn't know you were going anywhere."

"I need to go to Friday Harbor. I was going to drive, but now I'll take my boat. I'll be back in a few days and I'll fix your truck then. You can use mine."

Turning away from me, he continued his trek down the dock to his boat. My heels made it difficult to keep up with his long stride, so I waited until we reached his boat to continue the conversation.

"When are you coming back?"

He stepped into a forty-foot fishing boat and answered, "In a few days. I need to help my sister with the customer. They changed the scope of the project, but not the budget. I think they thought that since we left her in charge, they could bulldoze her and take advantage. I just need to give her some support."

Riley's boat was so beautiful I found myself stepping in after him. It swayed and I grabbed his arm for support.

He laughed. "Are you coming with me?"

"This boat is gorgeous. What is it?"

He paused, as if he was gauging my motives, then said, "It's a Scout 420."

I wandered along the sides of the deck, admiring the caramel, faux leather seats.

"Does it have a cabin?"

He tilted his head to an entryway. I stepped carefully down into a cozy galley, with a sleeping berth and small dining area.

Following me down, he ducked his head and scooted past me to toss his backpack on the bed. It was difficult to maneuver around him, and I regretted my decision to step in.

Riley took a seat at the tiny table, his legs stretched out in front of him, watching me with amusement, and I had to step around him to leave.

He reached out a hand to steady me, and I inhaled sharply at the feel of his palm on my leg.

"I…I should get going."

His voice was husky when he spoke. "You could come with me if you want. The lumber won't be delivered until later this week. Not much is going to happen on site."

He hadn't shaved and I briefly imagined him kissing my inner thighs, the soft hairs tickling me. His eyes sparkled with humor, as if he knew what he was doing to me.

Abruptly, I pushed his leg to the side. "I really need to get back. Thank you for letting me use your truck. I'll make sure I put gas in it. And text me when you get back, I'll come get you."

I'd scrambled to the boat deck and then out onto the dock before he reappeared from the cabin.

He shouted after me, "Don't crash it, Juliette!"

I gave him my middle finger.

11

For the past few days, while Riley was away, I'd spent my time working outside, cutting the unripe branches off the vines and checking for bacteria and viruses. My time alone had been cathartic and peaceful, which was probably why my mind was wandering.

Today I found myself sitting in the swing, legs pulled up underneath me, staring out at the vineyards and reminiscing about Jason.

The memories of that time in my life were so much sharper lately. They were cutting through the foggy barrier I'd built up between the truth of what I'd seen, and what I hadn't been able to bring myself to believe.

I'd chosen not to believe the truth, preferring to bury my feelings under bad behavior and false relationships. It was easier than moving on alone.

My time in France, when my parents had sent me to live with my Grandparents, had been idyllic – until it wasn't.

Evie, Jason, and my dad had driven me to the airport a few days after my high school graduation. They talked exuberantly about all the things I was going to learn, the fun I was going to have, and the new friends I would make.

The closer we got to the airport, the harder my tears fell.

Evie chuckled softly, but I saw her eyes were wet too. "Julie, it's only a year."

Reaching back from the front passenger seat, Jason grabbed my hand. "And I still have one more year of school, so we'll be together before you know it."

My tears fell once again.

In the driver's seat, my dad remained stoic. But I caught his eyes in the rearview mirror. His love gave me courage, knowing he would miss me too.

I hated that they had to leave me at the curb, and as my Dad unloaded my luggage, my sobs came uncontrollably.

Jason was holding me, trying to hold his laughter in. "Julie! It's fine. You're going to be fine. We'll talk and you'll be so busy, you won't even miss us."

We hugged and hugged some more, until my dad finally broke us apart and softly told me I needed to go. Evie crushed me to her, her love giving me strength to go as well. It didn't even occur to me until much later that Jason hadn't actually said he would miss me too.

The first twenty hours of my travel passed in a blur, my eyes tired from crying, the flight long, the food passable. At one point I cried to the flight attendants, and had a lengthy discussion about true love that turned into more tears and then a long nap.

By the time I landed at Charles de Gaulle airport, I was wrung out and disoriented. My face was splotchy, and my hair desperately needed a brush.

My grandmother's foreman, Samuel, met me at the airport,

covering my face in kisses, and telling me what a *belle fille* I had become. Squeezing my arms, he pulled me to him and chuckled, "Ta grand-mère sera si heureuse de te voir."

I responded, in French, that I was looking forward to seeing her too.

The drive to the vineyard was long, and I found myself falling asleep to Sam's incessant chatter about the grapes and the local sheep herders. But if I thought I would get any rest, or time to recover from the flight, I was sorely mistaken.

The moment Sam pulled in front of my grandparents' house, it was one cousin after the other pulling me into their arms, one neighbor after the other kissing my cheeks, and then straight to work.

My grandparents had never quite forgiven 'The American' for taking their only daughter away, and they were going to make up for it by showering me with love and attention.

The first week was a whirlwind of work, and learning, and eating. I texted Evie and Jason when I had time, but there was a nine-hour difference between us, and it was hard to find time to call each other.

After that first week, I settled into a routine with Sam. He seemed to always be laughing about something, making the lines around his already squinty eyes more pronounced.

I loved to watch him work, and talk. His love for the grapes was evident in the gentle way he touched them, as if they were something to be revered.

Sam was instructed to start with the basics with me, although I already knew a lot because I'd grown up on a vineyard.

"But you must build on your knowledge, absorb it all, and add to it. We will teach you the right way," he said, throwing in a jab at my father, as if he'd done it the wrong way.

And so, we did.

We started, literally, from the ground up. He taught me about the soil, and the weather, fungus and bacteria. Everything was about the earth, and nothing about the grapes.

"When you have the soil, the grapes will grow," he said, wisely.

Just when I felt like I'd finally settled into a routine, I received a text from Evie.

Jason left. He dropped out and took Trouble. Call me when you can.

My heart raced and I panicked. I was confused. Trouble was his horse. Why would he do that? Why would he go without me? It didn't even bother me that he dropped out of high school, only that he left without me.

Taking my phone outside, I ran into the vineyards. The setting sun cast golden hues across the acres and acres of grapes.

Facetiming Evie, I paced through the vines back and forth until she answered.

"Evie, what happened? Where did he go?"

I saw Evie was on the beach in front of her parent's house, the gray morning fog framing her tear-stained face.

"Oh, Julie. It was awful. He got in a fight with my dad last night, and the next thing I know, he was tearing out of the driveway. He didn't come home last night, and then he texted me this morning and said he was on his way to Billings, Montana for an event."

I sighed heavily. Jason and his dad had always had differences. "What were they fighting about?"

"The same thing as always. 'The rodeo isn't the place for a Reid. Blah, blah, blah.' He isn't answering my calls." She teared up again.

"Okay. Evie. Keep it together. I'll try him and I'll call you back."

I immediately called Jason's number. He answered after a few rings. His truck cab was visible behind him and his sparkling blue eyes lit up my screen. "Hey, Babe! What's up?"

"Uh, are you serious?"

He laughed. "Did Evie call you?"

"Yeah, but more importantly, why didn't you? What are you doing?"

"Give me a second."

The picture on his phone bounced around for a minute as he secured it in the holster on his dashboard.

"Okay, that's better." He glanced at me and then back at the road. "We talked about this, Jules, and I just couldn't wait. The execs wanted me now and I need to take advantage of being in the spotlight. I can get lots of sponsors and may only need to do this for the next three to four years. We'll have tons of money to build up your vineyard."

I knew what he was saying was true, but I felt deserted. "You said you'd wait for me."

"Jules, I don't want to fight with you. You do your thing, and I'll do mine."

I felt like he'd slapped me, and I jerked my head back and shook it. Angrily I asked, "What is that supposed to mean?"

He clenched his jaw. A tell I knew all too well. He was withdrawing from me. I still had months here, and the last thing I wanted to do was push him away, so I conceded. "Never mind. I'm happy for you. This will be great!"

Doubt clouded his eyes. I knew he didn't believe me, but neither of us had the energy to fight when we were five thousand miles apart.

"We'll be fine, Jules. We'll be fine."

Those words were starting to bug me. He'd said them in the barn the last time we made love, and I was starting to think they were the words he used when he wanted to placate me.

I nodded. "I know. Listen, I gotta go. My grandma is having a family dinner. Drive carefully, okay? I love you."

"Okay. Love ya, Jules."

I nodded and hung up. Not, 'I love you too, Julie,' but, 'Love ya.' I felt my world slipping away.

The next few weeks, I found it hard to concentrate. The call of social media and its representation of perfectly happy people, and the pictures I saw, were making me sick. Logically, I knew I was only seeing half-truths. But since I couldn't see the other half, it became my reality, to the point that I couldn't sleep or eat.

With each new town, and each win, new girls showed up at his side, holding on to his belt buckle, intertwining their arms, smiling up at him with infatuation.

I had to see him.

My savings account held enough to cover a plane ticket, with plenty left over for when I landed. I prayed my parents weren't monitoring my account.

Checking the rodeo competition schedule, I found one in Colorado. I thought to myself, 'I could make that one.'

I made my flight reservations. On the day I left, I wrote an apology note for my grandparents, telling them I would be back in a few days, and not to worry.

Samuel's grandson, Ismael, worked as a tour guide for our wine tasting tours. I enlisted his help in getting to the airport, under the pretense of picking up a package.

By the time they found my note and realized I'd left, my plane was already over the Atlantic Ocean.

Road weary and a little nervous, I tried to call Jason when I landed, but he didn't answer. Hailing a cab, I made my way to the rodeo grounds and bought a ticket. I knew I needed to sleep, since

I hadn't gotten much of it on the plane, but I needed to get to Jason first.

When he entered the arena, my heart stopped. I was so in love with him, I felt like I was whole again just watching him work. He was a cutter, and I'd never seen anyone cut the herd as elegantly as Jason.

His Wrangler jeans hugged his thighs, and I felt my body flush at the thought of making love with him our last night together. Cheering erupted from the crowd when Jason won the event, and I jumped from my seat, running down the breezeway to get to him.

Fans had crowded around the gate to get autographs of the bull riders and cutters, and I tried to wiggle my way to the front of the group. Jumping up and down, I saw him and screamed his name, waving frantically. "Jason! Jason!"

Inching my way along the steel barrier, I tugged on a burly guard's arm. "Can you let me back there? I'm his girlfriend."

His stare was cold and unwavering. "You and all the others."

"No really. We grew up together. I'm his girlfriend."

The guard ignored my pleas and continued monitoring the crowd.

I screamed for him again, my voice drowned among all the others.

Jason was signing autographs, and then I saw him lift a girl over the railing. He wandered off with her, arms over her shoulders, waving behind him at the remaining fans.

The world began to spin, and I wobbled in the crowd, unable to hold myself up. A faceless stranger asked me if I was okay and I stared at him with eyes full of shock. I couldn't even speak, and he pulled me out of the crowd so I could breath.

Sitting me on a bench, he asked, "Where are your friends? Do you need me to call someone for you?"

I sat stone still and just shook my head. My remaining clarity told me I needed to snap out of it, that I was probably frightening him.

"Uhm, I'm okay. I'm just dehydrated. Thank you for helping me. My friends are in the crowd. I'll text them."

"You sure?"

"Yes, thank you."

He stayed for just a moment, gauging if I really was okay, and then he wandered back to the crowd.

My chest started to shake and I willed back the tears. I had to find him. I couldn't leave like this.

Wandering the grounds in the dark, I made my way to the cattle and horse trailers. It was quiet, with only soft country music playing from one of the trailers in the distance.

The night had grown cold, and I wrapped my arms around me, weaving in and out of the trucks until I spotted his. His live-in trailer was still hitched to the back, and light shone through the cracks in the curtains.

Palms sweaty, heart racing, I reached for the door handle and gently turned it. Deep moans and high-pitched whimpers reached me before I actually saw them, but I couldn't stop myself from stepping into the trailer.

Jason had her bent over the small fold-out table, his jeans around his ankles, his ass flexing as he thrust in and out of her. I must have let out a scream, because Jason stopped his movements abruptly, accidently shoving the girl to the floor.

"Julie! What are you doing here?"

I was shaking uncontrollably. "What the fuck, Jason?"

He awkwardly buttoned up his jeans, and the girl scrambled to the bed, hiding behind the curtain.

"I don't know what to say."

He stood stoically in front of me, void of emotion, almost motionless, as if he'd turned to stone.

"Say, I'm dreaming, or I'm sorry, or something along the lines of...I don't know, Jason, something that eases the pain that is breaking my heart right now."

He said nothing, and I felt my pain rise up out of me like a monster, building like a boiling pot of water until it erupted. Pushing towards him, I lashed out at his chest, beating him, screaming at him. He just took it.

My sobs merged with my screams, and he finally gripped my arms and pulled me towards him. My pain was so deep my sobs turned silent as I grappled with this loss.

Numbly, I stepped away from him, the tears in my eyes threatening to spill over again.

Softly, he said, "Julie."

I put my hands out in front of me. "Don't."

"Julie, please."

"No."

I backed out of the trailer, and he followed me to the door. "Julie, stay."

In a daze, I just shook my head and kept walking. I walked until I found a cab in the parking lot and directed the driver to the airport.

My phone started blowing up. Jason, Evie, my mom. I turned it off.

Heartbroken and alone, I made my way to the ticket gate and tried to get on the next flight back to my grandparents. With hours to wait, I curled up on the floor in the boarding area and fell asleep.

A ticket agent gently woke me when it was time to board.

The flight attendants felt sorry for me and fed me snacks and sandwiches. By the time I landed and turned on my phone, I had thirty missed calls and texts.

I humbly called my grandmother, and was subsequently lambasted. It went on for what seemed like hours before I finally heard her say she was sending Ismael for me. Then she added that I owed him an apology, because his grandfather had boxed his ears for letting me get on the plane.

Protecting myself, and my heart, I put on a fake face, apologized daily, and kept my head down, closing off any possibility of feeling that kind of pain ever again.

I started a clandestine love affair with Ismael. We would sneak off into the fields and barn and anywhere else we wouldn't get caught.

He was lean and dark, and a very attentive lover, allowing me to make love without inhibitions. Our lovemaking was carnal and free, completely devoid of any long-term delusions.

My transformation into a cold, unemotional person happened so fast that I never really considered going back to the young, sweet, naïve girl I'd been when I arrived.

A year passed, then two, and finally three years passed before I finally started missing home. Three years of building the hard shell around my heart. Three years of learning absolutely everything about running and managing a vineyard. Three years without any contact with Jason. Three years until I received the text from Evie that I knew would change that.

He's coming home

Therefore, so was I.

12

Riley had been away now for almost three days, and I found myself thinking about his words to stop treating men like toys, or dogs. For a long time, it had been easier to keep men at a distance. The pain of young love had cut so deep, I hadn't had the strength to do it again.

But things were changing now. Maybe I should give Dax a chance. A real chance. Opening myself up to a real relationship was difficult for me, but maybe it was time. Maybe I needed to try opening my heart and letting Dax in.

While I drifted back and forth in the swing, I sent Dax a text, letting him know I was looking forward to the gala. He would not be coming back to the island for a few weeks, and I wanted him to know I was thinking of him.

He responded right away. *I've thought of nothing else*

His response made me flush, and I smiled to myself, giggling like a schoolgirl. See, not so hard.

A few seconds later I received another text.

I'll be back tomorrow, pick me up at the dock

Riley.

My mood deflated, and I texted back. *I'm sorry, I am currently out of the country with limited cell service. I'll respond in a few days.*

I laughed to myself. I could almost feel him stewing, and that made me laugh out loud.

A hot flash of unwanted lust shot through me at his next words. *You should be spanked*

I decided to tease him back, *I might enjoy that*

9AM Julie…we have lumber trucks coming tomorrow

His curt response had me smiling, and I texted back, *Yes Sir*

I knew he wouldn't respond to that, so I uncurled my legs and swaggered back to the office, practically skipping with mirth.

The keys to his truck were hanging inside the door, where I'd left them the day before. Swinging them around on my finger, I went back out to his truck and headed down to Nick's law office to pick up a desk he said I could have for the home office.

Slowing the truck to almost a coasting speed, I waved at the tourists in the village as I passed through. It was busy with summer people now, milling around the bakery and local shops. They loved admiring the hand-blown glass in the art studio, and commenting on how lovely it would look in their beach themed bathroom.

The law office was on the other side of the quaint town, and I parked in front of the antique building.

A bell rang above the door as I entered the office, announcing my arrival. Suzi stepped out from the back kitchen, her pace slowed with age, but her smile still bright. She had a bowl of fruit salad in her hand. "Hello, darlin', what brings you here?"

Her eager expression caught me off guard, and I blinked my eyes a few times before responding pleasantly. "Hi, Suzi. Nick said I could have an old desk he had in the storeroom. We're using card tables right now, and it's just not working for us. Riley has piles of invoices and catalogs in stacks on the floor. I wanted to try and get it organized before tomorrow."

"Oh, that's great! I was going to take it home and refinish it, but I'm glad it will have a good home." She put her bowl down on her desk and said, "Let me see if I can get Nick and Ethan to help you."

I watched as she picked up the phone to call Nick, and I heard her say, "Okay, I'll let her know."

To my right was the conference room where we had signed all the contracts just a few short weeks ago. I noticed through the glass that it was clean and tidy, the leather chairs all tucked in tightly and evenly. Outside the window, the water sparkled in the summer sun, and the boats bobbed elegantly in the bay.

I heard Suzi clear her throat, and I turned to see her sitting back behind her desk, eating her fruit. "The two o' them'll be down in a few minutes to help you. Do you need anything while you wait?"

"No, I'm good. I think I'll drive the truck around back so we don't have as far to carry it."

I turned to head back out the front door and her tentative voice stopped me, forcing me to face her. "Julie."

"Yes?"

Her face softened, and she said with sincerity, "I'm real proud of you, girl. You've been alone for a long time, battling the town gossips, keeping that wall up. But you've come through, and I'm excited to see this beautiful resort you're going to build. It's going to be something special for sure."

Suzi was all of five feet tall, but her love for Evie, and Shaye, and all her family, made her seem larger than life. I'd always wondered what it would feel like to be on the receiving end of all that love, and now I knew. For fear of choking up, I simply gave her a small smile, and a nod, and went out the front door.

It wasn't until I was in the truck that I let the tears fall. The shell I'd built up was cracking more and more every day. It hurt, but I was feeling like I could finally breathe again.

I turned to the back seat to see if Riley had any Kleenex in the truck. When I turned around, Nick was standing in the doorway of the building. With his arm raised, he pointed at his wrist. I heard him shout, "Don't have all day, Julie."

I was so tempted to flip him off. Instead, I started the truck and backed up as Nick went back into the building.

When I met him around back, the desk had been broken down into three pieces. I stepped aside as Nick and Ethan carried them out the back door and loaded them into Riley's truck.

Ethan asked, "Do you need help unloading it?"

"That would be great! Thank you!"

We agreed that they would both come up in about twenty minutes, and I headed back through the village towards the Vineyard.

The sun was setting as I sat on the front porch of the house, now office, and waited for Nick and Ethan to come help me. Arriving in a cloud of dust, they were both still in their suits, and anxious to get this over with and get home to Evie and Shaye.

When they carried the heavy pieces into the living room, I had them set it up under the large whiteboard. Taking off their suit jackets and rolling up their sleeves, they looked a little more human, and I appreciated their manly efforts. After they were finished, Nick ran back out to his truck and came back in with a small filing cabinet. "Thought you might need this as well."

Just when I thought Nick wasn't capable of being nice to me, he went and did something kind. "Thank you, Nick. That was thoughtful of you."

He shrugged and looked around as if he was uncomfortable.

"Do you guys want a beer or something?"

Ethan leaned in to kiss me on the cheek before he left. "I can't Julie, but thanks for the offer. You up for dinner at the house soon?"

"Yeah, that sounds great. I'll call Evie."

I followed him out and watched as he jogged down the steps, his muscular frame moving elegantly. He honked his horn as he drove away. I gave a little wave, not really knowing if he saw me or not.

When I went back inside, Nick was standing expectantly in the middle of the room. I raised my eyebrows and asked again if he wanted a beer. He didn't immediately respond, and the silence between us stretched longer than what I was comfortable with.

To break the silence, and hopefully draw some semblance of a conversation out of him, I said, "I saw Shaye the other day. She was taking flying lessons. She looked really happy."

"Uh-huh. Yep."

I crossed my arms protectively around me. "Do you want to talk about something, Nick?"

His eyes bore into mine, making sure I was paying attention. "I have been…I have been unkind to you, Julie. And I'm sorry."

His apology was the last thing I expected him to say, and it caught me off guard. My arms fell slowly to my side. I was speechless as he continued, "You were so much younger than me, growing up. I didn't really pay much attention to you and Jason. When he died, it was my pain I wallowed in, and it was hard to see beyond that."

He cleared his throat and shifted uncomfortably. "When we…" He took a deep breath. "When we got together, I never considered that I was doing more damage than good."

"Why are you telling me this?"

"Shaye and Evie love you. I know you've trusted me and Ethan over the past year to help you, and we may not have given you the same respect and trust."

I felt a sting in my eyes, and I willed it away.

"I wanted to say I was sorry, and that I think what you're doing is pretty remarkable. You should be proud of yourself."

"Thank you, Nick. That means a lot to me."

He made his way across the room and opened the front door to leave. With his hand resting on the doorknob, he nodded sternly at me. "Well, you've earned it."

As he stepped outside, I tried to add some levity to our conversation and asked, "Don't you want to tell me not to fuck it up again?"

With a boisterous laugh, he responded, "I do, actually."

My grin spread across my face. "Don't worry. I'm on my best behavior."

Before he stepped into his truck, he turned serious. "You're alright, Julie. Don't let anyone make you feel otherwise. Even me."

I shut the front door with a smile on my face. This day had been full of surprises, and now I wanted to get the desk ready.

It was a beautiful, double-sided executive desk in a deep walnut finish, with drawers on both sides.

Under the kitchen sink, I found wood polish and a rag. I spent the next hour polishing the desk, making sure I reached every crease of the crown molding trim around the drawers.

When I was finished, I took two of the folding chairs and put them on either side, tucking them in neatly. They would have to do for now.

Tomorrow, when the polish was dry, I would put the laptops and various other office supplies that were littered around the main living area, into tidy, easy to find places.

In the filing cabinet, I slid the invoices in colored folders, labeled them by contractor, and placed all of the fixture catalogs in the bottom drawer.

When I was satisfied I'd done all I could do to make the living room look more like an office, I turned off the lights and drove Riley's truck back to the tasting room and my studio apartment.

Today had turned into one of the best days I could remember in a long time.

I woke the next morning and bounded out of bed. Knowing the lumber was going to arrive today had me practically skipping out the front door to go get Riley.

Because I was feeling exceptionally happy, I stopped at the bakery to pick up some treats. Sadly, I was kind of getting used to driving his shiny, although mostly dirty, dually truck. It was going to be hard to give it back.

The width of the truck wouldn't allow me to park in the packed lot in front of the bakery, so I pulled into the grass lot next to the building and left it there while I walked over.

Visitors dressed in their khaki shorts, water sandals, and expensive Eddie Bauer vests filled the small bakery. I had to wiggle my way to the front to get Evie's attention.

She finally saw me and raised her chin in acknowledgement. I made a face that said, 'Get me out of here quickly.'

She jerked her chin towards the back, and I stepped behind the counter. We went around behind the loaded bread racks where she kept extra baked goods. It smelled so good in here, I almost wanted to lick the pans, just to taste the leftover sugar.

She pulled off her bandana and wiped flour from her face. "Holy cow! I guess summer is here."

I let out a quick chuckle. "This always was your craziest time of year."

"What are you doing here?"

I grabbed a paper bag from her shelf and started packing it with ham and cheese croissants, chocolate chip cookies and a couple of slices of strawberry banana bread. "I have to pick Riley up at the Islander dock. He went to Friday Harbor this week and I borrowed his truck."

"Did you want some treats to take to him?"

Her sardonic tone did not escape me. "No."

It was her turn to laugh at me. "Ethan said we should do a dinner soon."

"Yeah, he mentioned that last night. I was thinking we should invite Dax."

Evie's silence forced me to look at her. I saw affection, and concern, in her eyes.

When I made eye contact with her, she asked, "Do you like him?"

I shrugged. "I do. I think maybe it's time that I take someone seriously, and he seems nice."

She raised her eyebrows. "Nice?"

"Yeah, c'mon, I need nice."

"Okay." She drawled, indicating she didn't quite believe me.

"And he's sexy."

"And he's city," she reminded me.

"And he can kiss."

"You've kissed him?"

"C'mon, Evie, I like him."

We stared at each other in silence.

"I need to get back to work."

"Are you angry with me?"

She continued putting her bandana back on her head to cover all of her thick, dark hair.

"Of course not. I just…I just don't want you hurt."

"Again?"

"Again."

I put the bag down on her cutting board and hugged her. "I like him. I won't get hurt."

"Fair enough." We both went back out to the front – her to work, me to leave.

I made one last stop at the coffee shop across the street to get two large coffees. The quirky beatnik shop was less crowded than the bakery. I was grateful for the soothing environment and the musty, floral scent of the burning incense.

Reaching the counter, I ordered my regular mocha and a black coffee for Riley.

The barista behind the counter said, "He takes it with cream."

"Who does?"

"Riley does. Riley takes it with cream. That's his truck, right?" The earthy, supermodel look-alike snapped at me, and I felt my back tense.

Nope. Not going to respond. I'm going to be nice. Well, as nice as I can be.

I smiled serenely at her and dramatically sighed. "It is. I thought I would let him sleep in today. He's been working so hard. And thank you so much for adding the cream for him. I was going to do it when I got home, but you might as well, since I'm here."

Her look turned dark, and I just kept the sweet smile on my face. Inside, though, I was wincing. When would I learn?

Thanking her politely, I left the coffee shop, my good mood slightly marred. I hated being provoked.

The bag of treats sat next to me on the seat, and I put the coffees in the cup holders. Then I drove the short distance to the resort to get Riley.

His boat wasn't in the slip he'd left from, so I sat on a nearby bench and sipped my coffee. Periodically, I reached absentmindedly into the bag and broke off bits of the bread, shoving it in my mouth.

The low frequency sound of an outboard motor caught my attention, and I turned to see Riley's boat coming around the side of the dock. He was standing at the center console, his broad frame at ease behind the wheel, slowly maneuvering the boat into place.

On the bow of the boat was a young woman wearing a heavy knit sweater and a baseball cap. Her curly, tawny, gold-blond hair was pulled through the back of the cap, and she was covered by a down blanket.

Sunglasses masked her eyes so I couldn't make out the color, but the drawn look on her mouth told me she wasn't happy.

When Riley saw me, his face lit up. As hard as I tried not to, I smiled right back.

As the boat lined up with the dock, the buoys bounced off the planks, and he instructed the sour faced girl to jump out and grab the tie lines.

Shouting to me he said, "Juliette, hold the railings until she gets it tied up."

Quickly, I put the coffee down and did as he asked. I still didn't know who she was, but I was starting to think it might be his sister.

When the boat was secure, he came directly to me. He smelled like salt water, and wind, and I realized I'd missed him.

"Is that for me?" His hands were on his hips as he nodded at the coffee.

I handed him the other cup. "Oh, yes. Your girlfriend added cream for you."

"You became my girlfriend while I was away?"

"No, jackass, the barista."

"Oh, right, Heather."

"Her name is Heather? Figures."

His boisterous laugh reverberated and he drank from his cup. "This is good, thank you."

I held up the bag of baked goods. "I brought you treats, too, although I don't know now if you deserve them."

"There are only two reasons you would do that. You either crashed my truck, or you're starting to like me."

"I didn't crash your truck."

His look turned a little wicked, and his voice lowered as he whispered, "Was it the spanking? Is that what turned you?"

Grumpy-girl interrupted us. "Riley, I'm hungry. Can we please go eat?"

"Julie, this is my sister, Maggie. Maggie, this is Julie, my boss."

Eek, was this the sister I reminded him of? She looked like a petulant girl, but I knew she was in her mid-twenties. "Hi, Maggie, nice to meet you."

"Oh, hi. I'm sorry I'm being rude. My brother kidnapped me and I'm kind of hungry. It's nice to meet you, too."

"I brought ham and cheese croissants, if you'd like one."

She glanced at Riley. "May I, jailor?"

Riley explained. "She's mad because I thought she needed more experience running a job. She's going to work with me over the next week or so, if that's okay."

"Oh, sure. Uhm, is she staying with you?"

Through a mouthful of croissant, she said, "I'm right here."

I snapped my head back and blinked my eyes a couple of times in shock. I had no response for her.

"Knock it off, Maggie. Just because you're pissed at me, and yourself, you don't need to take it out on Julie."

She had the decency to look embarrassed, and apologized to me. "I'm sorry. I screwed up the job in Friday Harbor, and Riley's kind of pissed at me."

"Apology accepted."

"Maggie will sleep on my old air mattress. I was thinking she could use the front bedroom, if that's okay with you."

"Sure, fine."

I don't know why I felt deflated, but I did.

He saw the blankness in my eyes, and told Maggie to go up to the resort and wait for us by his truck.

Reaching for my hand, he tried to catch my eye. His hand was warm and soothing. I felt a zing all the way to my chest. "Hey, are you sure it's okay? I didn't really think about it until we were here. I don't want you to feel put out."

My fingers were loosely wrapped in his. "No really, it's fine. It is the office, so it's fine."

"Oh, Juliette, you did miss me." He teased as he pulled me along the dock up to the resort.

"Not really. But you should know, I might have given *Heather* the impression we were sleeping together."

His chest rumbled with laughter. "Thank God! She's a persistent one. Maybe now she'll leave me alone."

"Poor sexy, manly Riley, with all the girl troubles." My sing-song voice had him laughing again.

"Between you, Maggie, *and* Heather, I might not survive the summer."

I started skipping backwards up the dock, my light-hearted mood having returned. "I have a present for you back at the office."

"Does it involve you, naked?"

I couldn't resist. "No, but it involves a hard surface."

He stumbled for a minute, and his mouth dropped open, then shut.

"Boys. You're all the same."

13

All opportunities for peace went out the window the moment we returned to the vineyard.

If I thought the pouring of concrete was a monumental back-breaking task, I was sorely incorrect.

Flatbed semi-trucks loaded with lumber and steel beams were lined up alongside the road to the entrance of the winery. Goosebumps rose on my arms, a shiver of anticipation boiling in my chest.

As soon as Riley parked his truck in front of the office, he shifted from friendly banter to business mode. He jumped out of the cab, his long stride taking him to the first of the trucks waiting for direction.

He said over his shoulder, "Maggie, let's go."

She jumped obediently from the back of the cab to follow him.

Not wanting to be left behind, I ran swiftly to the office. Clumsily, I put on my construction boots, bouncing on each foot as I pulled them on. As I ran back out the door, I grabbed three hard hats and jogged to catch up with them.

Riley was all business, easily directing the trucks and getting his crew to work with the drivers to efficiently unload. I stood behind Riley and Maggie, watching with fascination as Maggie paid rapt attention to her brother. He seemed to get larger as I watched him, commanding respect and admiration from his team.

When I extended the hard hat to Maggie, she turned and whispered, "Thank you." A genuine smile crossed her face and her observant eyes reminded me of Riley, always taking in everything without being intrusive.

A few hours into the off-loading process, Riley found me and asked if I could help Maggie get set up in the front bedroom.

"Sure. Do you know where she is?"

We both scanned the horizon and saw her sitting on the swing Riley had built.

"I spy with my little eye."

"Maggie." I responded, and chuckled. "I'll go get her."

'Thank you. I'll be out here the rest of the day checking the quality of the lumber, and then I need to go over the schedule with the crew after dinner. Do you want to stay?"

"For dinner?"

"For both. Dinner and the meeting?"

I was momentarily taken aback by his offer of inclusion. Standing a little taller, my back a little straighter, I smiled. "I would, thank you."

Logically, I knew I could insert myself anywhere I wanted to, but his invitation warmed me.

He started off, saying over his shoulder, "Okay. I'll see you back at the office."

"Should I start dinner?" I shouted after him.

"Make Maggie cook."

I mumbled to myself, since he was already trekking back to the building site, "Oh, that'll go over well."

Quietly, I approached Maggie, and asked if I could join her.

"Oh, sure. It's your bench."

She scooted over a bit, and I joined her on the swing.

"It's so beautiful here." Her voice was a quiet interruption to the moment of easy peace we were having.

"It is, isn't it? I love this swing. Riley put it up after my friend Evie's wedding. I love being able to look out at the vineyards and the water. It's peaceful. It's become my place."

"I can see that."

We swung back and forth, each absorbed in our own thoughts.

I felt her eyes on me, and I turned towards her. "You're staring."

"Just trying to see what Riley sees."

I chuckled. "What do you mean by that?"

"He told me all about you in Friday Harbor. How beautiful your vision is, how strong you are, mentally. Not physically, because you're obviously a tiny thing."

I blinked my eyes and laughed at her. "You certainly aren't shy, are you?"

"Not really." She turned to stare back at the vineyards. "I have adored my brother forever. He was always my idol. I followed him and my dad around to every building site. Our older sister is beautiful and elegant, but all I wanted to do was build something. This project that Riley gave me? I screwed it up."

She lowered her head and I reached out to touch her arm. "You don't have to tell me if you don't want to."

"It's not really a secret, and Riley will send me back soon, but for now, he's making me pay."

"Pay how?"

"He put my foreman in charge. Pulled me right off the site in front of everyone." A tear dropped into her lap.

"I can't pretend to know anything about construction projects, I rely on Riley for that, but I can't imagine anything could be that bad."

Her sardonic laugh caught me off guard. "Oh boy!" She wiped a finger under her eye, swiping away a tear. "Well, the client wanted to change the scope of the project. They wanted to build out the master bath and make a private outdoor patio and shower. You know? Something all 'at one with the forest,' is what they said. When they came to look at the plans with the architect, I'd been using the wrong set of blueprints. I wasn't even building the right house. What I mean is that the plans were not the originals, the ones that had been filed with the county."

I covered my mouth in shock, and tried not to laugh. "Maggie! Oh! He must be furious."

"He is…disappointed. My dad is furious. But Riley? I think he's just sad. He trusted me. At first, he was coming to help me with the client, to talk about the changes. When he arrived and we looked at the plans, he scolded me up and down, reminding me how much paperwork would need to be done to get the new permits. Of course, the county office will move mountains for Riley."

I rubbed her back and whispered, "I'm so sorry."

"Don't get me wrong, I admire him just as much as everyone else. I think I'm just embarrassed. And he put my foreman in charge, which is a double hit."

We sat like that a while longer before I poked her gently and told her we were going to make dinner together.

"Riley's idea?"

"Actually, he said you were to make it."

"I thought he was trying to punish me. I guess he's trying to punish you." She laughed a bold laugh that made me smile, and I looped my arm through hers as we walked back to the office.

Our conversation came easily now, and I realized she *was* a lot like me. Fiercely independent, a little rough around the edges, but I could also tell she had a good heart, and loved her brother dearly.

That last thought caused me to catch my breath, and I shoved it back down as quickly as I thought it. As I inspected the contents of the refrigerator, Maggie set up the mattress and unpacked her clothes from her bag, stacking them on the floor instead of using the closet.

It appeared that Riley was an extremely clean eater. Fresh fruit, vegetables, and plain yogurt filled the shelves. I decided on asparagus as a side dish.

Pork chops had been left thawing, and I pulled those out to cook, scanning the pantry for applesauce.

Riley hadn't been specific about what time he would be back, so I simply sat on the couch with a sparkling water, waiting, and watching Maggie get settled.

"How long are you going to stay?" I asked her nonchalantly as she went back and forth from her 'room' to the bathroom.

"Probably a week or so. Or, until Riley lets me go back. I really wanted to be here for the framing, and that usually goes pretty fast. All the interior stuff, like the drywall and fixtures, I don't really want to wait around for."

She passed by me, into the kitchen, and I saw her put her head down into the refrigerator. "Do you know if Riley has any beer?"

Before I could answer, she said, "Never mind. I found it."

She popped the cap and took a seat at the other end of the couch from me, curling her legs up underneath her.

I was amused by her. I waited until I sensed I had her full attention and that she was fully relaxed before I asked her what she had planned next.

"Grovel for forgiveness. Then Riley might give me a treehouse to build."

"I have a dollhouse that needs restoring."

"Har-har." She laughed and took a drink of her beer.

"I picked out all the lighting fixtures and bathroom hardware, but there's a chandelier I really wanted that might be on backorder."

"For the dollhouse?"

It was my turn to laugh. "For the resort."

She took another drink of her beer. "He'll get it for you. He always pulls through."

My phone pinged with a text. *The guys are on their way. There's a full case of beer on the back porch in the second fridge.*

Second fridge?

Beer, Julie. See you in a bit.

"Apparently, we have been relegated to servant girls." I stood from the couch. "C'mon, help me with some snacks for the crew."

Maggie rolled her eyes and stood to help me. "I wonder who I can sleep with on his crew to get back at him."

I paused, and looked at her in shock.

"I'm just kidding."

Telling her how much she reminded me of me was not the impression I wanted to give her. It was bizarre being on the receiving end of that kind of humor, and I started to see what my friends saw in me. I didn't like it.

I simply nodded. "Right."

By the time we had the chips and salsa and chilled beer out, most of the six-man crew had filled the living room, straddling the folding chairs and reclining on the sofa.

Riley came in last and took a seat at the desk I'd set up for him. I couldn't take my eyes off of him. His work jeans hugged his thighs and ass, and I was finally appreciating how built he was. It was becoming an annoyance.

He started talking to the men, and I heard nothing. He stood and pointed at the project plan and I heard nothing. All I could think about was his strong hand gripping my thigh under my dress at the wedding, and how I wanted him to lay me down on the desktop and put his mouth on me.

"Julie?"

I was brought from my daydreaming by Riley's voice. "I'm sorry, what?"

He smirked at me, his eyes sparkling mischievously. "Is there anything you wanted to add?"

Crap! Riley had invited me to the crew meeting and I hadn't even been paying attention.

"I'll just say that I'm really excited about the progress you guys have made, and if you ever need anything, please let me know."

The crew all nodded and thanked me for the beer. Riley chuckled and shook his head at me.

By the time they all left, the three of us were ready to eat. I set the folding table, using the silverware I'd brought over from the tasting room.

"Where'd you go tonight, Juliette?" Riley was leaning against the door jamb to the kitchen, holding a beer.

"What do you mean?"

He laughed, "You looked like you got caught with your hand in the cookie jar."

"I was timing dinner. I didn't want it to burn."

He turned back to the kitchen to plate up his dinner, saying, "That was kind of awkward. Did you not want to say anything?"

Maggie came out of the bathroom and pushed Riley out of the way, cutting in front of him to take the best pork chop. "She was probably daydreaming about one of your guys. They are all smokin' hot, Riley; which one can I have?"

I sighed with gratitude, silently thanking her for taking the focus off of me.

"Maggie, stay away from them. This is Julie's project, and I don't need you messing it up for her. I do not need a distracted crew."

"Fine. I will be the dutiful side-kick. I won't wear makeup and I'll wear the same lumberjack flannel everyday so it gets stinky and nasty."

I thought Riley would laugh. Instead he said, "Thank you."

After dinner, the three of us sat on the front porch in the dark, staring out at the building site and the vineyards. Riley sat on the railing, while Maggie and I sat on the porch swing, sipping on our beer.

The night was quiet and clear, the cool summer breeze brushing over our arms.

I pushed us back and forth with my toes, lulling myself into a peaceful state. It was comforting to sit here with the two of them, different from Evie and Shaye. I felt content, like I wasn't being sucked into my past.

Maggie interrupted my musings. "Can I just stay here and work on this project?"

"No," was all he said.

My phone buzzed, lighting up the darkness.

"It's Dax," I said enthusiastically.

Riley raised his beer to me. "You should get that."

I stood and answered, opening the screen door and stepping inside to talk.

"Hello!" I greeted him cheerily.

"Hey, how's your day?" He sounded so cheerful.

"It is *so* good." I proceeded to tell him about everything that had happened; the lumber trucks arriving, everything I could remember about the meeting with the crew, and how excited I was about the accelerated schedule. "I think we might actually meet our October opening date."

He chuckled with amusement. "That all sounds great, Julie, but I really just wanted to call and talk to you."

His tone warmed me and I relaxed a little, knowing it wasn't just a business call.

"Oh, I'm really good. I'm really happy, and I'm excited to see you in a few weeks." The last part was a reach, and I wasn't sure I should have said it. I was rewarded with agreement.

"Me too. I was going to try and come up before then so we could spend some more time together. Unfortunately, I have another project that is not progressing as well as yours, and I need to re-evaluate my commitment."

"Yikes! That doesn't sound good." I cringed.

"No, it's not. But I don't want to bore you with the details."

I pretended to snore.

I heard him laugh robustly on the other end of the phone. "Exactly."

We talked for a few more minutes about the schedule. It was hard not to talk about work, since we didn't know enough about each other to talk about much else. He ended the call with a promise to call again in a few days.

"Do you want a report from me?" I asked him hesitantly.

"No, Julie, I get that from Riley. I just want to get to know you."

I felt my insides flutter. I smiled, whispering coyly into the phone, "Me too."

"I'll talk to you soon."

We said goodnight, and I went back out to the front porch, smiling what I am sure was *way* too big a grin.

Maggie was still sitting on the swing, although she wasn't pumping it back and forth anymore. "Please do not tell me that was Dax Bentley."

My smile dropped. Her tone was laced with anger. "Uhm, yes?"

"Is he your boyfriend?"

Her hostility was confusing me. "No, he's my investor."

She stood abruptly from the bench. Her eyes shot daggers at Riley. "Seriously, Riley?"

"It has nothing to do with anything, Maggie. It's just a job."

I snapped my head back. "What do you mean, 'just a job'?"

Riley sighed, "I'm sorry, I didn't mean it like that."

I crossed my arms. "How did you mean it?"

"Dax and I have known each other for a long time. He had a lot to say on a project, a big project, and recommended that it not be awarded to me. It was a long time ago."

Maggie scoffed. "Really, that's what you're going with?"

He cautioned her, "Maggie."

Now I was worried. "Is he shady?"

Riley was now standing. "No. He's a brilliant businessman and only invests in projects he believes in. You have nothing to worry about Julie."

His tone was calm and reassuring.

Maggie just mumbled, "Whatever, I'm going to bed."

The screen door slammed behind her, bouncing a few times before settling against the frame. Riley settled himself in the swing, letting out a breath as if he was carrying the weight of the world.

Settling in next to him, I said softly, "Riley."

He rolled his head to me, his eyes almost sad.

I scooted closer. "Riley, should I be worried?"

Reaching out, he patted my knee. "No. Dax is a good guy. You have nothing to worry about."

I wanted to ask why Maggie was so upset, but I had a feeling he wouldn't tell me. He was rubbing his hand back and forth on my leg, almost absentmindedly. When I looked down at it, he paused, and then slowly pulled it back.

I stood slowly, and cleared my throat. "I'll go clean up the dishes."

"Leave 'em. I'll take care of them."

The silence that was stretching between us was uncomfortable, forcing me to stay in place, hoping for something more from him.

His voice was strained and flat, almost a whisper, "Do you want me to drive you home?"

An invisible wall had been erected between us. He was keeping something from me. I wanted to stomp my foot and demand that he tell me what it was, but his face was passive and I knew he wouldn't.

I set my beer on the railing, crossed my arms in front of me, and went down the steps.

"I can walk."

His goodnight was barely heard, as I walked into the darkness, back to my apartment.

14

FALLING INTO A routine over the next week, the three of us established a pattern of work that was comfortable and easy. Maggie's bad mood over Dax seemed to disappear, and her snarky, sarcastic personality was back in full force.

Every morning I would walk up to the home office and have breakfast with them. A pot of coffee was always on, compliments of Riley, since Maggie was slow to wake.

We would talk about the construction plans for the day, and then we would go our separate ways: me to do winery business, and Riley and Maggie to work on the resort.

In the afternoon, I would meet them back at the office for dinner. Each of us took turns cooking.

Maggie teased us one night, asking if we were going to keep up the communal living when she left. The question caught both me and Riley off guard.

I responded, covering my unease. "I'll invite the crew for dinner so I don't have to endure Mr. Grump's criticism."

Both Maggie and I laughed like sisters. For a moment, I thought I saw a flash of hurt in Riley's eyes, but I put that right out of my mind and went back to mixing the stir-fry.

The framing of the resort seemed to go up in hyper-speed. One day it was just a foundation, and seven days later, it looked like a resort – from the outside anyway. Inside it was still two-by-fours and open doorways to guest room decks.

On the day that all the plumbing lines, pipes and wires, and ductwork for the HVAC system arrived, Riley came down to the tasting room and handed me an updated schedule for inspections.

Taking a seat at the bar, he rested easily, almost too big for the bar stool. Leaning forward, arms crossed on the bar, he waited for me to acknowledge him.

I'd been counting bottles behind the bar, and I intentionally took my time marking the inventory sheet. When I was finished, I turned and smiled at him, put my clipboard down, and said in surprise, "Hello, I didn't see you come in."

Teasing me, he said, "You're a pain in the ass, Julie."

"Ah, I thought we'd grown so close."

He handed a slip of paper to me. I took it from him, but not before I saw the smile on his face.

Reading the schedule, I looked up at him in surprise.

"This has accelerated quite a bit!"

"It's good news, Julie. The county had some other projects halted, so they were able to free up one of their inspectors. The drywall will arrive as soon as the next inspection is complete."

I put my hand to my chest and let out a deep breath. "This is so fast. I can't believe it."

"We'll need to finish your cabinet and bathroom vanity orders.

I have a whole list of decorative accessories, countertops, bedding, all kinds of things we need to finalize. We'll want to have all the flooring and guest rooms almost completely finished before the final inspection."

His eyes were dancing with excitement. "It's pretty real, Juliette. It's pretty real."

A flash of acceptance, and a feeling of togetherness passed between us.

Like a puppet I repeated it back to him, almost in a whisper. "It's pretty real."

He tapped his palm twice on the bar as he stood to leave. "Are you joining me and Maggie for dinner tonight?"

"I can't tonight. Evie and Shaye are coming over for girls' night. You know, wine, food, slutty girl talk?"

He laughed in understanding, while simultaneously communicating that he didn't really want to hear any details.

I almost asked him if he wanted to send Maggie down, but he spoke before I had the chance. I realized I was grateful I hadn't invited her. Shaye and Evie and I hadn't seen much of each other in a while, and I missed them.

"I'm taking Maggie back to Friday Harbor tomorrow. Do you want to go with me?"

His invitation surprised and delighted me. "On your boat?"

He shrugged. "It's faster."

"Okay. I could use a day off."

His hand on the door handle, he turned to me and said, "At 6:00 a.m. we'll be here to get you."

"At 6:00 a.m.?" I exclaimed. "Will I never sleep again?"

"Maggie needs to go back to work, and I want to put the crab pots out." He stepped outside and said, as he shut the door, "I'll see you in the morning."

I groaned and heard him laugh as the door clicked shut behind him. I finished with my work, and then cleaned up the tasting room, making it cozy for Evie and Shaye.

The stone fireplace made the coziest corner, so I situated three oversized, high-back chairs in a half moon shape in front of it. A wrought-iron, glass-top table was set evenly spaced between the three chairs.

I placed battery operated candles on the bar and mantle, and dimmed the lights before going up to my apartment to change.

When I came back down, both Shaye and Evie were making themselves comfortable. Evie was behind the bar opening the wine, and Shaye was just coming out of the kitchen with an antipasto platter.

"Hey! There you are! We didn't think you would mind if we got snacks out." Shaye said energetically as she came through the swinging door.

"Of course not." I turned to Evie. "Is that the Chardonnay I put in the cooler for tonight?"

"I think so." She turned the label towards her. "Yes. Yes, this is Chardonnay."

I shook my head in mock exasperation and laughed. Evie was so undiscerning when it came to wine.

"I'm so glad you guys came over tonight. I feel like I haven't had a second to breathe these past few months." I took a seat in the middle chair and reached for a slice of salami and a cracker.

Balancing the three wine glasses, Evie set them on the table and went back to the bar to get the bottle.

"I've heard so many great things in town about the progress. I'm just sorry I couldn't get here when it was still light out so you could show us around." Evie curled herself up in the chair to my right.

"It's probably best you waited a few more weeks. It's dirty, and it's hard to visualize it right now if you don't know what you're looking for."

Shaye took her wine glass and sat down to my left. I watched as she sipped it slowly, and I joked, "Pregnant again?"

"Ha! No. I'm flying again tomorrow and I don't want to be too cloudy."

"I still can't believe you're going to be a pilot. It's just *so far* from the girl we met waiting tables."

"A lot is *so far* from the girl I was when I was waiting tables."

Evie was always watching us together. I often wondered if she was waiting for the other shoe to drop between me and Shaye. She reached out and touched my arm. "You doing okay?"

"Yeah, I'm actually doing really well."

Sitting up on the edge of her seat, Shaye asked, "What's wrong?"

"It's nothing." I rushed out my words. "A few months before Evie's wedding I found a box of Jason's clothes. I had kind of a meltdown."

"I'm so sorry, Julie."

"I'm fine. It's strange. The more progress I make on the resort, the less pain I feel. It's like…It's like everything Jason and I had talked about was put on hold and my dreams died with him. I know that's hard to understand, given that I was so angry with him. But it feels like I'm finally starting to live again and be who I was. At the same time, though, I feel like I'm cheating on him." I laughed sardonically.

Shaye asked, "With Dax?"

"Not really Dax, but living the dream without him. Which is even more bizarre, since he was the one that cheated."

"You know, Julie, you've never told me what happened."

Evie sat silent, knowing it was my story to tell.

"Another time. I don't think I have the energy tonight." The truth was, I didn't want Shaye to know the truth. Not yet anyway. I could live with what Jason had done to me, but not what I'd done to him, and to Nick and Shaye.

The rest of the night unfolded the way I'd wanted it too: laughter, and a great deal of fun. We laughed about all the good times we'd had that first summer together – fourth of July; camping with Nick's 'girlfriend' Jackie, who had dissolved into a drunk mess; campfires on the beach; and all the late nights at the local bar.

When Evie was sufficiently buzzed and Shaye started to nod off in her chair, I ushered them both out and told them I would see them soon. The gala was in just a few weeks, and I was really looking forward to a fancy night off this island, in the city.

After their tail-lights disappeared into the darkness, I looked up at the stars and inhaled the sharp, clean, cold air. There wasn't a moon out tonight, and all the stars seemed to shine brighter in the cloudless sky. There were so many stars.

Out of the corner of my eye, I saw a flash of light up at the resort. At first, I thought I imagined it, and then I saw it again, flashing around in the framed structure.

Jumping into the golf cart, I drove to the building site, parked in what had become the front circular drive, and went through the open doorway to the main lobby area. The lights were flashing around to the right, where the guest rooms were located.

I shouted, "Hello?"

"Julie?" Riley's voice echoed in the frame of the resort.

"Riley, what are you doing up here?"

"Stay where you are. I'll come to you."

The flashlight shone on the ground as he approached me. "What are *you* doing up here?"

I crossed my arms, realizing it had become a bit chilly. "I saw a light and thought someone was trespassing."

In the shadows, I saw him scowling at me. "And you came up here anyway?"

My temper flared. "I'm sure no one would hurt me."

I heard him sigh.

"And what are you doing up here?"

"Fire watch. Now that we're starting to do hot work, one of the crew needs to check it every night. We don't want your building going up in smoke before it gets finished."

I wasn't even going to pretend I knew what he was talking about. "Well, thank you."

He gently took my elbow and guided me through the building, down the circular framed steps, to the restaurant space down below. "Come with me."

Tentatively, I walked alongside him towards the wall where the floor-to-ceiling windows would look out to the vineyard and ceremony site. It was open now, until the glass was placed. We sat down against the framing to stare out at the fields; the lights from the tasting room, and my apartment were visible in the night.

"It's so beautiful up here," I said, as I absorbed the view. I sat down, my back against the frame of the building.

Riley's voice was soft and deep when he responded. "You picked the perfect location."

I watched as he sat down across from me. Then I giggled. I'd had just enough to drink that I felt flirty and bold, but not drunk. I said, "We should make out."

He choked, "What?

"You should kiss me again," I heard myself purring.

"Are you drunk?"

"No." I laughed.

"Because you shouldn't be on a construction site when you've been drinking."

I mock-scowled at him. "Oh, so serious."

His response was a chuckle. I came to my knees and crawled towards him. "C'mon.... Then I can say I made out with a stud in the studs."

"I don't think Dax would appreciate that very much."

His response froze me in place. I shifted back to the beam. "Yeah, since he doesn't like you."

He shrugged. "But he seems to like you."

It was my turn to remain silent.

"Do you really like him?" Riley asked.

"I do. He's different. He's not..." I was worried he would judge me, but I also didn't want to lie to him. "He's safe. He feels safe."

"So, you're hiding?"

I said, with a little too much vehemence, "I'm not hiding."

His legs were stretched out in front of him, ankles crossed. I extended mine alongside his, facing him from the other wall.

The silence stretched between us, and I started telling him about Jason. I told him about what happened when I was gone, and how I stayed much longer than planned because I didn't want to face the island alone.

"I never knew a life without him. All my plans were wrapped up in him. We felt like one person. At least, I felt like we were one person. Everyone loved him, and by default, everyone loved me. My identity had been all wrapped up in being a de facto Reid, and I'd thought it would always be that way."

He listened patiently, and I continued. I told him about how I caught him with the other girl, and how I stayed with my relatives until Evie told me he was leaving the rodeo circuit and coming home. "When I got back to the Island, I thought I could fix us. But I was still so hurt, I started acting like I didn't care. I'm ashamed to admit that I acted like a tramp, pretending I was okay with the little attention

Jason gave me. I took whatever he offered and thought it would be enough. Despite all that had happened, I still thought we could make it work."

"Did he know how you felt?"

I shook my head and shrugged. "He thought we were just casual. I don't know, maybe? It's difficult to put whatever we were that summer into words."

"You wanted more." It was a statement, and I agreed.

"But then Shaye showed up, and he was smitten and kind of stupid about her. I felt like he was breaking my heart all over again. People had started seeing me as the town tramp, and I'd worked too hard to protect myself from getting hurt again, so I perpetuated the image. I mean, even you made that comment at Evie's wedding."

"I apologized for that, and I am truly sorry. I think you're being too hard on yourself, Julie. You're building your dream on your own. That's something to be proud of."

My eyes glassed over. "Maybe."

"Do you still care what people think?"

The tears dropped. "Kind of. This is my home. It's…challenging to keep up a tough façade, to preserve people's impressions. I'm tired."

I started to cry and he reached out to pull me into his lap, my head resting against his chest. Riley held me while I gently cried, years of putting up a wall starting to crack. I wanted to stop fighting. I wanted to let go and love someone again. I just didn't know how.

Then he asked, "Do you think by dating Dax he'll give you esteem?"

His chest vibrated as he spoke, my head tucked under his chin.

I opened my eyes and stared out into the night. I relaxed against Riley's chest, feeling it rise and fall. The soft fabric of his flannel shirt felt like a blanket and I wanted to wrap it around me.

"I hadn't thought about it that way. I just like him. And, he's..." My voice trailed off.

I heard him whisper, "safe."

My tears had stopped. Both of us were quiet now, the air around us thickening with sexual tension. I became more aware of where I was sitting. His strong thighs tensed beneath me and my breathing accelerated.

I thought about moving, but then he asked, "Are you afraid of falling in love, Julie?"

"No." I paused. "Maybe. I don't know."

Then he asked me the real question, the one I'd been struggling with for weeks now. "Are you afraid of falling in love with me?"

Still trying to keep him at an emotional distance, I asked quietly, "Is there a difference?"

"Sure." His hands were stroking my back. "I'm not a player, Julie. Falling in love means you risk getting hurt. Falling in love with me means you're safe."

"Are you...are you falling in love with me?"

Riley tilted my chin up towards him and looked at me the way no other man had. His eyes burned into mine. Not even Jason had made me yearn the way he was.

With painstaking slowness, his hand came to rest on my cheek. His thumb caressed my cheekbone, tenderness in his eyes.

Reaching up to clasp my hand behind his neck, we gazed at each other, both of us questioning what was happening. I felt fused to him, cradled against him, my heart thudding in my chest.

I watched as his eyes closed and he lowered his forehead to mine, softly rubbing our skin together, our faces tentatively drawing closer. My eyes closed and all I could do was feel – his soft breath, the thick waves of his hair at the nape of his neck.

My senses were overcharged.

His lips hovered over mine, tenderly waiting for permission.

I wasn't ready for this. And I had Dax to think of…I think.

With as much strength as I could gather, I pulled back from him, and slowly stood from his lap.

He was motionless, his arms resting at his side. In the darkness, I could tell he was restraining himself. Tension settled between us; the air was still with unanswered questions.

Dusting off the sawdust from my bottom, I said uncertainly, "I should go."

Extending the flashlight to me, he told me to take it.

"What will you use?"

His response was curt. "My phone."

I stuttered a bit. "Okay. Well, I'll see you in the morning?"

"You still want to go?"

His insecurity warmed me, and I responded softly, "Of course."

He nodded. "See you in the morning, then."

I left him behind to make my way back to my apartment. My thoughts rattled around in my head like a maraca. I was going to have a headache in the morning.

15

"I WAS KIND of getting used to sleeping in. Now I have to go back to a real job." Maggie spoke from the back seat of Riley's truck.

The morning air was still damp, and the sky had the lavender gray hues of early dawn.

Riley looked at her in the rear-view mirror and grinned cheekily. "You've hardly been sleeping in. And I'm proud of you for working so hard."

She leaned forward and rested her chin on the back of my seat, looking at his profile. "Aw, my big brother is proud of me."

I took a sip of the hot coffee they'd brought me and added, "I'm just glad the plans weren't as bad as you originally made them out to be."

Relaxing back in her seat, she said, "Yeah, I might have exaggerated a bit."

Riley added gruffly, "But you still made a mistake that cost us. I'm sure you won't do it again."

She saluted him. "No, sir. I've learned my lesson, sir."

We laughed at her silliness, and I stared out at the passing fields and trees, reflecting on how much I would miss her.

When we approached the resort and marina, I commented on the placid water. "It looks like glass this morning. I can see the reflection of the trees across the bay." I sighed. "It's so beautiful."

Maggie added, "It'll be a smooth ride back to Friday Harbor."

After Riley parked alongside the resort, he jumped out, and reached into the bed of the truck. Pulling out the orange buoy, he handed it to me as I came around the back. "I'll carry the crab pot."

Maggie had her backpack on and was already headed down the dock to Riley's boat. Riley followed behind her, the crab pot hitched up towards his shoulder, his long strides closing the gap.

I trailed behind, wondering if he was intentionally trying to make me struggle. The buoy wasn't heavy, but it was awkward. Eventually, I dropped it alongside of me, and started dragging it.

Finally, after much frustration, I left it on the ground and continued to the boat.

When I reached the boat, Riley's smile told me all I needed to know. "Where's the buoy?"

"You're a jackass. You go get it."

His chuckle trailed behind him as he went back up the dock to get it.

Tossing the buoy into the back of the boat, he stepped over the railing and said, "You're just so much fun to tease."

I ignored him and joined Maggie on the bow, settling in on the seats and reclining against the front of the wheel house. Maggie smiled at me and extended the blanket over my legs.

We watched as Riley untied the dock lines and then said to us, "I'm going out just a little way to put the pots out, then I'll take you home, ok, Maggie?"

She gave him a thumbs up. Over my shoulder, I watched Riley start the engine and slowly pull away from the dock. He smiled at me, and I felt myself blush. Maggie had been watching us, and I saw her laugh, shaking her head.

Riley kept the throttle of the boat at a speed that wouldn't cause very much wake. I scooted in next to Maggie, curling my arm through hers, and tucking the blanket in around us.

As we left the bay, we watched the sunrise over the mountains of the other islands, turning the sky to shades of purple, pink, and orange. It reflected off the glassy surface of the bay, and I inhaled the salty cold air, looking forward to a day on the water.

When we left the channel, Riley turned up the throttle and the boat shot out along the shore. The cold wind nipped my face. Maggie lifted her arms and shouted exuberantly, "I love this!"

Skirting just off the shoreline for a distance, he pulled into a cove and killed the engine. We drifted for a bit while he got the crab pots ready. "Maggie, will you go down below and get the bait for me?"

I watched as Maggie went to the cabin below, and I asked Riley if there was anything I could do to help.

"Can you get the buoy for me and hook it to the pot?"

For a moment, I just stared at him, raised my eyebrows, and asked if he was serious.

He laughed. "Yeah, actually, I wasn't teasing you this time."

"Oh, okay, I'll just roll it over."

"It's only, like, two pounds," he said on a laugh.

I pouted, "But it's big and awkward."

Riley stood and ambled to the front of the boat laughing and saying over his shoulder, "Oh, Juliette, I'm disappointed. Helpless girl doesn't suit you."

He came back with the buoy and hooked it effortlessly to the pot.

Crossing my arms, I scolded him. "I think you could have done this all on your own to begin with."

He remained silent but the corners of his eyes crinkled.

Maggie returned with bait, and I watched as Riley put the chicken breasts in the bait trap, secured the pot, and threw it over with the buoy. "We should have something by the time we get back. And if not, I brought lunch. We can eat while we wait for the pots to catch something."

Settling herself back on the front seats, Maggie mumbled, "I wish I could have crab for dinner. See, he continues to punish me."

I had come to know her tone and knew she was just kidding, but I responded anyway. "Maybe you should learn."

Her eyes popped wide open, and she laughed. "Look at you, all smart mouth Mary. Now I see what Riley sees. You're a challenge."

I had settled in next to her, and Riley had returned to drive the boat. "Maggie, Riley and I are just friends. He works for me. Well, technically, me and Dax, but there's nothing more."

She eyed me skeptically. "And, I see you are both stupid. I will say no more." She ran her finger across the seam of her lips, indicating she was done talking.

Throttling up the speed of the boat, Riley took us out into the ship channel and towards Friday Harbor. The sound of the engine drowned out any more opportunities for me and Maggie to talk, and for that I was glad. I didn't want to examine this any further. Then there was Dax, who I'd barely begun to get to know, but felt excited about nonetheless. I turned my head to the sun, closed my eyes, and relaxed.

The ride took less than thirty minutes. By the time we arrived in Friday Harbor, the docks were bustling with tourists leaving their boats in search of coffee, and breakfast. Riley circled for a bit, waiting for a spot to open at the marina fueling station. When a yacht pulled out from the other side, Riley expertly maneuvered into the vacant spot.

"I always forget how much busier Friday Harbor is than Lopez. It's kind of exciting."

Maggie abruptly grabbed her bag and jumped over the side before Riley could finish tying up the boat. "Thanks for the vacation, Riley, but I really can't stay and play tour guide."

Riley looked momentarily hurt. He stopped what he was doing, still holding on to the rope and standing on the dock, looking a little confused. "Oh, okay."

"Jules, I'll see you soon, okay?"

I stood, feeling a little perplexed myself. "Sure. It was good to meet you."

She waved at the two of us and then made her way quickly up the dock.

'That was odd." He said almost to himself. He looked at me and asked, almost as if he wasn't quite sure what to do with me, "Do you want to go walk around town for a bit?"

I patted the driver's seat. "Why don't we just head back? We can enjoy the quiet morning, eat the lunch you packed, and see if we have any crabs for dinner."

When he didn't immediately respond, I patted the seat a little harder. "C'mon. Otherwise, I'm going to leave you standing on the dock looking like a guppy. C'mon."

Riley threw the rope back in the boat, jumped in, and came to stand at the wheel. After a moment, he turned the engine back on and slowly trolled out of the marina.

I grabbed the blanket from the front seats and sat next to him under the awning while he stood and drove, his eyes shielded by his Ray-ban sunglasses. "Don't you think that was kind of odd?"

"I don't know. Maybe she saw someone she knew and didn't want to introduce us."

He looked at me with furrowed brows, "What are we? The old, judgmental parents?"

Putting my feet up on the console, I tucked the blanket around my legs. "Maybe she was just done with us."

He glanced back as if he thought he should return. I placed my hand on his arm. "Riley, she's a grown girl. Leave her be."

His face finally softened, and he smiled mischievously when we came out from the Harbor. "Ready?"

Judging by the wicked little-boy-enthusiasm smile on his face, he was going to go full throttle. I braced my feet, held on to the arm rests and smiled up at him, "Ready!"

Smiling broadly, he pushed the throttle forward, and the boat's four engines launched us out over the open water, the spray of the ocean flying up alongside us. When I looked down at the console, I saw we were going almost fifty miles an hour, and it was exhilarating.

For fun, Riley took turns and zig-zagged his way back to where he'd put the crab pots, periodically looking down at me and making sure I was okay.

As we approached the cove, he slowed it down and gently came to a stop alongside the buoy.

"It's still early. Do you want to anchor and eat…" His voice trailed off as he looked at his watch. "Brunch?"

I got up from the bench and walked to the front of the boat. "Sure. I'll get the food out while you anchor."

Setting up a picnic of sorts on the front seats, I settled down on the inclined bench and leaned back against the front of the wheelhouse.

Turning my head to the sun, I closed my eyes and waited for Riley to join me.

Shortly after the clanging of the anchor dropping stopped, Riley laid down on his side next to me.

"I've missed this." He sighed as he reached for the grapes and popped one in his mouth.

"Eating?" I smirked at him.

"No, Juliette," he said sardonically. "Getting away and being totally disconnected." He grabbed another grape and put it in my mouth.

I chewed slowly and watched as he continued to eat. He placed slices of cheese on crackers and shoved them in his mouth.

Laughing at him, I asked, "Were you raised in a barn?"

He settled back against the seat and closed his eyes. "I didn't eat breakfast. Maggie was useless, and my usual wench wasn't there to cook for me."

I punched him softly in the arm. He laughed without opening his eyes.

Quietly we sat together, enjoying the lulling of the boat and the gentle breeze blowing over the water. The sun was hot enough to warm, but not so hot that it wasn't a perfectly peaceful day on the water.

I sat staring at Riley, garnering the courage to talk about last night.

As if he sensed me staring, he said without opening his eyes, "Out with it."

I took a deep breath and said, "About last night."

Opening his eyes, he rolled his head towards me, his eyes gleaming playfully. "You mean when you almost kissed me?"

I knew he was teasing me, but his words hurt and embarrassed me. "You are not a gentleman. Stop teasing me."

He rolled to his side and propped his head on his elbow. "Whoa, I'm sorry. I wasn't sure you wanted to have a deep conversation today."

I was sitting crisscross and I wove my fingers together nervously. "I didn't think I did, but…I don't know. I feel like we should be… friends."

"We are friends." He reached out and grabbed my fingers. "We are friends."

"Thank you for listening to me last night."

He smiled again. "You're welcome."

Our fingers stayed connected and we stared at each other thoughtfully.

"So, despite your pining for Evie, how come you don't have a girlfriend?"

He groaned and laughed simultaneously, pulling his fingers from mine and leaning back against the seat. He put his forearm over his eyes and said sarcastically, "Oh, here we go. Poke, poke. The girlfriend-talk."

Laughing, I pulled his arm from his eyes. "Seriously. I spilled the beans last night. It's your turn."

"First, I'm not pining for Evie."

I raised my eyebrows at him, questioningly.

"I'm not. And if I'm honest, I think Evie and I would've been boring together."

"That's not very nice. Evie isn't boring."

"I'm not saying *she's* boring. I'm saying that I think we would have been boring together. Ethan adores her, and she toys with him, I've seen it. She knows he's wrapped around her finger."

I had to laugh at that because I'd seen it too. Ethan was totally in love with her and would do whatever Evie asked of him. She played damsel in distress often.

"So, why are you still single? I remember you said you had a girlfriend last year. She took your Sonics t-shirt?"

He laughed. "That wasn't really anything." Then he let out a heavy breath and stared out over the water. "I loved someone...once. And, she died."

He looked at me pointedly, waiting for my response.

His words felt like a punch in the gut. I opened my mouth to say something and then closed it again.

"It was a few years ago. We met on the first day of college. She was like a bright light that just lit up a room. Everyone was drawn to her. But she sat down next to me in Economics 101 and said, 'Hey, you look super smart, we should buddy up this year.' And that was that. I was hooked. Her smile, her laugh, her kindness – she lifted everyone up."

I tried hard to hide my jealousy of this seemingly perfect girl. Keeping my tone neutral, I said, "She sounds perfect."

He scoffed. "Far from it. She was a pain in the ass." Pensively, he continued. "She ate off of paper plates because she hated to do dishes, she left her dirty clothes on the bathroom floor, she bit her nails, and she was *never* on time. For anything. But she was kind, and always excited for whatever a day would bring."

"How did she die?"

"She had leukemia."

"Is that why your family supports Seattle Children's Hospital?"

He nodded.

"Did you know she was sick?"

He shook his head. "Not until our junior year. I wanted to marry her, and she kept saying that she couldn't. I kept bugging her and then she finally told me that she'd been in remission and was sick again."

"What about her family?"

"She hadn't told them. I started thinking that she must have always felt as if she knew she would die young. It explained her exuberance for life, and her recklessness with my and her family's feelings."

"I'm so sorry." I reached out to take his hand, and he laced his fingers with mine.

"I'm fine now. But I did wonder for a long time whether she really loved me. Her family hated me for keeping her from them, but I didn't know she was sick until close to the end, and then she wouldn't leave me. She said, 'I want us to be together, please don't make me go back. They'll just put me back in the hospital for more tests and experiments. I'm tired, and I just want to be with you.'"

"I don't think you should question if she loved you or not. She must have loved you very much."

He was looking at me intently, trying to convey that he understood my own pain. My eyes welled up when he said, "And she would want me to know that it's okay to eventually love someone else."

I whispered, trying not to choke on my tears, "At least you got to say good-bye."

He pulled me towards him, cradling my head on his chest and tucking me into his side. My tears came freely again, but this time they were for him too.

When the tears finally subsided, I jokingly said, "I have *really* got to stop crying in front of you."

"Or at least on my shirts."

I chuckled and sat up so I could see him.

"Why did you kiss me at Evie's wedding?"

"I thought it was the other way around."

I didn't answer, not wanting to joke about it.

He sighed, "You looked like you were sad."

"You pitied me?"

"No!" He sat up and looked me in the eyes. "I would never pity you. You are too strong and too beautiful to be pitied."

"Then why?"

I waited patiently for his response, and inhaled sharply when he said, "Because I wanted to."

I leaned towards him. "Do you want to kiss me now?"

Reaching towards me, he held my head and kissed me softly on the cheek, trailing kisses down my neck to my collar.

I was melting, wanting nothing more than to feel him kiss me all over. My head lolled back and I relaxed into him.

Between kisses along my neck and chin, I heard him say, "From the very first day I met you, when Ethan got punched at the bar, you started getting under my skin. Your sassy mouth and the way you pretend things don't bother you? You are challenging, to say the least. But I can't help feeling like I want to be the guy that makes you fall."

With my eyes closed, I begged, "Please kiss me, Riley, please."

Slowly, he pulled back from me. "I want to. But I can't."

It took a moment for it to register that he denied me. "Why not?"

"Because you aren't ready."

I pushed at him. "What do you mean I'm not ready? What the hell is that supposed to mean?"

His eyes flared angrily. "Are you, or are you not, dating Dax?"

"Uhh…"

"And, are you, or are you not, still reeling about Jason?"

I shouted back, "That's not fair! You can't use that against me. No one thought about me after he died. No one! I can still be grieving if I want to!"

He shouted, "It was years ago!"

I stood from the bench and shouted back at him. "And yet no one has allowed me to move on."

Standing, he reached for me. "Julie."

With strength I said, "I was a good girl. I came home from my family's vineyard knowing everything, *everything*, about making wine; from the soil to the grapes to how to label the bottles. When I got home, I thought Jason and I would be together again. I was willing to overlook what had happened. But the people of this island expected me to be one way and after a while I just got tired of fighting them. I did things I'm not proud of, and I'll make amends for them, but when Jason died, I was just forgotten. No one took me seriously."

I continued softly, "Even Evie let me bury my pain. She accepted my behavior as if it was funny. As if…as if my pain didn't count."

With his hands-on hips, he dropped his chin to his chest. "I'm sorry. That was unkind of me."

I was embarrassed by my outburst and simply wanted to get home.

"I need to get home."

"I'm really sorry Julie. I shouldn't discount your feelings."

"It's okay. I really do need to get home though. We have a busy week and I have lots to do."

Nodding once, he added, "I just need to pull the pots up. Give me five minutes."

I sat back down and stared blankly out at the water, the sun creating momentary glitter on the waves.

The chain from the pot banged against the boat, and I heard Riley laugh.

I turned and saw there weren't any crabs in the pot. "Well, maybe we should have left it out longer."

He looked at me as if I'd lost my mind, and he said sarcastically, "Really?"

I knew he was referring to my outburst. I simply shrugged and turned back to stare out at the water.

A few minutes later, I heard the anchor come up, and then the engine started.

Riley kept the boat at a slower speed on the way back, allowing me to think more clearly.

Our conversation went terribly wrong today. He'd confided in me and I'd turned it into something about me. I owed him an apology.

When we pulled back into his boat slip, he left the pot and the buoy in the boat, saying he'd take care of it later. We walked quietly to his truck, and he held the door for me as I climbed in.

As he pulled out onto the main road, I asked, "Do you want to stop and get a coffee?"

"I can't. I have some things I need to do today, too. I'll drop you back at your place, and then I need to head out for a bit."

I desperately wanted to ask him what things he had to do, where he was going, and when he'd be back. But his tone and the fact that he wasn't making eye contact with me led me to believe that they would not be welcome questions.

He stopped in front of my apartment and left the engine running as he waited for me to get out.

"Thanks for the beautiful morning."

"Mmhmm."

I turned to face him, and said softly, "Riley."

His eyes were sad. I felt as if I'd forced him to open wounds he didn't want to explore. "Thank you for telling me about…I don't know her name."

"Harper. Her name was Harper."

"Thank you for telling me about Harper."

He nodded once.

I opened the door and stepped out. "I'll see you tomorrow?"

"Yep."

Gently, I shut the door and walked around the front of his truck to the porch. I watched him drive back out of the vineyard, away from the office. I had a feeling I wouldn't see him for a while.

16

Gary, Riley's construction foreman, was standing in front of me in the office looking sheepish and uncomfortable at the news he'd just delivered.

Calmly, I asked, "Do you know when he'll be back?"

"Not sure, Miss. He just told me that I needed to step in as construction manager for a week or so."

It wasn't Gary's fault that I was seething. "Do you know where he went?"

"I believe he went to Seattle. You know, his family has a number of projects in the downtown area. Maybe he needed to check in?"

He was fiddling with his hard hat, and I felt bad for interrogating him. "Thank you, Gary. I assume you're caught up on the progress and the upcoming inspections?" Tap, tap, tap on the desk went the pencil in my hand.

"Yes, Ma'am."

"You can call me Julie." I threw the pencil down in frustration.

"Yes, Ma'am. I mean Julie, Miss."

"Thank you, Gary, for letting me know," I said as politely as I could.

He bowed his head to me respectfully. "Yes, Ma'am."

I almost groaned out loud. Picking up my phone, I texted Riley. *Chicken Shit!*

He didn't respond.

The gala was next weekend and I had a lot to do to get ready. Now that I knew Riley would be gone this week, I spent most of my time going over orders for linens and towels, soaps, and other toiletry supplies for the guest rooms.

The local products were as good as any, in any hotel chain across the country, and I wanted to use as many of them as possible. I made sure I had enough for the gift shop as well as the guest rooms for at least a month after opening day.

I chose lavender rose soaps, shampoos, and conditioners for the rooms, and a variety of other scents for the gift shop: jasmine tea, cucumber shea, and sandalwood citrus. The samples I'd picked up earlier were on the construction desk, their earthy scents permeating the entire room. I giggled briefly, thinking that I ought to feminize the office a little bit while Riley was gone.

The day before I left for Seattle, I drove to the hardware store and picked up some lavender paint.

Then I stopped at the fabric store and picked up some floral print curtains in pinks, yellows, and blues.

When I got back to the office, I called Gary on the walkie talkie to come meet me as soon as he had a minute. Less than three minutes later he came through the front door. "Ma'am? You wanted to see me?"

The Ma'am thing was growing on me. *Maybe I should let him continue*, I thought to myself.

"I'm leaving for Seattle tomorrow morning. I won't be back until Sunday night, and I need the house painted."

"Ma'am?" He sounded confused.

"The inside of the house. The office part." I stood from behind the desk and walked towards the door, where I'd left the 5-gallon container of paint. "I bought some paint at the hardware store, and I think there are enough rolling thingies. Five gallons of paint should be enough. If you don't have the supplies you need, just use Riley's construction credit card to cover it."

"Ma'am, you have fiberglass and insulation comin' tomorrow. I'm not sure if I'll have time to get this done for you."

Crossing my arms in front of me, I remained silent.

"And you have an inspection next Friday – we're gonna need to make sure all the drywall is hung."

My eyes never wavered from him.

He shuffled his feet a little. "I guess I could take care of it this weekend."

I uncrossed my arms and put a smile on my face. "Excellent. And when it's dry would you please hang these curtains in the front bedroom, and on the windows in this room looking out to the porch?"

"I don't know if Mr. Riley is gonna like those curtains too much, Ma'am."

I grinned boldly back at him. "Well, it's not Mr. Riley's house, is it?"

He bowed his head. "No, Ma'am."

Grabbing my purse, I left the office after asking Gary to lock up before he left for the night.

I drove my golf cart back to my apartment and started the daunting task of packing for the weekend. Shaye and I would go dress shopping tomorrow night for the gala on Saturday, and I would definitely need something nice for dinner out. And then an outfit for

Sunday, just in case Dax wanted to have brunch before I flew back to the island.

I tossed hanger after hanger of clothing on my bed that just wouldn't work for me. After ten minutes of trying to figure out what I should wear, I finally threw myself down on top of the pile on my bed and stared up at the ceiling fan spinning around and around. This dressing up thing was exhausting.

Turning my head, my cheek brushed against cream wool pants, and I took that as a sign that I should pack them. Feeling a little more inspired, I sprung back up off the bed, folded another couple of lightweight sweaters, and placed an A-line dress into my travel bag.

After squishing down the top and holding the sides together, I zipped the bag closed. I stood on the scale, tried not to cringe, and then stepped off, stepping back on with the bag to make sure I wasn't over the weight limit.

Satisfied that I'd done a good job, I set the bag by my door and got myself ready for bed. Shaye wanted to fly out early, and I didn't want to piss her off by being late.

Dressing in a T-shirt nightie, I snuggled under the covers and set the alarm on my phone. Holding onto it, I turned over onto my back, propped pillows under my head, and ran my forefinger up and down over the screen.

I missed Riley. I shouldn't, but I did. His quirky tooth that was so sexy when he grinned sideways, his too-long hair that he hadn't cut since Evie's wedding, his seriously sexy long legs that I loved to watch when the fabric of his jeans would stretch over his thighs…

Scrolling through my contacts, I texted him, *I miss you*

I covered my mouth, shocked I'd actually sent it.

I watched as the phone indicated he'd read the text, and then the dots started bouncing. *I think you have the wrong person*

My smile dropped and I quickly went back through all the texts between us. The shit-head. It *was* him.

My apologies, I was fantasizing about a hot construction worker... must have typed the wrong number.

Julie?

Who's this?

You're a brat

I texted back a bunch of laughing emojis.

He responded; *I thought the text was for Dax*

My heart felt like it had been stabbed. I hated that Dax was coming between us, even as friends. It was hard not to imagine that Riley had left because of him.

Still, I couldn't help but tease him. *Me and Gary had a nice night tonight. I put him to work. He really knows how to swing a hammer.*

Poor Gary...I hope his wife doesn't mind the boot marks from you walking all over him.

I giggled as I typed. *I found this stimulating sex site on the internet...it gave me some interesting ideas*

He didn't respond for a few minutes. I was just starting to think I might have gone too far when he responded. *Maybe you should send the link to Dax; he looks like he has a lot to learn*

His response made me laugh out loud. *I think I might.*

I was just getting ready to put my phone down when his text came through *What are you wearing?*

So bold! I could hear his voice in my head. *Wouldn't you like to know?*

My phone rang, startling me. He was face-timing me.

I rolled to my side and answered, "Why are you calling me?"

"I wanted to know what you were wearing," he said huskily, laughing at the same time.

The image behind him was dark. I saw light reflecting on water, and the wind blowing his hair around.

"Where are you?"

"I'm down on the waterfront. Out with some friends."

"Why did you leave this week?"

I watched as he looked over the top of the phone and mouthed "Two minutes." Then he turned his attention back to me. "Did you miss me?"

"I missed someone managing my project, instead of being a pussy and running off, all butt-hurt, at a small argument."

He laughed boldly. "Language, Juliette."

"Whatever."

"Are you thinking about me?"

This was so dangerous. "Yes."

He continued when I didn't say anymore. "I'm thinking about you too."

We were both silent for a moment, staring at each other through the phone.

Then I whispered, "I really do miss you."

His low chuckle wrapped around me like a blanket. "Goodnight, Juliette."

In my half-asleep state, I whispered back, "Goodnight, Riley."

I woke in a languid state, stretching, and smiling to myself. A few seconds later, I sat straight up in bed and said out loud, "Oh no. Did I really tell Riley I missed him?"

In the light of day, me and Riley looked different. I should not have teased him.

I checked my phone to see if he'd called or texted. Nothing.

This was going to make things complicated.

Throwing back the covers, I quickly dressed in comfortable travel clothes, made my bed, and took my bag downstairs.

I scribbled a note to the weekend bartender who would be managing the tasting room, telling him Gary and his wife could drink for free. I would call Gary later and let him know he should bring his wife out for a nice evening.

When I arrived at the resort, I parked in the long-term parking next to the side of the building, and went inside to wait for Shaye.

Ten minutes later, she came through the front, juggling the car seat and holding little baby May, who was peeking out from under a blanket. Her big blue eyes, so like Evie's and Jason's, stared up at me in wonder as she sucked furiously on a pacifier.

"Do you need some help?" I reached out for the handle of the car seat.

She sighed. "Yes, thank you. I need to get a few more things from the car, and then we'll head down to the dock."

Sitting back down at one of the tables by the window, I put the car seat on the table and played with May's feet. She kicked excitedly, and I grabbed her little hand, bringing it to my mouth to kiss her tiny fingers.

Out of the corner of my eye, I watched the float plane approach and land. Shaye came back in, wearing a backpack and pulling a rolling suitcase behind her.

A diaper bag was slung, messenger style, across her chest and I couldn't help but laugh at her. "You look like a Sherpa."

She rolled her eyes. "I *feel* like a Sherpa. You ready to go?"

I nodded and followed her out to the dock, carrying the baby in the car seat, and rolling my small suitcase behind me.

When we reached the plane, the pilot jumped out to help us, and I watched as Shaye efficiently loaded all of our things behind the mesh screen separating the seats from the cargo hold in the back of the plane.

This was the smaller of the floatplanes that provided service to the islands. It only carried six passengers and two crew-members.

Shaye asked me to wait to get in until she had May settled. "It will be easier for me to get her out when we land."

After May was buckled in, Shaye jumped out onto the dock and smiled at me. "Okay! Your turn."

"Is it just us today?"

"Yep. It's technically a training flight."

"Right. You're flying us."

Her grin grew. "It's just for practice."

I just stared at her and then pointed my thumb over my shoulder. "I have no idea what you are saying, so how about I just get in, buckle up, and enjoy the ride."

She added, "And take care of May."

"And take care of May."

Shaye shut the door behind me. I watched as the pilot settled himself in the right seat and Shaye settled in the left.

She turned back to me and asked if I wanted a headset to listen to them talk. I shook my head no. "I'll just put the earplugs in."

My attention went back and forth between baby May and Shaye. I was fascinated with my friend's laser sharp focus on the task at hand, namely to get us safely to Seattle.

As the plane taxied out from the dock, she referred to a notebook that was resting on her right thigh, secured with a Velcro strap so it wouldn't slide off. Her hands went back and forth from the dials to the control yoke, and before she pushed the throttle forward, she looked back at me and smiled.

I nodded to her, held on to May's hand, and felt the plane shake from the thrust of the engine. The plane bounced and bobbled across the water, until, finally, I saw her pull back on the yolk and we were airborne.

She quickly adjusted some of the dials above her, and then scanned the sky below and above us.

Watching her command the plane was quite possibly the sexiest thing I'd ever seen her do. I felt a new appreciation for her as my friend, and I realized that I wasn't alone in being mis-judged. Shaye had weathered her own storms. It was that thought that alleviated my worry that she would be pissed when I told her what I'd done.

And that's what I get for thinking.

I was terribly wrong.

Later that day, after we'd landed and settled in at her mom's house, I asked her if we could sit outside and talk for awhile before we went shopping.

She handed me a bottle of white wine and two glasses and told me to head out to the patio. "I'm going to put May down to nap, and I'll be right back."

The living room in the house looked out towards a rectangular swimming pool and the Seattle skyline. It was built on the top of Queen Anne hill, so the views were unobstructed by other homes.

Taking the wine and the glasses out onto the deck, I sat down under a covered pergola. Scarlet-orange honeysuckle wrapped around the support beams, trained to follow the upward path.

A hummingbird feeder hung from the rafters, and I watched as the little birds came and went, their tiny wings flapping furiously to keep them aloft while they drank.

The sliding door opened behind me and Shaye stepped out. Holding a baby monitor in one hand, she looked refreshed and pretty in a flowery sundress and sandals.

I handed her a glass of wine after she sat down. Exhaling loudly, she closed her eyes. "Ah, quiet."

"It must be nice to have a little break from the island."

"Honestly? Every now and then, yes. I think JT is destroying every piece of furniture we own. I'm so glad we only have one boy."

After taking a sip of her wine, she asked, "Was Jason always rowdy?"

Her eyes bore into mine, patiently waiting for me to share. She knew something was going on with me.

Tucking my legs underneath me on the cushioned wicker patio chair, I took a deep breath and said, "Ever since Evie got engaged, I've been feeling…I've been feeling lost."

She was quiet, so I continued. "It's almost like I've been asleep for years, and when I woke up, nothing was as it should be. I can't figure out if I miss him, or if I just never processed losing him."

And then she asked me the question I'd never wanted her to ask me. "Julie, were you and Jason still…you know. Were you …" She paused. "Were you still having sex that summer?"

I could tell she already knew the answer, but we had to get this out. "Yes."

She didn't respond and I rushed on. "But he wasn't in it like I was. I still loved him, despite what he'd done, despite us being apart for so many years. He was trying to break it off…again. I still loved him and I was so jealous of you."

"But not anymore, right? I thought things between us were really good. Honestly, I feel like we talk more than Evie and I do, and she's my sister-in-law. Are we okay?"

I put my wine glass down on the table in front of me, and said adamantly, "We are. Yes! We are. But, actually, about Jason, there is something else I need to tell you."

Her eyebrows raised. "That sounds ominous."

"It's not, but then again, it might be. I don't know. All I know is I need to tell you. I need you to know."

We sat staring at each other.

I took a deep breath and said, "The night that Jason died – *Woo*! This is hard." I shook my hands to shake off the nerves.

"Just say it, Julie."

"Okay. The night that Jason died, I sent him outside."

"What? When?" She sounded confused.

"I was so mad at him. I knew about you and Nick. I could see it. I couldn't believe that Jason couldn't."

"I kind of remember that. I remember you made a comment about seeing what's right in front of you. But then I thought maybe you were just referring to my trying to push him away."

"Wow! You have a good memory."

"Not really. I was just super wound up that night, so everything is still sharp."

"I know what you mean." I continued, "when you left the table that night, I watched Nick follow you. The bar was so packed, no one was even paying attention except me. Jason fell on the floor. Do you remember? He was trying to laugh it off?"

She nodded.

"I helped him up and took him to the kitchen to wash his face – put some cold water on him. I was trying so hard to be kind, and he kept slapping my hand away. He called me a slut, said my behavior was ruining his reputation, and that he was trying to start a new life. He was awful and mean, and I hated you for turning him against me."

I started to cry, the tears falling down my face. "Everything just bubbled up, and I told him you two were outside. He didn't believe me. He never believed me. So, I said, 'If they're not out there, and I'm wrong, I will leave you alone forever.' He stood up from the kitchen stool and said, 'I hate you, Julie. You have become a horrible, petty person, and I want you to leave me alone forever regardless.' And he left. Those were the last words he said to me."

I wiped my tears with my fingertips and saw that Shaye was just staring at me, eyes wide with surprise.

"Please say something," I whispered.

"You let me believe all this time that it was just a random twist of horrible fate. But you sent him outside to catch us." Her voice was low and calm.

"Shaye," I almost pleaded. "I didn't do it to you, although it might look like it. I did it to him. I wanted him to hurt like I had."

"It's the same thing Julie. You did it to *us*!"

I started to cry again. "I'm so sorry."

She got up and walked away, coming back a moment later with a box of Kleenex.

Pulling a few from the box for herself, she handed the box to me when she was finished.

Together, we sat in silence. Me, crying. Her, trying not to.

With her head bowed, she spoke softly. "I was going to tell Jason that night, but he was so drunk. I was pleading with Nick to give me another day or two. I was…" She cleared the lump in her throat and looked up at me. "I was so afraid of what Jason would do."

I choked on my tears and dropped my head in my hands, weeping.

When my tears turned to shuddering breaths, I wiped them with a Kleenex and looked at Shaye. "I'm so sorry. I was a horrible friend to him. To you. To Nick and Evie."

I continued. "Please forgive me, Shaye. Please." I never imagined that I would be begging, but I was. "I want to let this go. The guilt has been like an albatross around my neck and I need to move on. I need to somehow let him go."

Her chest was rising and falling with the deep calming breaths she was taking. "Julie, you are the most exasperating person I've ever met. I will forgive you. But you also need to forgive yourself. We've certainly had our challenges, but I can't imagine us giving up the past few years of digging our way back to a friendship. I love you too much to not forgive you. But I love Nick more, and I'm not going to carry the past around in another secret. You have to tell them. You are going to tell them otherwise it will emotionally kill all of us. We will gradually crack, and then break apart. And then we won't be friends. You need to tell them."

I nodded wordlessly.

We sat in silence awhile longer: Shaye staring absentmindedly out at the city in the distance, me looking anywhere but at Shaye.

Finally, with resignation, she added, "In the meantime, we came to Seattle for a purpose, and we need to get you a dress."

"You still want to go?"

She pressed her fingers to her temples and mumbled under her breath. "Yes, but then I need a nap. Sometimes you are just too much."

17

SHAYE TOOK ME to see a personal shopper, and they brought me dress after dress after dress. Eventually, they all started to look the same, and when I could no longer focus, I selected the last one they showed me and called it done.

Her mom kept May so we could have a girl's day out, and I was thankful for the time with just her.

I didn't mention our conversation from earlier in the day. But, by the end of our shopping experience, she had thawed enough that I could bring it up again.

We were driving home after having dinner at a quiet Italian restaurant in Pike Place Market, and I told her I would talk to Nick and Evie next week.

She said as she drove, "I won't say anything to them, but they're going to know that I know something."

I stared solemnly out the window at the quiet neighborhood street as she pulled into the driveway and turned off the ignition. I said quietly, "I know." Turning to look at her in the driver's seat, I added, "I'll find the right time, I promise."

Reaching out to take my hand, she smiled serenely at me and squeezed my fingers gently. "Let's go inside. You have a big night tomorrow."

I followed her into the house, dress bag over my arm, and settled in to get ready for the next day.

When I woke the next morning, I momentarily forgot where I was. The pale green walls of the room were so unlike the distressed wood walls of my apartment.

My phone buzzed on the nightstand, and I saw that it was Dax calling.

Scooting up so I was sitting against the headboard, I answered the phone. "Hello?" I said with a smile on my face.

"Good morning, beautiful!" His endearment was sweet, and I could hear the smile in his voice.

"Good morning."

"I'm so glad you're in Seattle. I've really been looking forward to spending time with you off the island."

"Me too. It's a nice change." I realized that I meant it. The past few weeks had been confusing, but now that I was off the island, I was really excited to see him.

"The gala starts at eight o'clock but I need to be there a little early. I'm the opening speaker, so I hope you don't mind if I pick you up around seven?"

"Of course not. I'll be ready." I couldn't stop the smile from spreading. "I'll see you then."

We said our good-byes and I leapt out of bed.

Shaye was downstairs feeding May, and I sauntered into the kitchen, a huge smile on my face.

She paused the spoon mid-way and said, "Uhm, did someone sneak in last night?"

May hit her fist on the tray, demanding to be fed, and I laughed. "What do you mean?"

"You have an 'I just had sex' smile on your face."

The coffee was on and I saw that she'd put out a mug for me. I talked while I poured. "I just got off the phone with Dax."

"Ah, of course."

"He'll be here at seven to get me."

I took my mug and sat down at the counter, blowing on the coffee while I watched her feed May.

"Where's your mom?"

"Her and Tom went for a walk." Tom was Shaye's co-worker – her much older co-worker – and her mom's boyfriend. He'd helped Shaye through her darkest time after leaving the island, and when her Dad passed away, he had become a pseudo father figure.

"Is he always here now?"

"I think so. My mom won't actually say so, but all of his things are in the bathroom so…" She shrugged and her voice trailed off.

"I always liked him."

She paused and looked up at me. "Me too. I just wish they would tell me. They keep acting like it's a big secret, and I think they should just get married and get it over with."

"Maybe she thinks it will disrespect your father."

"Maybe."

I watched her cooing and laughing at May. "She's so cute."

Shaye smiled. "She's my favorite."

"They're all your favorite."

Smiling wistfully, she said, "No, she's going to be special. She's watchful and calm. She's so good and quiet – well, when she isn't hungry. It's like she already has us all figured out."

It was futile for me to disagree with her.

I excused myself and told Shaye I needed to plan for the day.

"The makeup artist and hair stylist will be here around three, and I need to work for a bit."

"Okay. I think I might take May down to the floatplane office. Lots of people want to meet her." She looked at May and said in baby talk, "Don't they? Don't they want to meet you? Yes, 'cause you're so cute! Yes, you are." Shaye kissed her cheeks and May giggled.

"You're a good mom, Shaye."

She looked up at me and paused before saying, "Thank you, Julie."

The rest of my day seemed to pass quickly.

I worked on the opening day schedule for the resort, I confirmed some early-bird reservations from people that were regular buyers of our wine, and I reviewed applications for chefs and resort staff.

My hair and makeup were complete by 6:00 p.m., and by then I felt like I needed a nap.

Shaye came into the bathroom where they were styling me and whistled. "Damn! You look good!"

"We didn't even work this hard for Evie's wedding."

"But it is so worth it! Have you seen yourself?"

I was sitting in a director's chair with my back to the mirror, and I shook my head.

She sat down on the edge of the tub. "Dax isn't going to recognize you."

"That bad?" I chuckled.

"No, that good."

"Well then, he should feel damn lucky!"

Laughing she said, "Yes, he should."

The makeup artist finished with the final touches and I stood. Still not looking in the mirror, I asked Shaye if she would help me get into my dress.

She stood. "Of course."

Turning to the makeup artist, Shaye asked if she needed any help packing up.

"No, I'm good. I'll just meet you guys downstairs?"

Shaye nodded and followed me into the bedroom.

Unzipping the dress bag, I gingerly took the dress out and placed it on the bed.

I removed my button-up, oversized flannel shirt and reached for the dress. Carefully stepping into the sapphire blue ball gown, I tried not to catch my toes on the layered tulle at the bottom.

The sleeveless top was embellished with hand-sewn crystals all the way up the high-neck collar. My hair had been styled in a sleek updo with a deep part so the crystals around my neck could shine.

Shaye delicately zipped up the back and fastened the hook at my neck, asking me if I'd brought earrings.

When I realized I'd totally forgotten, she told me to wait while she ran down the hall to see what her mom might have.

She returned a moment later, smiling exuberantly. "I found these crystal chandelier earrings. They are perfect!"

Watching me closely while I put the earrings in, she said, "You clean up very nicely, Julie Hunter. Very nicely indeed." She smiled kindly at me. "Dax is lucky to have you."

"Please don't make me cry, Shaye."

"Fine!" She walked towards me and turned me towards the full-length free-standing mirror. "But you should look now."

The girl staring back at me, with her refined posture and strong features, was a vision of who I'd clawed my way to becoming. I suddenly felt like all the judgement, and all the whispers behind my back had made me resilient.

From behind me, I heard Shaye say quietly, "I forgive you, Julie."

I took in a shuddering breath and tried not to ruin my makeup by crying. “Thank you.” I said through a lump in my throat. I saw, in the mirror, the understanding and compassion in her eyes.

“You are going to leave them speechless.”

Not wanting to continue down this rabbit hole of emotion, I turned from the mirror and said, “Enough with all these feelings, I need a glass of wine.”

“And there she is. I knew she hadn’t gone far.”

“I need to relax a little before this shindig thing.”

Halfway through my glass of wine, my phone buzzed with a message from Dax. He was ten minutes away and was looking forward to seeing me.

I held my phone up to Shaye and waggled my shoulders. “See there? He’s looking forward to seeing me.”

Her laughter bubbled up and she almost choked on her wine. “Well, yes he is.”

I toasted her one more time before tipping back the rest of my glass. “To new beginnings.”

“To new beginnings.”

I was hiding in the bathroom when the doorbell rang and my stomach fluttered.

Shaye opened the door, and I heard her greet Dax pleasantly.

“Hi, Dax, how are you?” She opened the door wider. “Come on in. Julie’s just grabbing her purse, I think.”

“Thank you. I don’t mind waiting for her.” I heard Dax’s laugh as I came down the hall. His eyes grew wide when he saw me.

“Wow! You are stunning. I am going to have to keep you close tonight.”

“Hi, Dax.” I twirled around in the entry-way and fluttered my eyes. “Will this work?”

“If I wasn’t the opening speaker, we wouldn’t be going.”

I laughed at his flirtation. “I guess that’s a yes?”

"Definitely a yes."

I turned to Shaye. "I have the key you gave me. I'll see you in the morning?"

She smiled at me. "I'll see you in the morning."

When I turned back to Dax, he held his elbow out for me to grab. "Shall we?"

I hooked my arm around his, gently resting my fingers on his forearm, and said, "We shall."

When we reached the stretch limousine, he held the door for me and I cautiously stepped in, careful not to catch my dress.

After I was situated, I looked at the seat across from me and noticed someone else.

"Hello." Her angelic voice practically sang out to me. She looked familiar but I couldn't place her.

"Hello," I responded warily. I hadn't expected someone else on our date.

"I'm Wren." Long arms extended to shake my hand.

"I'm Julie."

"I know. Dax has been talking about you all evening. It's a pleasure to meet you. I hear you're building an extraordinary resort."

Dax had gone around the other side of the car, and when he opened the door he said, "Oh good, you met."

He sat down next to me, and took my hand in his, placing it in his lap. Wren's eyes glanced briefly down at our clasped hands, and quickly back up to mine.

I was so confused. I had no idea who this woman was, but her guarded eyes told me she wasn't happy about me and Dax.

Trying to hide her contempt for me, she laughingly said, "Dax ditched me when you said you would come. Now I've been relegated to sitting with my brother, who doesn't even like these events to begin with."

The car started to move, and Dax blew off her statement, asking us both. "Would you ladies like a glass of champagne?"

"No, thank you," I said.

"Yes, please," Wren said at the same time.

Dax poured her a glass, and she said, after he handed it to her, "Tell me about your resort, Julie."

Her posture was regal, controlled. And she barely moved from the seat as we drove to the venue. I was bursting to ask how they knew each other, but since I didn't want to appear jealous or catty, I stuck to the topic of the resort.

I highlighted the plans, keeping out a lot of the details. I didn't feel as if she really wanted to know, so I kept my story light and almost boring.

When the car came to a stop, the driver opened the door for us; Wren and I stepped out and she quickly excused herself.

"It was nice to meet you, Wren."

She smiled bitterly, "You too, Julie."

She leaned over to give Dax a kiss on the cheek. "I'll see you inside."

As she walked off, I felt my phone buzz in my bag. I pulled it out and read it. Riley.

Did you review the delivery schedule for the lighting fixtures?

I put my phone back in my bag without responding, and, once again, held on to Dax's arm as he led me into the building.

The large, warehouse-style structure was an intriguing blend of elegant and industrial, surrounded by an outdoor courtyard that was decorated in fairy lights and extensive greenery.

We walked along a sapphire blue carpet, fitting with the theme of the gala, and were welcomed at the door with smiles, and a flute glass of blue champagne.

As we entered the building, Dax was greeted by so many people, my mind became a whirlwind of names and faces. I smiled, nodded, said, "Nice to meet you," so many times I lost count.

He never let go of me. Once, he pulled me in close to let other couples pass us by.

My phone buzzed again and I ignored it.

The sequins on my dress reflected the light from the chandeliers. I watched as they sparkled over the walls and tables as we walked through.

The ceiling was made of skylights, and the pinks and blues of the setting sun were visible above us. I was entranced and simultaneously overwhelmed.

Dax was still talking to everyone and introducing me as 'the visionary behind his next great project.'

My phone buzzed again, and I excused myself to check the messages.

Stepping into a candlelit alcove, I placed my bag on a black and chrome cocktail table and pulled out my phone.

Remind me, did you want New England White Pine flooring, or Vintage French Oak

I texted back, *Vintage French Oak*

I had just reached for my bag to put my phone away when it pinged again. *And I was able to get you the chandelier you wanted*

When I glanced back out towards the party, I saw that Wren had clawed her way to Dax.

I quickly responded to Riley, *Great! Can we talk about this tomorrow?* And then I grabbed my bag and quickly went back to Dax's side.

When I reached them, I was slightly winded. My phone pinged again and Wren looked down at my bag. "Do you need to get that?"

"No, I'm good."

She smiled serenely at me and then turned to Dax. "Dax, it's almost time for the opening speech. Are you ready?"

He'd been talking to an elderly couple, and he excused himself from the conversation. "Oh, right. Julie, will you be okay for about fifteen minutes? I need to start the event, and then I'll be right back to get you."

Wren had her arm looped through his.

I responded with as much calmness as I could muster. "Of course. I'll get another glass of champagne and wait right here." My phone pinged again and I tried to hide my exasperation. "I'll be fine."

I waited until the two of them had walked away and then ran back to the alcove.

Three more texts.

Gary said thanks for the invite

The guest room lighting fixtures arrived

I'm ordering a King Size mattress for 'my room'

I texted back furiously, *Riley! I'm on a date. Can we talk tomorrow?*

You aren't on a date…you're arm candy

I inhaled. Oh my God! *That was mean!*

But true

I didn't immediately respond, instead looking out at all the glamorous people. Glitz and glamour weren't part of my plan, but I had been enjoying myself – kind of – and now Riley was ruining it.

My phone buzzed again, startling me. *Not that it isn't effective* and he added a winking emoji.

I texted back, *Don't use emojis, it's beneath you*

I could almost hear him laughing.

I was about to text him back when his last one came through. *You look beautiful tonight, Juliette. Blue's your color.*

I gasped. That jerk! *Where are you?*

18

I SHOVED MY phone back in my bag, not waiting for a response, and skirted my way through the crowds.

Looking around wildly, I wove through people, periodically stepping up higher on my tippy-toes to look for Riley over the tops of people's heads.

A set of stairs along the back wall led up to a second story balcony and I made my way to them.

When I reached the top, I followed the railing, looking down into the room to see if I could see him.

Not finding him, I took out my phone to call him.

"Hello, Juliette." His laughing voice answered immediately.

"Where are you?" I barked.

"You're getting close." He added, "This is fun. When you get here, we can play sardines. Did you ever play that as a kid? When you find the person, you have to squeeze into the spot until the last person gets there."

I continued walking, peeking into small private alcoves, candle-lit for more intimate conversations. "Why didn't you tell me you were coming?"

As soon as the words left my mouth, I saw him in one of the rooms and stopped abruptly, feeling as if the wind was knocked from me.

He whispered into the phone. "It would have ruined this moment."

His custom, blue and black velvet tuxedo fit his body perfectly, accentuating his broad shoulders and tapering to his lean hips.

Clicking off my phone, I placed it back in my bag, and stepped into the room. "What are you doing here, Riley?"

He sighed heavily and scooted over on the couch, patting the place next to him. "Sit down."

"I'll stand."

He stood and came towards me. "I told you weeks ago that my family supports the Children's Hospital."

"But I kept mentioning that I was coming. You could have told me at any time."

He reached out to brush his thumb across my cheek. "I didn't know I was coming until a few days ago. My sister needed a date."

I slapped his hand away. My head clanged with warning bells and I stepped back from him. "Please don't tell me Wren is your sister?"

He laughed. "You met her." It was a statement.

Putting my fingers to my temples, I closed my eyes. "She rode with me and Dax in the limo on the way here."

His bold laugh erupted from him. "Oh, isn't she clever? She told me she didn't need a ride, but I had no idea she would worm her way into accompanying you."

I opened my eyes. "She doesn't seem to like me very much."

"No, she wouldn't. She's been in love with Dax for years."

My head was starting to pound. I said, almost to myself, "God is punishing me."

"What was that?"

I shook my head. "Nothing."

A moment of silence stretched between us, and then he said softly, "You really do look beautiful."

My eyes connected with his. "Thank you. You look very nice yourself."

He smiled his sexy smile, that made me want to kiss him desperately. Instead I commented on his hair. "You cut it again."

"My mom said I was starting to look like a homeless person. Said I should at least cut it for this party."

We were less than a few feet apart. "It's too short, again," I said petulantly.

He stepped close, and I could feel his breath on my face when he whispered, "Julie."

I could feel myself starting to shake, and I turned to leave. "I have to get back. Dax is giving his speech and I told him I would wait for him. Have a lovely evening. I'm sure I'll see you downstairs."

As I fled, I heard him say, "Save a dance for me."

Dax spotted me the minute I hit the bottom of the stairs and he smiled at me. His face lit up with genuine pleasure. "There you are! I looked around for you after the speech and couldn't find you."

"Oh, I needed to use the ladies' room."

He picked up my hand and kissed it. "Are you ready for dinner?"

He tucked my hand over his arm, and I responded that I was.

Large, round tables filled the main room. Waiters dressed elegantly in white tuxedos served the crowd, effortlessly moving in and out.

Dax and I were seated at a table with a number of doctors from the hospital and their spouses, who were intrigued with my resort.

One of the doctors' husbands commented that he'd been looking at property in Eastern Washington to start a vineyard, but that it just didn't seem to be his thing.

"It certainly takes a lot of time and commitment."

"How did you ever get started?" He asked me as he took a bite of the succulent filets that had been served.

"I was born into it. I don't know any different."

One of the wives interjected, "Well, I am very impressed with you. It takes a lot of courage to do what you're doing, and it looks like you brought in the perfect person to help you realize your dreams. Dax is one of the best investors on the west coast. All of his ideas turn to gold."

"Thank you. I have a lot of friends who support me, so I feel very blessed."

Dax reached for my hand under the table. "The vineyard is beautiful, the views amazing. But I can't say that I would have taken a chance on her idea had I not heard her speak. She is truly in love with her land, and she captured my heart as soon as she spoke."

A few awes could be heard, and then Dax continued. "Of course, she spoke in French and I had no idea what she said, but it was lovely."

Everyone laughed. I turned to look at Dax, looking for sincerity. Had he really started falling for me, or was he just playing to the table?

The evening was thoroughly enjoyable, and I found myself having a really nice time. Despite my earlier thoughts about the glitz and glamour, I discovered most of the partygoers were just like me: hard-working individuals who cared about their community.

I did my best to avoid Riley, but didn't have much luck avoiding Wren. I later found out she was the public relations director for the hospital. Since Dax and his family were some of the highest contributing benefactors, she made a point of hanging on him.

When the dancing began, many people took to the floor, while

I watched from the sides. Wren had swooped in and taken Dax to 'meet some people.' I'd smiled sweetly, giving him my permission to leave me.

A short time later, Riley came and stood next to me. He offered to share his glass of whiskey. "Need something stronger?"

I took it from him and took a heavy drink. "God bless you."

I was rewarded with a throaty laugh. He took the glass and put it down on the cocktail table next to us. Taking my hand, he said, "Dance with me."

He pulled me through the crowd. He turned towards me on the dance floor, pulling me in close.

"Can you dance, Riley?"

Swaying back and forth, he had one arm wrapped around me. The other held our hands out to the side. "No, but I can sway."

"You're ridiculous."

He put his check down close to mine. "Yes."

When he pulled back, I couldn't help but smile at his cheesy grin.

Dancing with Riley was fun. Swirling me around and dipping me, he was quirky and silly, laughing often.

When the song ended, he pulled me in and held me tight. The next song was a slow one, and he didn't allow me to escape his embrace.

Neither of us spoke. We just stood close together and swayed to the music.

My mind wandered, thinking about his hair, and how I'd wanted to feel the soft curls brushing his collar. I reached up to touch them, only to realize they were now gone.

I lifted my head quickly, and looked up into his face, realizing what I'd done. I was met with a knowing smile and a tightening of his arm around me.

I'd just relaxed back into him, resting my head under his chin, when I felt him stiffen and pull back from me slightly.

A moment later, Dax appeared and asked if he could cut in.

Riley released me, "Of course."

He turned back to me, giving my hand to Dax. "Thank you for the dance, Julie."

"You're welcome."

Dax took me in his arms and expertly moved me around the floor. His movements flowed with grace and elegance, and we glided from place to place, flowing effortlessly with the music, weaving in and out among the other partners.

Like a butterfly I floated, and when the music finally stopped, I grinned at Dax with sheer joy. "Dax, you're a beautiful dancer."

He kissed my hand and bowed before me. "Blessed with a beautiful partner."

I curtsied, giggled, and laughed at his outlandish behavior. Batting my eyelashes, I put my hand to my chest, "You're too kind, sir."

He took my hand, and pulled me towards him, whispering, "I'm ready to get out of here, how about you?"

With feigned surprise, I said, "Don't you need to stay and ask people for all of their money?"

"I've already taken it all. I'm ready to take you home."

He must have seen the look of shock on my face because he quickly added. "Your home, Julie. To Shaye's. As much as I would love to take you to my place, I think we need more time to get to know each other."

He leaned in close, whispering, "And I would really like to kiss you."

"And I would really like to kiss you, so we certainly should leave."

Rubbing his nose to mine, he kissed it and led me off the dance floor, making our way to our table.

I intentionally kept my focus forward, not wanting to make eye contact with Wren or Riley, wherever they might be. I smiled politely and received a few hugs from the ladies I'd met at our table. I was told to expect emails requesting rooms for our opening weekend.

"I would be happy to host you. I'll look forward to your email."

Graciously, Dax excused us and expertly maneuvered us to the door. People seemed to part the way for him, and he glided through them as if it was expected they would move.

The driver was holding the door for us when we reached the limousine, and as soon as the door was shut, Dax pulled me to him and kissed me.

Firm lips pressed against mine, and when my brain finally caught up with my body, I relaxed. He deepened the kiss, slanting his head to get closer to me.

His hand ran down my back and squeezed my hip, and I moaned softly, melting into him. His mouth left mine and began trailing kisses across my cheek.

In my ear, he whispered, "You are so gorgeous. I have been wanting to do that since I picked you up tonight. Julie! I am spellbound by you."

I was surprised. "Really?"

He gave me a quick peck on the lips and lifted me onto his lap. "If I was honest, I've wanted to do that since I saw you at the wedding. You are an angel." He said, alternating kisses on my cheeks.

I curled into him, wrapping my arms around him. "I've wanted to kiss you too."

The car started rolling and he slid me off of him, slanting in his seat to look directly at me. "Julie. Next Weekend. Come with me to San Francisco. We'll tour some wineries in Napa Valley, we'll ride bikes, we'll drink good wine, I'll let you choose, of course. Come with me. Just the two of us."

"Next weekend? Isn't our inspection on Friday?"

His eyes lit up. “Yes! I was thinking I’d fly up Friday morning and then you can fly back with me on Saturday.”

My head was spinning. “Wow! That’s a lot.”

He gripped my hands. “Say yes, Julie. Say yes.”

Laughter bubbled up. The decision felt a little crazy, but I said yes anyway.

He gripped my face in his hands and kissed me hard. “I’ll make all the arrangements. You just show up looking beautiful.”

My joy dropped a little at his statement. I pushed the feeling down, commenting that it had been a long time since I’d had a proper vacation.

“Then it’s time, don’t you think?”

I looked down at his lap, my hand rested on his thigh, squeezing it gently and noticing the strength of him.

When my eyes came back to his, I could see he was trying not to laugh. “Don’t tempt me tonight, Julie,” he warned with a grin.

I continued flirting. “I have no idea what you’re talking about.”

We kissed some more until we reached Shaye’s house, and then he walked me to the door. “I’ll call you tomorrow.”

“I’d like that.”

“Good-night, Julie.”

I said good-night and quietly let myself into the house.

A light was on in the living room, and I quietly went in to turn it off, only to notice Shaye curled up in one of the oversized chairs.

“Shaye?”

She turned at my voice and put her mug of tea on the coffee table in front of her. “Oh, hey, you’re home earlier than I expected.” Her voice sounded sad.

“Are you okay? Is May okay?”

She laughed softly, and I saw her wipe a tear from under her eye as I sat down across from her.

"What's the matter?"

She continued staring out the window. "It was right here where Nick gave me my Dad's letter. The one he wrote me about the house on the Island. That he hoped I'd found my way back to Nick, and that everything they did, they'd done for me."

"I remember." I reached for her hand.

"It's funny how parents always know what's best for their children when they can't even see it."

Shaye wasn't really talking to me. It was more like she was talking at me, lost in her own reminiscing.

Her words gave me pause about my own parents. Why did they send me away? Why did they leave the resort to me and move away? I hadn't imagined there was anything deeper than that they'd wanted to move to Eastern Washington. But, as Shaye talked, I wondered if they'd really wanted to break me and Jason apart so I could be someone stronger. And I had become someone stronger; the people of the island just hadn't been ready to accept me that way.

Turning her head back to me, she choked on a cry. "If my dad hadn't died, I never would have gone back to the island. I would have never found my place, and I would never have known how much he loved me."

"Oh, Shaye." I got down on my knees in front of her. "Of course, he loved you."

"And Nick?"

I chuckled. "I have absolute faith that Nick would have come to get you eventually. He was miserable."

"I want to go home, Julie. I miss my family."

I stood and pulled her from the chair. "Me too. But can we sleep first? I've had three glasses of champagne and a whisky. I need an aspirin and a good night's sleep."

I turned off the lamp, and we walked arm in arm down the hall, using my phone to guide us.

"Did you want to tell me about your night?"

"Well, Dax invited me to San Francisco next weekend."

She stopped abruptly. "He did?" I grinned broadly and she laughed. "WOW! Are you going?"

"I said yes."

"Good for you." She started walking again.

"And Riley was there."

She stopped again. "Why was Riley there?"

"His family supports the hospital. His sister is apparently the public relations director, so Riley went as her date."

"I have a hard time imagining Riley at a gala."

"He actually cleans up very nicely. He cut his hair and shaved and looked moderately respectable." I didn't tell her that I missed his longer hair, but I did tell her he was wearing a very cool tuxedo. "Most of the men were wearing basic black tuxedos but his was blue and black velvet. Very retro. It was kind of comical, really – arrogant. It felt like kind of a snub, but he was never lacking from female attention."

We'd stopped outside my room and Shaye was smiling at me oddly.

"What?"

"You told me more about Riley than you did Dax."

"Because Dax was my date, and Riley wasn't supposed to be there."

"What was his sister like?"

"Snarky, possessive of Dax, apparently she's been in love with him for years. She wasn't very nice to me, and took every opportunity to keep him away from me."

Shaye covered her mouth and laughed quietly. "Oh my."

"What do you mean, 'oh my?'"

"This sounds awfully familiar don't you think?"

"We aren't in high school, Shaye. She doesn't need to fight me for him."

"Were you willingly going to turn Jason over to me?"

For what seemed like the millionth time tonight, I pressed my fingers to my temples. "Oh my God! What am I doing? Are you saying I should walk away from Dax?"

"I'm not saying that at all. I'm saying that you know how she feels, and you have an opportunity to make a friend, not a rival."

To myself, I muttered, "I probably won't ever see her again, but you're right. I could have been kinder, more amiable to her tonight." I groaned. "Why does this drama follow me?"

She hugged me and said, "Because you're not settled. You'll get there."

"I'm going to bed. I thought I might have breakfast with Dax, but he didn't mention anything, so I'm ready to go whenever you are tomorrow."

"What about a 7:00 a.m. flight?"

"Lord, no! How about noon?"

"Eleven."

"Fine. But I want pizza from Foolish Amy's when we land. I'm going to need something greasy."

"Deal."

We hugged again. "Good night, Shaye."

"Good night, Julie."

19

THE FLIGHT HOME was uneventful. The weather was calm and the company quiet, allowing me to sleep off the residual champagne from the night before.

Evie met us at the dock with Ellie on her hip. Smiling and jovial, she hugged us both and asked me about the gala.

Noah was bouncing around at her heels, and JT was leaning over the dock to trail his fingers through the water.

Shaye handed Evie the car seat carrying May, and reached out to yank JT back from the edge by his life jacket.

I responded vaguely. "It was…shiny."

"Shiny?"

"Yeah, you know, Nick's kind of people," I said jokingly.

Shaye rolled her eyes and shoved my suitcase at me.

I laughed. "What? He would've loved the event."

Linking arms with Evie, we walked up the dock. Shaye turned

to wave to her pilot friend as he taxied back out into the bay to head back to Seattle.

Noah and JT ran ahead back towards the resort. I saw them immediately remove the life jackets, throwing them to the ground when they met the grass.

I titled my head back as if to groan and said, "I need pizza."

"Nick and Ethan are going to meet us there."

I almost asked if Riley was joining us too, but I didn't want to give Shaye any more reasons to question my affection.

I picked up the life jackets when we reached the end of the dock, hung them on the dock hooks, and said, "Okay, I'll meet you guys there."

Evie left me at my Scout and went to help Shaye with all of her kids.

Foolish Amy's Pizza Garage was crowded for a Sunday, but Nick and Ethan had already taken a large table out on the deck. We joined them under the umbrella.

JT and Noah ran around chaotically, until Ethan grabbed them both by the back of their shirts and settled them down in their seats, handing each of them a matchbox car.

He spoke authoritatively when he said, "Sit still for lunch, and I'll take you to the beach this afternoon."

"Yes, sir." JT said respectfully.

"Yes, Dad," Noah spoke confidently. Pride for his father resonated from his words.

Shaye's little girl, Ellie, snuggled up in Nick's lap. Shaye worked to secure the car seat in the modified high chair, while I sipped on my iced tea, watching in fascination at the choreography of being part of a family.

Multiple conversations took place throughout lunch, piling on top of each other as one ended and another was picked back up.

After we'd eaten our fill of pizza, and the kids were given ice cream bars, I excused myself to make my way home. "I am absolutely exhausted and need to get ready for the week."

A chorus of hugs and goodbyes sounded around the table. I made my way to my truck, sighing loudly at having some peace and quiet.

As soon as I made it back to the vineyard, I drug my suitcase inside, left it by the front door of the tasting room, and, with heavy footsteps, carried myself up to my apartment.

The combination of champagne, a late night, greasy pizza, and rambunctious kids caught up to me. I was asleep a minute after falling on my bed.

When I woke later and looked around the room, I couldn't tell whether it was morning or night. The shadows in the room could have been either, but the clock said it was evening, so I got up and groggily went downstairs to retrieve my suitcase.

Through the windows of the room, I saw the porch light on up at the main house and thought I would walk up to see if Riley had returned. Changing my mind about the suitcase, I grabbed my jacket and a flashlight and strolled up the hill. I was still a little bleary from my nap, and wasn't in the mood to drive the golf cart, craving a calm, quiet walk.

Reaching the front porch, I saw Riley through the window glass. Hunched over the construction desk, he looked deep in thought as he scribbled on a pad of paper.

He was so gorgeous. Over the past few weeks, we'd grown so much closer, but I had no idea how he really felt about me. We were friendly, flirty, and I was definitely attracted to him. He just seemed... out of reach.

I'd teased him about Evie, but I didn't really think he was pining for her. He also seemed to be over his former girlfriend, but he never talked about anyone since then.

Everything about him was just…solid.

Staring at him through the glass, I questioned my intentions towards being here.

Lately, every time I was near him, I wanted him to flirt with me. When he did, I barked at him and pushed him away. When he didn't, I pouted like a child. He was making me crazy.

He was the kind of guy that when he loved again, it would be forever, and I wasn't sure that girl was supposed to be me. I still felt unfinished, and I didn't know how to get to the other side.

I saw a half-eaten sandwich, a bag of chips, and a beer sat on the table next to him, and my stomach churned from the pizza.

I quietly opened the door, and he smiled sweetly at me when he looked up. "Hey, you're home."

His voice washed over me. He sounded genuinely glad to see me.

Gently clicking the door shut behind me, I wandered to the desk and sat down in the folding chair on the other side.

"Yeah, we flew back this afternoon. I just woke up from a nap and saw your light on."

He stood and asked if I was hungry.

"No. Sit back down. I'm fine. I just wanted to say hi."

Lowering himself back into the chair he said, "I love the new color scheme. Plum, is it?"

He was making fun of me, and I chuckled. "You can say purple."

"Purple it is then. It matches the curtains."

I looked around at the walls, seeing them really for the first time. "I think it turned out lovely."

He laughed out loud at me. "How was your weekend?"

I looked at him from under my brows and he laughed again.

"Well, it was lovely, but I kept getting interrupted."

"I really needed some decisions to be made."

"I'm sure you did," I said sardonically.

We sat smiling at each other across the table.

I jerked my head towards the paper on the desk. "What are you working on?"

His grin grew. "I'm designing a glamp-ground."

"A what?"

Tilting the paper, a little to his left, he slid his chair over, making room for me to see. "Here, come look."

I stepped around the desk and looked at what appeared to be a plot of land, with large tee-pees and common areas with big fire-pits.

He pointed with his pencil. "Each fire-pit is set in the middle of 2 – 4 tents. The tents will be elevated over a wood base, and will have all the comforts of a hotel room, even running water for a sink. They'll need to share a communal shower room, one for the men and one for the women, but for the most part, each room will have what they need. Even a coffee pot."

I looked down at him and his eyes were sparkling. Teasing him, I spoke softly, almost with wonder. "A coffee pot?"

He laughed at me, and I wanted to reach over and touch him. "For the not so rustic individual."

"Glamorous camping."

"Glamping."

His word made me laugh. "Glamping?"

He looked down at his drawing again and pointed to a larger building as he spoke. "Yeah, it's a thing now. I've designed a large eco-friendly common building for family style meals and nightly events. You know, so all those rich folks can pretend they're roughing it."

I leaned back against the desk and crossed my arms. His leg brushed up against mine as he leaned back in the chair, swiveling it side to side. He smiled at me.

Playfully, I said, "Rich folk? I thought they were coming to my resort?"

"Maybe you can offer this as an alternative?" His tone was teasing.

My smile dropped a little bit. "Are you suggesting we build this here?"

He shrugged.

I looked back down at his drawing, feeling a little more serious. "How many acres do you need?"

"Five."

We stared at each other pensively. This project suited him, and oddly, I felt like it suited me. I wasn't willing to sacrifice one project for the other, but maybe there was a way to do both.

"We should take the golf cart out to the tree line tomorrow. There's an access road that connects to the main road on the other side of the property. It might be a..." I shifted on the desk when he rolled closer to me. "It might be a good place to plot this out."

His grin grew. I stood and walked back around to the other side of the desk.

"I'd like that."

Left with not much else to say, I walked towards the front door. "Well, I'm glad you made it back safely."

He stood. "You too."

The space between us felt like it was filled with questions. Questions that neither one of us was willing to ask, but desperately wanted to know the answers to.

"We have our inspection Friday."

"We do."

"Will we pass?"

"We will." He was so confident, standing a few feet from me, hands shoved in his front pockets, legs spread slightly.

"Dax is coming up."

"I figured he would."

I shifted uncomfortably in front of him. "He asked me to go to San Francisco with him next weekend."

Riley didn't move a muscle. Had I not noticed the tensing of his jaw and the darkening of his eyes, I wouldn't have thought he even heard me.

"He thought it would be nice for just the two of us to go away, get to know each other better."

"Sounds fun."

I felt tears stinging my eyes. These feelings were making me crazy. Turning quickly, I yanked open the front door to leave before he saw me make a fool of myself.

"I'll see you in the morning, Riley," I said over my shoulder as I went out the door and walked quickly home, not even sure if he replied or not. I hadn't cried over a boy – a man, really – since Jason.

When I reached my apartment, I immediately undressed. Without even washing my face, or brushing my teeth, I crawled into bed, my tears coming freely, until I fell asleep whimpering.

For the remainder of the week, Riley ignored me. Whether it was intentional or not didn't really matter; we had an inspection in five days, and the crew was serious and focused on making sure we were ready.

The resort was almost looking like a finished structure, exactly how I'd envisioned it.

From the outside, the cedar shingles matched the lap siding. The faux gas lights on the rails and jutting beams cast warm glows on the pathways and windows.

Only the interior painting, furnishings, decorations, and landscaping would be left to do after this week.

Friday morning, Dax called me to say he was getting ready to get on the float plane, and asked if I was excited for our trip.

"I am. I've done some research on the wineries I'd like to visit, and I'm looking forward to it."

I could hear his smile through the phone. "Can't wait to see which ones." His voice softened when he said. "It will be peaceful Julie, just the two of us."

His voice was like honey, and I couldn't deny that it was incredibly attractive.

"I'll see you in a few hours. Do you need me to pick you up?"

"No, Ethan is leaving his truck for me. Or some kind of truck that I guess everyone on the island uses?"

I laughed. "Yes, it's an old truck that belonged to Nick's dad. Most of the time it's left at the dock, but sometimes it gets left in really random locations, like the post office, or a beach."

"Well, in that case, I'll call if it's missing."

"I'll see you in a few hours."

We said our good-byes and hung up.

His plane was supposed to land at 9:00 a.m., and our inspection was scheduled for eleven. We were told to plan on four to six hours for the inspection, and two hours after that to get the approval.

Riley had been staying closely connected to the county, and he assured me we'd done everything right.

I waited until I knew Dax had arrived before I went up to the construction office, desperately needing a buffer between me and Riley. When I saw the county truck, followed by the old truck Dax was driving, I made my way up to the office.

Men's laughter and bold voices greeted me as soon as I stepped in the house. Riley and his crew were standing around the room, coffee mugs in hand. They looked rugged and rough, their clothing worn from work, and not from manufacturing.

I, too, was wearing my old jeans and boots. Riley looked me up and down appreciatively before asking if I needed a coffee. I shook my head no, and he nodded.

When Dax saw me, his face lit up. He greeted me enthusiastically, pulling me into the conversation with the inspector.

"Here's our little lady."

I grimaced when he said that.

Shaking hands with the inspector, I asked if he needed anything from me, and if he was ready to get started.

An oversized clipboard was tucked under his arm, and he reached for it, flipping to a page that needed my, Riley, and Dax's signatures.

"Just need your John Hancock and we can head over to the site."

I signed it, then the inspector passed it to Dax, who then passed it to Riley without making eye contact.

When the signatures were complete, we made our way out the front door, dutifully following behind Dax and the inspector.

Riley came up behind me and whispered in my ear as he walked. "You look adorable today."

I glared at him and did my best to look disdainful. "You look… bedraggled."

"Ha! I thought you would say sexy or kissable."

"In your dreams!"

"You left too early for me to have my dreams come true."

"You're always so bawdy in the daylight, and can't seem to deliver at night." I challenged him.

"Shhhh. Your boyfriend will hear you." He winked at me as he trudged up ahead, and I stomped behind him.

The day seemed to drag on and on. The checklist was never ending. The inspector checked the roof, the heating, the electrical, the plumbing, the quality of the wood.

Pizza was delivered later in the afternoon, and by the end of the day, I'd seen every crack and crevice of my resort.

When we were all back at the office, I suggested that everyone come back to the tasting room where I would serve them wine and snacks.

Dax gleefully said that sounded like a great idea. And he echoed that he would love for everyone to join us.

His enthusiasm caught me off guard. When I glanced at Riley, his eyes were wide, and he was trying not to laugh.

The inspector made apologies that he had to catch a ferry, but that my inspection looked perfect. Then he added that he was going to give me preliminary approval, and that I shouldn't expect to delay the project.

"Thank you so much! Let me walk you out."

Riley followed behind me. After the inspector drove away, he said, "You know, you didn't really need to invite the crew down for wine."

"I want to. They've worked really hard. They deserve it."

He looked a little embarrassed, struggling with his next words. "It's just…they're kind of beer guys."

I suddenly felt as if I really wanted them to join me, and I wanted to do everything to please them. "I think I have beer."

"Julie," he implored.

"I want to thank them."

"They know."

"Please go get some beer and meet me at the tasting room," I said stubbornly.

He looked at me tenderly and said, "I have some here. I'll bring it down."

"Thank you."

He reached out and gently held my neck, his thumb caressing my cheek. "You're welcome."

The wind had picked up and the clouds were moving quickly across the sky.

"I'm going to head back. Please tell the guys and Dax to come down when they're ready. I'll prepare some food and see you all in a bit."

I stepped away from him, feeling the first drops of rain splash down on my head. He put his hands back in his pockets and nodded at me as I drove back down the hill.

20

A DELUGE OF rain had started by the time I got back to the building. I parked the golf cart under the lean-to and ran through the mud, dragging dirt up the front steps to the door.

Under the covered porch, I stomped my feet to get the mud off, and then left my boots just outside the door, shaking the rain off my sleeves and out of my hair.

Once inside, I ran quickly up the stairs to my apartment and changed into clean leggings, a soft sweater, and a pair of house shoes. I headed back downstairs in time to see headlights coming down the driveway.

The construction crew was arriving and I needed to work fast.

In the kitchen, I quickly prepared a smoked cheese fondue, sliced up two loaves of French bread, and put some popcorn in the microwave.

While the popcorn was popping, I arranged roasted fruit and cheese on a pewter serving tray.

Riley might think they only wanted beer, but I wanted them to know how much I appreciated them. I wanted to serve them savory snacks.

I heard the door open, and I popped my head out from the kitchen to tell them to make themselves comfortable.

Riley and one of his crew were carrying in a cooler filled with beers. One by one, all six of them arrived, including Dax, and none of them took their shoes off.

I briefly winced at the thought of all the mud on the floor. Then I relaxed, thinking to myself that it was really no big deal and I could mop in the morning.

When the popcorn was finished popping, I added roasted pistachio nuts and seasonings. I proceeded to carry out all my appetizers, placing them on the bar next to the cocktail plates and napkins.

My parents had taught me to be a gracious host, frequently hosting wine pairing dinners and events.

The conversation was loud and boisterous. Everyone unanimously agreed that I would definitely pass inspection, and it would be just a matter of weeks before we would be ready to open.

Standing behind the bar, I raised my glass to them in a toast. "I couldn't have done it without all of you." I looked to Riley and Dax and thanked them equally, and one of the crew shouted out, "To a great team!" and a chorus of cheers went around the room.

The rain was coming down harder now, and the shutters on the house were banging back and forth against the glass.

Riley had been sitting at the end of the bar and commented that he would go out and secure them.

"Are you sure? I can do it later."

He smiled at me and stepped down from the bar stool. "I got it."

When he left the room, Dax reached across the bar and took my hand, saying softly, "Are you packed for tomorrow?"

"This weather is kind of bad, do you think we'll be able to leave?"

He glanced around the room to make sure no one was within hearing distance, and whispered, "If not, then maybe I could just stay here?"

I saw the shutters close across the windows and heard the latch from outside.

The weather was making me jittery, and the lights flickered. "Maybe we should talk about that tomorrow. This looks really bad."

Around the stone fireplace, the men started to stand, most of them commenting that they should probably get going.

"Hey, guys, thank you so much for your good work this past week. I agree this weather is getting pretty bad and I don't want you getting stuck on your way home."

Dax stood as well. "I guess I should head back to the resort as well."

I reached out my hand to him. "Wait just a minute, okay?"

He nodded and leaned against the bar.

I hugged the men goodbye, telling them to drive safely, and then turned back to Dax.

Sighing heavily, I sat on the bar stool next to him.

He leaned down and put his forehead against mine, and whispered, "This will pass. Meet me for breakfast before we leave. I promise tomorrow will be a beautiful day."

As he leaned in to kiss me, Riley came back through the front door. He was rain soaked and his cheeks were pink. "You're all boarded up. You should be protected tonight."

Standing from the bar stool, I wrapped my arms around the middle. "Thank you."

Neither man moved. Dax leaned on the bar, while Riley stood in the doorway.

Awkwardly, I shifted. "Well, thanks again."

Riley glanced briefly at Dax and then back at me. "Let me know if you need anything."

I hated the negativity passing between them, especially because I had no idea why there was such animosity. I wondered if it might be about me, but it was there before I'd started becoming more attached to Riley.

As soon as the front door shut behind him, Dax pulled me into his arms and leaned in to kiss my neck, mumbling, "I could stay?"

"No, go. I need to clean up and finish packing. I'll see you in the morning."

His kisses moved across my jaw and settled on my lips, tenderly kissing me, until I gently pushed at him and he released me.

Running his hands over his face, he said, "You are killing me."

We both laughed and I walked him to the door. "I'll see you in the morning."

Quickly leaning in, he gave me a sweet kiss on the cheek and reached out to squeeze my fingers. "See you in the morning."

I walked him out. The rain sprayed against us as we stood under the porch, and I ushered him off so I could get back inside.

He quickly ran to the truck, flashing his lights at me as he drove off.

With the door safely shut behind me, I took the food trays back to the kitchen. I started cleaning up, grateful that they'd enjoyed the food, and proud of myself for making an effort for them.

The wind had picked up. I heard it howling through the trees outside, the branches scraping the sides of the house. Back and forth they went, not letting up at all.

The lights flickered again, and I paused, waiting to see if they would stay on, giving myself a moment to think about what I needed to do if the power went out.

I took a flashlight from the kitchen drawer and carried it with me into the other room, keeping it close.

I had a generator that would automatically kick on if the power went off, but it hadn't been used in a while, and I wasn't completely confident there was propane in the tank.

A few steps into the tasting room, the power went out. I stopped in my tracks, allowing my eyes to adjust to the dark, and waited for the generator.

"Come on," I said to myself, adding, "Turn on."

After a moment, I realized it wasn't kicking on. I grabbed a coat and my flashlight to go outside and check on the tank.

Rounding the corner of the building, I shone the flashlight on the meter and wiped the rain from my eyes to see. It read half full.

Headlights were coming from the main house, and a moment later, Riley's truck came to a stop. He stepped out and ran towards me.

Shouting over the rain, he asked what I was doing.

The rain was hammering down on us, and I shone my flashlight on the tank, saying loudly, "My generator didn't kick on, but it has over half a tank of propane."

He put out his hand, and I gave him the flashlight.

I watched him go around to the other side and saw him turn a knob. When he looked back up at me, he raised his eyebrows. "It would help if you turned on the valve."

His eyes were laughing at me. When I saw the lights go back on in the tasting room, I stomped back inside, leaving him to follow, or leave, I didn't really care.

Slowly, after I'd slammed it shut, the front door opened and Riley stepped in. He took off his coat and shook off the water.

Leaving him standing in the middle of the room, I went upstairs to change out of my wet clothes, again. Taking my time, I hoped he'd be gone when I came back down, but I prayed he wouldn't be.

I was tired of the back and forth between us, and I intended to tell him so.

When I came back down the steps, he was squatting in front of the fireplace, a small fire building and turning the room intimate and cozy.

He stood and put his hands in his front pockets, gauging my mood, waiting for me to speak.

"Why are you here, Riley?"

He started to speak. I could tell by the lines crinkling at the corners of his eyes he was going to say something sarcastic, so I added, "And don't be smart."

His eyes turned warm. "I wanted to make sure you were okay. I didn't know you had a generator, and I didn't want you alone in the dark."

I took a chance and asked, "How did you know I was alone?"

His jaw tensed. "You try me, Juliette, you really do."

Stepping forward, I put my hand in the middle of his chest and felt his breathing change.

Not raising my eyes to him, I whispered, "Why haven't you tried to kiss me again?"

I was staring at his chest, patiently waiting for his response. His hands were still in his pockets.

Huskily he asked, "Do you want me to?"

When I looked up, I could see he was struggling not to reach for me. "I feel like…I feel like you're making fun of me."

He scoffed. "Hardly."

I whispered, "Then why am I so confused when you're around?"

"Can you elaborate on that confusion?"

His indifference and ability to be so thick-headed made me angry. I pushed at him, stepping back and stomping my foot.

"No, I cannot. You know what I'm talking about. You send me

sexy texts, you bring me coffee, you constantly interrupt me and Dax, you build me beautiful woodwork, and then you ignore me. Why?" I was almost shouting, and almost crying.

It was his turn to get angry. His brows furrowed and his eyes darkened. "How can you say I ignore you in the same sentence as everything else? I don't ignore you; I adore you. But you are so wrapped up in the shiny exterior of Dax, and the ghost of Jason, you can't see it. You think the people of the island crushed your spirit, but I've never met someone so driven and focused to be a success. You blame the past for your inability to love, but you compare every man to Jason. He wasn't a saint, Julie, and he didn't love you." His voice softened, and he added, "Not like you deserve to be loved."

His last words felt like a slap in the face. "Get out!" I said with quiet anger, desperately trying to control my emotions.

We were both breathing heavily, and he turned to leave, grabbing his coat off the rack. At the door he paused. "You want to know why I don't try and kiss you? Because you aren't ready. Open your eyes and your heart, Julie. Let go."

"I said get out." The tears were coming and I didn't want him to see me fall apart.

He came back to me and placed his hand on my cheek, his thumb caressing me. "You beautiful, crazy girl. I'll kiss you again, but not to help you make a decision. I'll kiss you when you can let everything go and kiss me back."

When he stepped away from me, I felt as if he took my whole heart and soul with him. Emptiness engulfed me, leaving behind a hole, I knew, only he could fill. My chest ached as I watched him leave, sucked away like a vacuum, gently closing the door behind him.

The wind and the rain raged outside, and I collapsed to the floor, emptying myself of years of pain, crying as if to exhume all the heartache from before.

Gradually, my tears subsided, and I was left in the quiet of the room, not knowing what to do next.

My only thought was that I wanted to be with Riley. Not someday, not later, but *right now.* I shot up off the floor, ran out the front door into the rain, and jumped into my truck.

A minute later I was parked in front of the office, my heart racing.

A dim light shone through a crack in the curtains, and I made my way to the front door, taking deep breaths of courage.

Soaked through, my hair hung in wet strands, and I nervously wiped my palms on the front of my pants, before I raised my hand to knock.

Thinking that maybe he couldn't hear the knock, I raised my hand again and the door flung open, my hand in mid-air.

Riley wasn't wearing a shirt, a dry T-shirt in his hands, his wet jeans unbuttoned at the top.

I opened my mouth to speak, and only a squeak came out.

Patiently, he waited, his hand on the door jamb, and I tried again.

Stepping forward, I said, "I'll kiss you back."

21

I THOUGHT HE would pull me to him and kiss me with all the pent-up frustration and energy that had been bouncing back and forth between us for weeks. I'd expected, almost wanted, a carnal attack on me at the front door – I felt like I needed him desperately.

But he didn't.

Opening the door wider, he stepped back, a silent invitation to come inside.

Humbly, I stepped across the threshold and wondered if I'd been too hasty. Adrenaline was zinging through me. Not fifteen minutes ago we'd been screaming at each other.

The air between us was thick with anticipation, intensified by the raging storm outside.

I moved towards the middle of the room and heard the door close softly behind me.

The generator here at the house was running, but the only light came from the kitchen: the solitary overhead that dimly lit the main room through the door.

"Wait right there." His voice was husky.

He threw his T-shirt on the couch, went into the bathroom, and came out a moment later with a towel.

Approaching me, almost cautiously, he reached out to dry my hair. Rubbing the towel gently across the top of my head and squeezing the water from the ends, he led me into the circle of his arms.

My body was shaking, and not from the cold. Eyes level with his chest, I watched his muscles flex beneath his smooth skin as he dried me off.

I knew that Riley would have an incredible body, he was so hard working. But seeing it in person was causing me to take deep breaths just to get air into my lungs.

Weeks ago, I'd caught a glimpse of his stomach, and knew he would have blond hairs on his chest. But I couldn't have imagined the golden smoothness of his broad shoulders, or the spattering of freckles that covered him. Valleys and shadows played across the muscles of his chest and arms, creating the definition of a body earned through manual labor.

I had to reach out and touch him – softly, gently – and I felt him tremble. He was nervous.

Slowly, I raised my eyes to his, and trailed my fingertips across his chest, tracing the freckles, making a map on his muscles.

Every part of my body ached with need to kiss him, to touch him, to be consumed by him. He simply stood there, patting my hair dry and wiping the mascara off from under my eyes, running from the rain.

"We match." He whispered it, and I almost didn't hear him for the sound of my blood pumping through my body.

"Huh?" I could barely get the word out. I could smell him

standing so close to me, and I leaned in to press my lips to his chest, inhaling the warm, woodsy scent of him.

I heard him laugh softly. "Our freckles."

"Mm-hmm."

I felt him lean down and press his lips against my head, taking his own time breathing me in.

When he stepped away from me, I got chilled. I saw him glance at my wet T-shirt, my breasts straining against the fabric of my bra, aching to be released.

Dropping the towel to the floor, he reached for the hem of my T-shirt and slowly rolled it up and over my head.

I felt the goosebumps on my arms and watched as my chest rose and fell. This was so unexpected. A dream. I was in the moment, but watching at the same time.

His hands went to the button of my jeans and unfastened it, grazing my lower belly with his knuckles, teasing me, and I inhaled sharply. Tremors of desire leapt through me, and I pulled in my stomach. He pulled down the zipper, and I caught my breath when he wrapped his hands around my back, sliding underneath the waistband and pulling my wet jeans slowly from my body.

As he knelt down in front of me, I tentatively rested my fingertips on his shoulders and stepped out of the jeans.

Neither of us was speaking, my mind still whirling with the desire for just a kiss.

His fingers went under the thin string of my thong underwear, and I felt them glide over my hips and thighs on their way to the floor.

Gripping my hips, he held me in place, and when his lips pressed against my inner thigh, my eyes closed. Luxuriating in the soft touch of his lips, I thought my knees would buckle and I would fall to the ground.

When he stood, his eyes were sparkling with unrestrained laughter.

I swallowed audibly. "I don't think this is very funny."

His big hands held my sides, his thumbs flicking over my nipples straining against my wet bra. "Nor do I, Juliette, nor do I."

With painstaking slowness, he reached around me and effortlessly unsnapped my bra. It fell to the floor, and a second later, his mouth was on my breast and I was holding his head in place. My head fell back in exquisite torture as he sucked on my breasts, gently nipping them, and then softly lapping at them with his tongue.

Abruptly, I was lifted in his arms and carried up the stairs. Holding on to his neck, I buried my head under his chin when he told me to watch my head. "The ceilings are really low."

"Old houses," I teased.

"Who built this thing, anyway? Hobbits?"

"Hey!" I was laughing. "My parents are not that short."

Laughing, he threw me on the bed, and I was suddenly nervous.

His bed was unmade, the sheets rumpled, and I wanted to crawl under them with him.

We'd been dancing around this since Evie's wedding, and now that it was here, I didn't want to rationalize it. He was giving me too much time to think.

I pulled my knees to my chest, crossing my ankles and wrapping my arms around my shins. "I said I would kiss you back. Are you going to get to it, or what?" I teased, trying to hide my nerves.

Standing at the end of the bed, his eyes bore into mine, and he slowly unzipped his jeans.

He never tore his gaze from mine as he stepped from the pants and stood before me. I tried not to look, wanting to stay connected to him, but I couldn't stop myself.

Everything about him was perfect. His thighs were thick and strong, covered with blond hairs, and I couldn't wait for him any longer.

Bringing myself to my knees, I crawled to him.

I wrapped my arms around his neck.

I ached, deep in my belly, my sex clenching, desperate for him. "Please. Please kiss me," I begged.

With both hands, he grabbed my bottom and lifted me, spreading my legs and lowering me back to the bed.

When he had nestled between my legs, I thrust my hips toward him and wrapped my legs around the back of his thighs, urging him to enter me.

He resisted, but I could feel his hard, smooth shaft pressing against me.

Warm skin, soft and smooth, pressed against me and he lowered his lips to my chest, placing soft, wet kisses everywhere, working his way up my neck to my ears, purring words of love and adoration.

I was being tormented and loved, writhing beneath him.

When I couldn't take it any longer, I felt him rise over me, lifting his hips. He was looking deep into my eyes.

With all the restraint I had left, I uttered, "I love you. Please."

My mouth opened in a silent gasp and my breath shuddered as I slowly felt him fill me, stretching me until he was fully inside me, touching the deepest parts of my soul.

When my eyes fluttered closed, he whispered, "Open your eyes, Julie."

His gorgeous eyes were so full of love, it was all I could do not to kiss him. I pulled his mouth to mine, no longer able to wait for him.

Our mouths merged, and I was melting. Our tongues clashed together, our mouths opening to take everything of each other.

Never had I felt so connected to another person. We could barely break apart. His deep thrusts were so rhythmic, calculated and intentional. With every movement, he rubbed against me, relentless in his efforts to claim me as his.

My arms moved frantically, trying to hold on as he continued to move against me, rubbing and thrusting as if he couldn't get close enough to me.

Our pace built, our bodies frantic for release, binding us together. His hands cradled my head and I buried my face in his neck.

I felt like I was having an out of body experience, the tingling in my body building, reaching all the way to my toes.

With a final thrust into me, he ground against me, my body tightening, my back arching and I screamed as I felt myself break apart, my orgasm shattering through me. His mouth met mine, capturing everything that was left in me, taking it as his own. He came, and I felt his guttural moan as he continued to kiss me, his muscles tightening above me, and then relaxing.

Slowly, sweetly, we both relaxed, my body languid beneath him. I threw my arms out to my side and started to laugh.

He rolled to my side and propped his head up with his right hand. "That's not a response I've ever had."

Rolling my head to look at him, I reached across and held his cheek with my hand. "Did you expect me to cry?" I said unsympathetically, a teasing lilt to my tone.

"No. That would be asking too much." He laughed, and I pushed at his chest, causing him to fall back. On his way, he pulled me with him, lifting me up and over to straddle him.

His eyes were filled with tenderness as he smoothed my hair back behind my ears.

Leaning down to kiss him, I felt him growing hard again, and I grinned wickedly.

"That's a pleasant surprise."

"It's you."

This time, I rose above him, guiding him into me. I closed my eyes, put my head back and set my hips in a thrusting rhythm that elevated me closer and closer to another orgasm.

"Touch yourself, Julie," he said softly, his words lighting me on fire, and I rubbed myself as he gripped my bottom, thrusting himself into me. My mind was frenzied, my moans loud as my body fought for release, climbing higher and higher, I pushed against his chest with my free hand and pushed my sex down hard on him one last time, taking all of him as deep as I could.

"Come for me, Juliette. So…fucking…beautiful." He pushed up into me with each word, as a firework of lights shot out behind my eyes and I convulsed on him, shaking from the force of our love making.

I flopped down on his chest, spent and exhausted. His chest rumbled underneath me, and I whispered, "Are you laughing at me, now?"

"Yes."

I raised my head, placing my hands on his chest and resting my chin on the back of them. I couldn't respond. I could only stare at his gorgeous smiling face.

His eyes roved over my face, and he stroked my hair back, lovingly touching me.

Silently, we stared, marveling at being together.

He opened his mouth to speak, and then closed it again.

I raised my eyebrows questioningly, a small smile playing on my mouth.

"C'mon, Bob. Spit it out."

He reminded me of what I thought a grown-up Jason would have been, but calmer. Now that I thought more about it, I'd never felt this safe with Jason. I felt as if Riley was my partner, that I could tease him without fear of him leaving me. I could fight with him, without fear of him closing up on me. I knew I could trust him.

"Where'd you go?" he asked.

Quickly I shook my head.

He rolled me to my side and tapped my temple. "You went somewhere. Stay with me. Don't go into that pretty little head of yours."

"I was just thinking…" It was so hard to admit to him that I was falling for him. "I was just thinking that I trust you."

Leaning down, he gave me a sweet kiss, and said softly against my lips, "I love you, too."

I put my hands to his chest and leaned back so I could see him more clearly. Squinting my eyes at him, I said, "I said I trust you, not I love you."

He leaned down to plant tiny kisses on my chin and cheeks. "You said it earlier."

"I did not!" I furrowed my brow.

My vehemence made him laugh. "Oh, my poor baby. You were so lost in passion you don't even remember." He jumped out of the bed, and smacked my bottom on the way out.

"Ow."

"I need food." He threw me a T-shirt from his dresser. "Put this on. I'll make us some eggs."

My head was spinning with the 'I love you' thing, and I couldn't keep up with his words. "I love you?"

"It's usually said as a statement, or declaration, not a question, but yes, you do." He gave me more kisses. "Hurry up, I'm hungry."

He left me staring after him, feeling an ache in my heart.

I pulled the T-shirt over my head and met him down in the kitchen. I jumped up on the counter, watching him pull eggs and green grapes from the fridge, setting them on the counter next to me.

Effortlessly, he cracked the eggs and let them cook while he made toast and poured me a glass of wine.

"Has this been an affliction of yours for long?" I asked as I popped a grape in my mouth.

He propped a hip against the counter and smiled, his eyes crinkling at the sides in humor. "What? This lurrrvve I have for you?"

I punched him in the arm. "You don't need to mock me."

He turned back to the stove and flipped the eggs. "But it's so much fun."

"Seriously. We've known each other for a long time, and you're always just so…just so laid back and Riley-ish."

He laughed. "Riley-ish?"

"Yeah, you're always so together, and calm, and happy. When did your feelings change?"

"Who said my feelings for you have changed?"

Every moment I'd spent with Riley before Evie's wedding ran through my head in a jumble of memories. "I thought you had a thing for Evie?"

Removing the pan from the stove, he turned the heat off and then stepped between my legs.

I hooked my legs around his waist, fully aware that I wasn't wearing any underwear.

His hands were rubbing the outside of my thighs and he was looking at me hesitantly. "Do you remember the first time we met?"

"The day Evie closed the bakery. The day Ethan got punched."

"Right." His look was intent.

Evie had just closed her bakery for the season, and we had all met at the resort to celebrate.

When Riley walked in, I remembered asking him how he knew Evie.

"But you said you asked Evie out."

"I did. But I didn't say it to embarrass Evie, or get Ethan's attention. I said it to see what you would do."

"Why?" My heart was fluttering.

He raised his hands to hold my face. "Oh, Juliette, you are such a mess. And I mean that in the most loving way. When I walked out onto that deck at the bar and saw you, I felt like I got punched in the gut. The bottom of my world fell out from underneath me. You were brighter than the sun, your smile bewitched me, and I almost just fell at your feet begging you to…to do whatever you wanted with me."

"But you really had asked Evie out, right?"

"I had." He paused. "And I did want to go out with her, at the time. But I think I felt like I needed to poke you in some way – get your attention. I almost felt like the universe was playing a cruel joke by putting you in front of me, after I'd already asked Evie out."

"When you walked out on the deck that day, you were so casual. You just walked in like you belonged with us, all cool and guy-like."

He laughed and kissed me sweetly. "If I'd started flirting with you then, you would have chewed me up and spit me out."

"But I liked you."

"You may have liked me, but I would have been just another toy to you then."

"You came to Evie's engagement party." I was trying to remember all the times he was with us, when he was near Evie.

"You invited me."

Had I? The party had been a secret, but now I remembered that he'd come into the tasting room one Friday night and sat at the bar talking with me. I hadn't thought anything of it at the time. I remembered that I'd invited him to piss him off, rub it in that Evie had chosen Ethan. When he'd said yes, I remember feeling like I was losing a best friend.

The realization that I'd had a thing for Riley for a long time was becoming very clear, and I whispered, "You came to family dinners."

He whispered back, "You invited me."

"You were always here on the weekends."

"'There's a band playing this weekend, Riley, you should stay.'"

I covered my mouth with my hand. He was always here for me, because of me, and I always wanted him here.

"You're building my resort."

"You told Ethan to hire me."

Riley had recently become the most stable person in my life. He had never pushed my buttons until recently, and even when I looked back at our kiss at Evie's wedding, I remembered that we were both surprised by it. Not because it was weird, but because it wasn't.

I may have spoken the words earlier out of passion, but when I said them again, I meant them with every part of my being. "Riley, I love you."

I felt tears stinging my eyes, as he pressed his lips to mine, saying, "I know."

22

RILEY TRIED TO carry me back upstairs, my legs wrapped around his waist. We only made it as far as the living room, when he set me down on the desk and made love to me on top of the construction plans.

I couldn't stop touching him, kissing him, loving him.

After another orgasm overtook me, I dropped my legs over the edge of the table, and closed my eyes, sighing heavily. "I'm done. You need to let me sleep."

He snorted and I cracked one eye open, watching him pull his jeans back up.

Reaching for my hands, he pulled me upright, and we climbed the stairs together.

Early the next morning, I woke with a start. The rain had stopped and a quiet peace had settled outside.

My mind, however, was not at peace when I realized I was supposed to be going to San Francisco with Dax.

I needed to talk to Evie.

Riley was sleeping soundly on his stomach next to me, his arms tucked under the pillow, soft snores coming from him.

Quietly, slowly, I stepped out of bed and searched the floor for something to wear. It was still dark outside and I had difficulty finding my way around, so I grabbed a T-shirt and a pair of joggers from Riley's dresser.

Creeping down the stairs, I quietly let myself out and started my truck. I winced when the engine came to life, hoping I didn't wake Riley, and I drove to Evie's house.

I sent her a text, hoping she would get it before I got there, but when I pulled into her driveway all the lights were out, so I assumed she hadn't.

Parking next to her Volkswagen, I went to their front door to let myself in.

When I pushed on the latch, it was locked. "What the heck?" I said out loud to myself, and then muttered, "Evie, no one locks their doors."

I looked under a planter box and above the door for a key and found nothing.

Placing my hands on my hips, I looked to the windows and saw the one to their master bathroom was open. Walking through their landscaping, I reached up for the ledge and pulled myself up, getting my stomach on the ledge before I pulled my legs in.

I had managed to get one leg through the window when Ethan came crashing through the bathroom door with a bat.

"What on earth are you doing?"

"Oh, hey, Ethan. I was hoping I could talk to Evie." I was stuck in mid-entry, trying to act like this was nothing unusual.

"Did you have to come through the bathroom window? You scared the fuck out of me."

I felt his hands on my hips as he helped me to the floor.

"The front door was locked."

"For a reason, Julie," he whispered.

I huffed at him. "It's no secret you're doing it. You're married."

"Seriously?" The look he gave me was a combination of frustration and respect.

"Look, I really need to talk to Evie. I know I should have waited until later this morning, but it's really important."

He stepped aside, extending his arm to the bathroom door. "By all means, what's one more drama between the two of you?"

I ignored his comment and went into their bedroom, crawling in next to Evie and pushing her towards the middle of the bed. I whispered, "Move over."

Sleepily, she opened her eyes. "Julie?"

I smiled, and snuggled up to her. "Hi."

She rolled her head to the other side, looking for Ethan, and saw him standing at the edge of the mattress.

He asked, "Is it always going to be like this?"

She answered sweetly, "I think so."

I batted my eyes at him. "Can you make some coffee?"

He glared at me as he left the room, and I commented to Evie, "He is really delicious, isn't he?"

She curled into me. "What are you doing here?"

I pulled my phone out of my pocket and texted Shaye. "First, we need to get Shaye here. Give me a second." I shot off a quick text and hoped she would get it.

"What time is it?"

As I sent the text, I saw that it was almost five thirty. I told her that as I hit send and turned back to her, snuggling deeper under the covers.

"It's so early, Julie. Seriously, she may not even be awake."

"She has a passel of kids, of course she's awake."

My phone pinged with her response, *Be right there.*

I flashed the screen to Evie, smiling smugly. "She's on her way."

Evie rolled over and groaned.

Snuggling up behind her, I said fervently, "It's important. I'll tell you when she gets here."

We both started nodding off and were startled a short while later, when we heard Nick bellowing from the front of the house. "Where is she? Is she okay?"

The next thing we knew, Nick and Shaye were both standing in Evie's bedroom, Nick with a baby strapped to the front of him, Shaye holding JT's hand, his eyes still puffy from sleep, Ellie on her hip.

"Evie, what's the matter? What happened? Are you okay?"

Evie pushed herself up onto her elbow and glanced back and forth between me and Nick, a bemused look on her face. "Nothing. Julie had something she wanted to share with me and Shaye. What are you doing here?"

Nick turned stormy eyes to me. "Shaye got a '911 at Evie's' text from Julie."

This time, Evie turned to look at me in a 'shame on you' kind of way, mouth thin, eyebrows furrowed. "Seriously?"

I shrugged, "Well, it is. Kind of."

"Oh, you're fucking kidding me." Nick stormed out of the room, exasperated with me.

JT looked up at Shaye. "Daddy used a bad word."

"Yes, he did."

Ethan came back into the room, "Coffee's ready."

If I hadn't really needed to talk to Shaye and Evie, I would have laughed out loud.

Shaye implored of Ethan, "Can you take JT and put him in bed with Noah? I'll keep Ellie with me."

"C'mon buddy, let's go have a sleep-in with Noah," Ethan said, as he grabbed JT's hand and gently shut the door behind him.

Shaye placed Ellie between her and Evie as she crawled in bed and tucked in tight with us.

Looking at me over Evie, she said, "This is the time you chose to tell her about Jason?"

Laying flat, her head resting on a pillow, Evie glanced quickly between me and Shaye. "What about Jason?"

"Actually, uhm, no, that's not it. But I will get to it." Confusion flashed in Shaye's eyes, and Evie looked worried. "I've done something else, and I need help."

Evie shot up and sat back against the headboard. "Are you going to be arrested?"

I tried so hard not to laugh, and failed. "No! It's nothing like that. Just give me a second to get it out."

The two of them waited patiently, and I said quickly, "I slept with Riley."

Silence hung between the three of us. Evie and Shaye looked equally perplexed and confused. Evie was the first to speak. "You mean, like, in a bed?"

My smile slowly grew. "Well, at first it was in a bed, and then it was on the construction office table after he made us some eggs. Which, now that I think about it, never got eaten."

I couldn't tell if Evie was mad or shocked; she just sat there staring at me.

With a little bit of awe, Shaye said, "You had sex with Riley?"

"Mm-hmm. Oh yes! And it was *very* good sex." I couldn't stop the laughter. And the longer Evie remained quiet, the harder I laughed. "Evie, say something. Are you mad?"

"Riley?"

"Yes, Riley, you know, your little lap dog."

Shaye just rolled her eyes and asked, "So, what exactly is the problem?"

At that moment, Evie began to laugh. "Shaye, Julie is supposed to go to San Francisco with Dax today."

Shaye's eyes grew wide. "Oh, right. Yikes."

"Actually, that's not really the biggest problem. I can take care of that." I didn't really believe that, since I hadn't quite figured that out yet, but I knew what I had to say next would shock them both.

Evie's laughter subsided and she whispered, "Then what is it?"

I took a deep breath and let it out in a big puff of air. "I love him."

Shaye looked perplexed and asked, "Dax?"

I shook my head slowly.

Evie's eyes went wide and she covered her mouth.

I nodded.

Evie turned to hug me and I looked at Shaye over her shoulder. "Riley. I love Riley."

Laughter bubbled up from Shaye, so much so that Ellie started to whimper and she had to soothe her forehead. Shaye whispered triumphantly, "I knew it!"

"How did you know?" Evie asked with an almost hurt tone.

"She was all agitated in Seattle that Riley was at the gala. She went on and on about him, and not a word about Dax."

Turning back to me, Evie said. "I was hoping you guys would get together, but I didn't want to push it."

"What do you mean, you were hoping?"

"He's so calm and grounded, and he doesn't put up with your crap."

Shaye jumped in. "I like it. I like you guys together."

I threw myself back against the pillows, and stared up at the ceiling. "Now what do I do about Dax?"

Removing herself from the bed, Shaye scooped Ellie up. "You

have to tell him you can't go to San Francisco, and I need some coffee. Please tell him before the flight. I'm flying today and I don't need your drama at the dock." She cooed at Ellie, "Mommy needs some coffee to cope with her crazy friend. Yes, she does, she needs lots of coffee."

Shaye looked back at me pointedly before she left the bedroom. "You have lots of clearing up to do today, don't you Julie?"

I understood what she was saying and was grateful she hadn't been the one to tell Evie and Nick.

"Yep. I sure do."

After leaving the room, I turned back to Evie. "You aren't mad?"

"About Riley? Oh goodness no! I like him. Like I said, he's good for you."

I couldn't stop the smile from spreading on my face. "I think so too."

"So, what about Dax?"

I sat up on the bed, crossing my legs underneath me and wrung my hands together. "I need to tell you something else first. And, please know – please, please know – that I am profoundly sorry and regret what I did."

Her eyes filled with fear. "Oh, jeez, Julie, what? You're exhausting me this morning."

I started at the very beginning, from the time I returned to the Island, and all my sneaking around with Jason, even when he was starting to hang out with Shaye.

I told her how Jason and I fought about Nick.

I told her that I desperately wanted him to stop seeing Shaye, to work things out with me.

I told her about the night he died, and I choked in the middle of the story, my tears lodging in my throat.

I told her how I watched and waited, and when Nick and Shaye went outside, the seeds of doubt I'd been planting all summer in Jason's mind forced him outside.

I told her that when I saw him drive away, I was planning on going to his cottage that night to console him, hoping he would see Shaye for what I thought she was.

Her lack of response gave me room to continue. The tears were running down my cheeks now.

"When the ambulances went by the bar and you and Shaye went running out, I watched from the window as you pulled her along and she followed behind you in a stupor."

"I knew, in my heart, he had crashed. I knew our lives were over. I went to the bathroom to throw up, and when I came back out, everyone in the bar was whispering about what had happened, and they didn't even see me leave. I went up the hill and parked when I saw the lights flashing. The helicopter was just taking off, and I stayed on the side of the road, crying. Everything happened so fast after that, and you needed me so much, I just couldn't bear it."

Evie was crying now, soft, sniffling cries that squeezed my heart. I felt it shatter and knew that if she didn't – if she *couldn't* – forgive me, I would be lost.

She wiped her tears with her sheet and said, "Go on."

I took a deep breath. "I kept wanting to tell you, but there was never a good time. And then so much time passed that I didn't think it even mattered anymore. I thought that we'd all moved on, but I hadn't. It has been slowly eating at me, forcing its way to the surface. I know now that I was keeping men at a distance because I thought I didn't deserve to be loved. That somehow, I needed to atone for what I'd done. But I couldn't keep it from you anymore, and I don't expect you to forgive me, but I desperately hope that you can."

Reaching out for me, she pulled me to her. "Julie, I am so sorry. I am so sorry for not being a better friend to you."

Holding on to my shoulders, she pushed me from her so she could see me. "I should have known what was going on. When you came back to the Island, I just thought you were so worldly about sex, and had become more sophisticated than all of us. I never even considered how much you might have still loved Jason. I'm so sorry I let you down."

I chuckled between my tears. "Did you hear anything I said?"

"Yes, and I don't blame you. It was an accident. You didn't make him drive away. You didn't make him speed. And you certainly didn't plant a deer in front of him." She started crying again. "You poor thing. All this time."

Hysteria bubbled up, and laughter with it. I couldn't really believe that she was so forgiving. "You are my best friend. I love you so much."

"I love you too."

I wiped my own tears with her sheet and she snorted. "Please don't blow your nose on my sheets."

"I won't, but I do need to ask a favor of you."

"What is it?"

"I really need to get back to Riley, and I need to talk to Dax. Can you tell Nick for me? I don't have the energy for whatever he has to say to me. He finally respects me, and I'm sure I will spend the next year or so trying to earn it back."

She gently pushed me off the edge of the bed. "Go! I'll tell him and Ethan. Go!"

I ran back to hug her. "I love you so much, Evie."

"Go!"

Her laughter followed behind me as I ran out the door, down the hall and out the front door, shouting to Nick, Shaye, and Ethan in the kitchen. "Bye guys! Sorry for waking you up so early."

Joy filled me as I drove down the hill, along the bay, and back to Riley.

23

I WAS SO focused on speeding along the bay road, that I almost didn't see Dax waving at me from the grassy curb of the resort.

His face lit up when I slowed at the crosswalk, and he came around to my driver side window. Glancing in my rear-view mirror, I saw a car come up behind me, and I waved it past.

"What a joy, seeing you driving by. What are you doing out this early? I thought we weren't meeting until later for breakfast."

It wasn't exactly early anymore. The sun was up, and I'd wanted to get home, shower, and change before we met. I was planning on telling him before the flight that I couldn't go to San Francisco with him. I guess now was as good a time as any. Except I was in Riley's clothes and I was going in the wrong direction.

"Hey! Yeah, I spent the night at Evie's." An imaginary angel kicked me in the side of the head, and the devil on the other side, laughed.

"Oh, that's good. I was worried about you in the storm."

"Right. The storm."

He looked over his shoulder at the restaurant and stepped back from my window. "Why don't you park and join me for coffee?"

My thoughts went to Riley and I wondered if he was awake yet. I was sure he was. I nodded and drove into the lot, parking near the front door.

When I stepped out of my truck, Dax laughed and his eyes widened in surprise. "Borrowing Ethan's clothes?"

My stomach knotted. "Yeah, I needed something dry."

"Well, you still look adorable. Come on, let's get some breakfast."

The hostess walked us to a table near the window. I shifted uncomfortably in my seat, gathering the courage to tell him I couldn't go with him.

"Dax…" I started.

"Julie," he said at the same time.

I chuckled awkwardly. "You go ahead."

He reached across the table and took my hands. "I'm so glad you were safe last night. I was really worried about you."

"I was fine. Storms like that happen a lot up here."

"Still, when I couldn't reach you, I was concerned."

I was starting to panic. "Did you come to the winery?"

"No. But I did try and call. You didn't answer. I was on my way out when the resort manager came by and said it was best if I stayed put. He was very dramatic that we all stay in place. He said, with a bit of a twang, 'Never know when a tree might fall and hit ya.'"

I laughed at his imitation of the resort manager. Inwardly I relaxed, knowing that he hadn't come out to check on me.

"Guess it was a good thing you stayed put, then."

"I guess so." His smile dropped, and he looked out at the marina. His tone was quiet, almost remorseful, when he added, "I'm sure Riley could have helped you. But to be honest, I don't really like you being so close to him."

I felt adrenaline rush through my body. "Why is that?"

He stared out the window for a moment longer, appearing to gather his thoughts. When he turned back to me, he looked sad. "I know he's really good at his job, which was why I let you hire him, but he's not a good guy."

I bristled at the idea that he thought he let me hire anyone. It briefly overshadowed his comment about Riley not being a good guy, and, to move past my brief flash of anger, I asked him how so.

"I didn't want to burden you with my family history, but I've known Riley for a long time, and he's arrogant and selfish. His family is very committed to the Children's Hospital, so it's difficult for me to avoid him, but I sure wish I could." He dropped his head, shaking it side to side.

My stomach was in knots, and I could feel my chest tightening. I felt my world slipping away from me. He was not going to be happy when I told him about Riley, and I wasn't sure I was even going to tell him now. I couldn't risk it, and I felt myself shrinking in submission to Dax.

"He seems like a good guy," I said quietly. I felt like I was walking a very thin line. I tried to act light-hearted when I asked jokingly, "What did he do, steal your girlfriend?" Which was probably not the best thing to joke about, given the circumstances.

"Worse. He killed my sister."

I inhaled sharply, and wrapped my arms around my middle. "What? How?"

My shock surprised him, and he said, "He didn't actually kill her. He just kept her isolated and away from her family so she couldn't get the help she needed. She was very sick. She had been in remission, and we thought she would be fine. But she wasn't. Riley was her college boyfriend and he never told any of us that she was sick again.

She could have gotten better. She could have received the care and treatment to survive."

I choked back the tears.

"Your sister," I stated. "Her name is Harper?" I asked.

The look of surprise on his face would have been comical if I wasn't on the verge of a breakdown. With frustration, he said, "Julie, you knew that."

"No, I didn't."

"I've told you her name, and I said it at the gala in my speech. We donate in her name."

Oh no! That was when I was with Riley upstairs. "Right. Of course."

My head was spinning. His voice droned on in the background. I couldn't make out the words because I was in my own head, replaying my conversation with Riley about Harper and her sickness. He'd seemed so genuine, so honest about it.

I opened my mouth to tell Dax that wasn't how it happened, that he had it all wrong. I wanted to defend Riley, but then I feared Dax would pull out of my project. I was trapped.

In a daze, I stood from the table. "Dax, I can't really stay. I need to get back and finish packing."

He stood abruptly and came to my side of the table. "Julie, I'm so sorry. I shouldn't have brought you down like that. We are supposed to be celebrating your successful inspection and going away for a beautiful weekend." Leaning down he kissed me softly on the cheek. "I'll make it up to you, I promise."

I nodded wordlessly, turned and practically ran to my truck.

The remaining miles couldn't pass fast enough, and I had to keep blinking back the tears. When I drove into the winery, I drove straight past the tasting room and directly to the office.

Charging through the front door, I saw Riley in the kitchen.

Turning at the sound of the door slamming shut, he said with a huge grin on his face, "Hey, there you are. I was wondering when you were coming back. Are you hungry?"

His smile dropped when he saw the anger and tears on my face. The spatula still in mid-air, he asked, "What happened?"

"Harper."

I saw the moment he realized that I knew. His face relaxed. He gently put the spatula on the counter and came to stand stoically in front of me. "What about Harper?"

My eyebrows raised. "What do you mean, 'What about Harper?' She's Dax's sister, and you never told me."

"I didn't think it mattered."

"Maybe not before, but it does now."

"I'm sorry. I should have told you, but I really didn't think it mattered. And I *really* didn't want to get you in the middle of it." He added, "I would have told you soon. I thought we would talk about it. About her."

I laughed, almost hysterically. "I'm kind of *right* in the middle of it, Riley. I was planning on telling him I couldn't go to San Francisco when he dumped that little nugget of information, that I was *apparently* supposed to have already known."

His eyes flashed anger. "You're not still going, are you?"

"Of course, I'm going. Do you know how hard you've made this for me? He hates you!"

"If you knew, would it have made a difference? Would you have stayed the night with me? Would we still be…whatever we are?"

I knew the answer and it made me sad. I knew I wouldn't have let it go that far. I would do anything to save the vineyard and the resort.

My heart was breaking. The knowledge of what I had to do cracked through me like a sledgehammer.

Calmly and collectively, I answered, "I don't know what we are, what this is." I pointed back and forth between us. "But I can't risk it. I'm sorry."

He gripped my shoulders and it was all I could do not to cry. "Are you kidding me, right now? Julie! Listen to yourself."

I stared at his collarbone and said, void of emotion, "Dax is better for me."

"Julie," he pleaded.

"Please let go of me. I need to go." My voice cracked. If he held me one moment longer, I was going to fall apart.

His hands move to my cheeks, forcing me to look at him. "You may think he's better for you, for your resort, but he's not. On the outside, he's pretty, and he has lots of money…" he took a deep breath and continued, "But that isn't what love is, Julie. Love is messy and complicated. It requires the ability to forgive and start over the next day. It means you risk losing the one person in your whole world you love the most, if they die first. But it also means that they do too."

I could feel my eyes watering and I swallowed the lump in my throat.

He continued softly. "It means you make every day important. I love you, Julie. I love that when you think no one's looking, you smile like you have a secret. I love that you want everyone to think you're a princess, when I know you would rather be in muck boots and dirty jeans working with the grapes. I love that you love your friends with your whole heart, even the one you thought wronged you. I love that you built this place because you want people around you. You want to take care of them, make them feel important. And I love that I can't get a breath until I see you every morning."

The tears were now flowing down my cheeks and I reached up to grab his wrists, gently pulling them off my face. "I have to go."

"I love you, Julie. I love you. Doesn't that mean anything to you?"

I whispered, "Please let me go."

He stepped back and nearly shouted, "Get out of your head! Let him go, Julie. Let Jason go."

"What are you talking about? This has nothing to do with Jason."

"It has everything to do with him. This was your dream together. If you lose it, you lose him. You are behaving exactly the way Jason did with Shaye. She was shiny, and new and different, and he thought that being with her would make him something other than what he was. Shaye wasn't for Jason, just like you aren't for Dax. Being with Dax is only going to kill you. Maybe not physically, but inside it will. You love me, Julie." He stopped and then added quietly, "But you have to let him go."

I felt like a caged animal, and I was running out of time. I had to get back to the dock. I said the only thing I thought would keep me safe, the only thing I could think of at that moment that would validate what I was doing.

"I want you out of the house by the time I get back."

He almost laughed, "Oh, you're firing me? That's rich!"

If I stayed a moment longer, I felt like my entire world would collapse. So, I simply nodded at him, turned, and left.

My head was aching, and as soon as I got to my car the tears were flowing freely. I wouldn't look back. I couldn't look back. I'd made my decision, and now I had to live with it.

24

Time was moving so fast. I wanted to scream, "Stop!" so I could try to find my way out of this. So many moving parts with no time to figure it out.

When I got back to my apartment, I mindlessly started putting clothes in my suitcase. I wasn't even aware of what I was doing, only that I needed to put one foot in front of the other and keep going.

The tears would stop. And then they would start again.

In the bathroom, I showered and then spent a few minutes with a frozen eye mask to reduce the swelling.

"Get it together, Julie," I ordered myself while waiting for the cold compress to work its magic.

I dressed conservatively and kept my makeup minimal. Fresh and pretty.

The clock on the wall indicated it was time to go. Riley hadn't come after me, and I didn't really blame him.

The drive back to the dock was slow and somber. The heaviness in my heart caused me to drive ever slower the closer I got to the resort and float plane dock.

I parked next to Shaye's SUV and took a few minutes to gather my enthusiasm, bury my heartache, and put a smile on my face.

Stepping from the car, I made my way into the restaurant, out the back door, and down the dock. Shaye was sitting on a bench, dressed in her pilot clothes, talking to Dax as they waited for the plane.

She stood when she saw me, surprise on her face. "Hey! You're here."

Smiling, Dax came to me and took my bag. "You look gorgeous." Leaning over, he kissed my cheek and took my bag to the end of the dock.

When Dax was far enough away, Shaye whispered, "What are you doing?"

Shame and embarrassment bubbled up. I pushed it back down, broadening my grin. "I'm going to San Francisco."

She moved her head, trying to catch my eyes. "What about Riley?"

"Yeah, no."

"Julie, what happened?"

Dax came back to wait with us. "Wow! It's a beautiful day isn't it?" He inhaled and closed his eyes. "I love the smell of the salt water. It's so fresh."

Shaye turned to him. "Dax, I need Julie's help with…" She stopped and I looked at her in warning. "I need her help with something. We'll be right back." She grabbed my elbow and led me back to the office, calling over her shoulder, "If the plane arrives, tell the pilot we'll be back in just a few minutes."

Not wanting to cause a scene, I walked alongside her, back to her office. She opened the door and waited for me to step inside before shutting it behind me.

I looked around and asked, "Are you ever going to get a real office? Wasn't this, like, the laundry room or something?"

"It was a storage closet. Julie, what happened?"

As quickly as I could, I told her everything that had happened since I left Evie's this morning. At one point, she covered her mouth and then muttered empathetically, "Oh, Julie."

"You can see why I need to go on this trip."

She reached for my hands. "Actually, I can't. You love Riley. Don't do this. You don't need to go. Don't martyr yourself. Dax won't pull the funding, but you will never forgive yourself."

"If I broke things off with Dax, he might still fund the project. But, if he finds out it's because of Riley, I don't know for sure that he would."

Shaye was quiet, her eyes sad.

"I see now that you're coming around to my side."

"No, Julie, I'm not. I'm sad for you."

"Please don't be. I can't handle much more of an emotional roller coaster today."

"Riley will not forgive you for this. If you sell yourself out for the vineyard, he won't be there for you when it's all over."

I turned to leave Shaye's office. "I'm done talking about this. You have a plane to fly."

Stalking off, I headed back to the dock, only to see Riley with his backpack heading towards his boat.

I looked away and made my way back to Dax just as the plane was pulling up to the dock.

"Are you ready?" I greeted him enthusiastically.

He smiled in return. "I am."

Shaye gave me a dirty look before greeting the pilot and then helping him with the bags.

A few other passengers were flying to Seattle today, and Dax and I settled in the back.

Shaye started to shut the door, and asked, while only looking at me, "Is everyone on board headed to Seattle?"

I glared at her and she shut the door, blocking out her view of my scowl. I watched out the window as she pushed the plane away from the dock, jumped onto the pontoon and climbed up into the pilot seat.

The other pilot put his headset on, and Shaye just sat there looking out the window. Following her line of sight, I saw she was looking at Riley standing on his boat. She gave him a quick wave and then turned back to look at me, over her shoulder, her eyes pleading with me not to do this.

I looked away from her and could feel myself starting to shake.

Dax reached over to grab my hand. "Afraid to fly?"

I nodded briefly. My leg began to bounce.

Shaye still wasn't starting the plane, and I saw the other pilot look at her questioningly.

She gave me one last glance and started the engines. Maneuvering out into the middle of the bay, she throttled the engines and I saw her shake her head like she didn't want to do this. She pushed the throttle all the way forward, the plane started bouncing, and I realized I needed to stop her.

As loud as I possibly could, I screamed for her to stop. With the second scream, she heard me and pulled back on the throttle. The drag in the water brought the plane almost to an immediate stop.

The second pilot looked back at me with murderous eyes. Shaye just dropped her head, but I could see her smiling.

Floating now, in the middle of the bay, Shaye turned and asked if I was okay.

"Yes, I just…I just need a minute." I looked out the window and saw that Riley was standing on the bow of his boat, watching us. Feelings of hope were bubbling up inside me. It was quite possible I was about to lose my resort but at this point, I didn't care.

I unbuckled my seat belt and turned to Dax. "Dax."

"Julie, are you okay?"

"Yes. It's just…oh my goodness." I rubbed my hands over my face and continued. "Do you love me?"

He almost laughed. "Uhm, no, but I kind of thought this weekend was going to be the start to finding out."

I sighed. "Okay. Because the thing is, I love someone else. And I can't go away with you and not be with him."

I heard the engines spool up again. Shaye was taking us back to the dock.

The look on Dax's face was pure surprise. "I had no idea you were seeing someone."

"Well, that's the complicated part. I wasn't, but I kind of have been, and didn't really know I was falling in love with him."

"Does he know?"

"Yes. And I'm hoping he still loves me after this."

He looked at me kindly, "I'm sure he does. You're a beautiful, courageous woman, Julie."

"I'm hoping you still think that when I tell you who it is." I grimaced and waited for his response.

Out the window, he saw Riley moving from his boat up the dock towards the plane. He looked back at me. "Riley?"

Shaye was turning the plane to line up, so I rushed the words out as fast I could. "It just happened. I didn't even know what was happening. He told me about Harper, but I hadn't put two and two together."

"I know you don't like him and I know you guys haven't gotten along in the past. But I really hope you can forgive me for this, and that you still want to be part of my project. I believe in it, and I believe in our partnership, and I am so sorry. I'm sorry I couldn't have been the one for you, but..." I took a deep breath and continued, "but I love him, and I can't imagine being without him."

The pontoons lined up alongside the dock and Shaye jumped out to open the door for me. I apologized one more time and scurried down the steel-frame steps to the pontoon. Shaye smiled at me, and I squeezed her hand.

She whispered, "Go get him."

"Will you tell Nick and Evie to meet me?"

"Where?"

"Tell them what happened. They'll know where."

She nodded and I started to run.

Riley saw me coming up the dock and picked up his pace. By the time he reached me, I was laughing so hard, I considered that I was, quite possibly, hysterical.

"You crazy girl, what are you doing?" He scooped me up in arms and swung me around. I held on tight and buried my face in his neck.

"I love you, Riley. I love you."

Putting me down gently, he held my face and kissed me.

I held onto his wrists and stood flush against him. "Please tell me you still love me."

"Of course, I love you, Julie." He kissed me again. "This isn't going to go well for the resort, you know."

I hadn't waited for an answer from Dax, so I wasn't sure, but Riley was probably correct. "I guess. I don't know. I can't worry about that right now. I have something I need to do first."

He grinned at me wickedly. "Yes, you do."

Gently pushing back from him, I said, "Later. There's something else important. Meet me at the vineyard. I'll be there in about an hour."

"An hour?"

"Yes. And could you grab my suitcase and take it back to the house?"

"Is it always going to be like this?"

"Like what?"

"You thinking you can boss me around?"

"Of course not. I fired you. I'm not your boss." I laughed at him as I ran up the dock to my Scout. I waved at him as I drove off.

Driving along the bay road, I watched the float plane taking off from the bay and knew Dax was on it, alone. I had no idea what would happen next, but I knew I'd done the right thing. I felt lighter, freer, and I just had one more thing I needed to do.

The pristine white church sat at the crest of a hill, its Gothic revival architecture still intact after almost a hundred years. A white picket fence surrounded the grounds.

I parked in the lot across from the cemetery and went through the iron gate, solemnly walking down the path that led down to Jason's grave-site.

It was quiet today. The air was still, and I tread softly, reverently, through the graves until I saw his headstone. Fresh flowers had been placed to the side – lilies. His mom had been here.

So much time had passed. My young love had been the anchor to what I thought love was supposed to feel like. I hadn't let anyone in. Until now.

I dusted off his headstone, for lack of anything else to do, and sat down to its side. Picking at the leaves, I started to talk to him.

"Hey there, I know it's been a really long time, and I'm sorry about that. I've been missing you, and angry at the same time. It's made it hard to come up and visit. I wanted to let you know that I've met someone, that I love someone. He cares for me and is everything I didn't know I needed."

The quiet surrounded me, my voice the only interruption to the serenity. "I'm sorry…" I wiped away a tear. "I'm sorry I wasn't a better friend to you. I'm sorry I couldn't help you with your demons. I'm sorry I couldn't move past what had happened and just be your friend. I love you, Jason. I will always love you. I hope you know how much we all loved you." I reached out my hand and touched the Earth. "Rest in peace, Jason."

I heard a crackle at the tree line and looked up to see a doe and her fawn lurking in the shadows. "Keep watching over him, okay?"

A few moments passed while the mama just stared at me. She finally turned and stepped cautiously back into the woods, the branches crackling, the fawn following behind her.

Behind me, I heard Evie's hesitant voice. "Julie?"

I turned to see her and Nick a few yards from me.

I stood and brushed the dirt from my dress. "Thank you for coming."

"What's going on?" Nick asked.

"I wanted to apologize. To both of you."

I turned to Evie. "Did you tell him?"

Evie nodded.

I stepped closer to the two of them. "I owe you a long overdue apology."

I told him everything I'd told Evie that morning, leaving out parts I knew Evie would have told him. I told him about Riley, and how much I loved him, and that I needed him and Evie to forgive me. "I didn't intend for Jason to die. I never wished that on him."

They had both been listening thoughtfully.

Nick's voice was quiet, his emotions simmering just under the surface of his words. "No one ever intends for someone to die, Julie."

I sucked in my lips, biting down on them so I wouldn't cry, and nodded.

He continued, "But you don't need my forgiveness. I think I've known for a long time. Jason wouldn't just randomly come outside unless he thought something was going on. I've played that night over and over again in my head so many times. You couldn't have known what was going to happen."

Evie came to me, wrapping her arms around me. "We're okay, Julie."

I hugged her back and then she opened one arm, extending it to Nick. "C'mon, hug her."

He groaned, and both Evie and I laughed. But he came to us and wrapped us both in his arms. "Okay. Love fest over. I'm more worried about the resort."

When he stepped back, I said to him, "Yeah, I might have screwed that up. I know you told me a million times not to, but I love Riley, and I'm choosing him."

He sighed and pinched the bridge of his nose. "I suppose I'll need to make some calls on Monday."

"It'll work out. Riley has this great idea for a glamping site."

Nick's eyes shot daggers, and he put up his hand. "Stop. We'll figure it out together, Julie, but I don't want to talk about any other projects with you. Not yet."

I made a zipper across my lips and Evie tried not to laugh.

"In the meantime, you're not alone."

They both hugged me and we walked back up to the parking lot.

Evie was smiling at me. "You look softer."

"I feel poorer."

She laughed heartily. "Oh, Julie. I'm glad all of you hasn't changed."

They walked me to my car, and Nick told me he would call me later, after he'd talked to Dax. "I'm sure I can smooth it over."

"Thanks, Nick."

They left, and I closed my eyes, breathing in the fresh air. I did feel lighter – as if I was on the right path.

My drive back to the resort was bittersweet. I had no idea what would happen Monday morning. I might still have a resort; I might not. But I still had my vineyard, the tasting room, a house, and an apartment I could rent out if I needed to.

I parked in front of the office and saw him down in the vineyard, sitting on the swing he made for me.

Taking a few minutes to admire him from afar, I smiled with contentment. I walked slowly towards him, knowing that everything was wrapped up with him now.

His arm was draped across the back of the bench, and I sat down next to him, one leg bent up on the seat.

"Hey."

He smiled his sexy, lazy smile. "Hey."

"I'm sor-"

He cut me off. "Shhhhh. You don't need to apologize. We'll figure it out together."

I simply stared at him. It felt so right, so easy to be with him.

"What now?" I asked.

He answered softly, "You and me."

I leaned over to kiss him, whispering against his lips, "You and me."

25

"JULIETTE. JULIETTE." THE husky timbre of his voice woke me from my peaceful sleep. His soft kisses grazed my stomach, while his body lay half on top of me.

I stretched, cat-like, extending my arms over my head. His lips worked their way up my body, and he bent his head to kiss the soft spot between my neck and my collarbone. "It's time to wake up."

"Mmmm, that feels nice." My eyes opened, and I stared up at Riley, a small grin on my face. "Can we sleep out here again tonight?"

"You like my yurt?"

I laughed. "That sounds funny."

"Don't laugh. You've already sold out the other ten for opening day, next Spring."

Sighing loudly, I said, "I still can't believe we finished the resort, *and* launched this project." I softly pushed him to his back and straddled him, placing my hands on him and admiring his bare chest. "You're so sexy."

He linked his hands and placed them behind his head, cradling it. Teasing me, he said, "And you were going to give all this up for Dax."

I swatted his stomach and he reached out to grab my wrists.

He was laughing at me, and I pouted. "Stop it. I've apologized a million times, and we didn't know if it would work out or not."

Pulling my face down to him, he gripped the back of my head and kissed me. The kiss ignited desire in me, and I pressed myself down on him, feeling his obvious desire for me. Slowly, the kiss eased, and he pulled my head a few inches away, whispering, "It's just so much fun to tease you. And I know you love me."

Against his lips, I whispered back, "And you love me."

Our eyes locked, and I realized how easily he'd fit into my life. He filled the emptiness I'd had for so long, settled me and made me feel invincible.

He interrupted my musings when he said, "In answer to your original question, yes, we can sleep out here tonight, and any night that you want."

"Since you've taken over my apartment…" I let the words hang between us.

With another kiss, he asked, "Why don't you just move into the house?"

We hadn't discussed where we would live long-term, but we hadn't spent a night apart since the day I'd ditched Dax at the float plane dock. I'd already decided I was going to move into the house; I just wanted to make sure he was going to stay.

Before I could ask, he flipped me off of him, lovingly tapped me on the bottom, and told me to get up. "Today is your big day."

"Today is *our* big day."

"No, Juliette. This is all you. I helped, but this is all you. Your vision, your dream. No one is going to take that away from you."

I paused before I said, "You do know Dax will be here, don't you?"

He laughed – a sardonic laugh that surprised me.

"Why the laughter?" I sat up and held the sheet to my chest.

He took his jeans from the small dresser against the fabric of the yurt and stepped into them, leaving the top button undone. "Well, not only do I know he's coming, but he's bringing my sister."

"Maggie?"

He looked at me with mock annoyance. "Really?"

"Wren?" I asked in shock.

He tapped his nose, and pointed at me. "That's how I responded."

"Are they…?"

"Together? I don't think so, but I find it interesting."

"I hope she's nicer to me."

His blank look and raised eyebrows, made me add sheepishly. "And I will be nice to her."

Kneeling back down on the bed, he pulled the sheet down from in front of me and I watched his eyes heat with desire. I asked, "Didn't you just tell me it was time to get up?"

He stood abruptly and took off his jeans. "I changed my mind."

Giggling, I tore off the rest of the sheet and lovingly embraced him as he fell down on top of me.

The resort was exquisite. Rustic, yet sophisticated. Cozy and classy. I'd walked the property and the rooms the day before and knew it was perfect.

Each of the rooms were minimalistic in style, with buttery walls flecked with watercolor art. The soaps and toiletries I'd meticulously picked out sat neatly in bamboo trays with the HM logo branded in the wood.

Outside, the landscaping was lush and green. Italian cypress trees lined the long driveway, leading in from the road and up the hill.

A three-tier castle fountain sat in the middle of the driveway illuminated with blue LED lights. Gas fire bowls flanked the heavy double wooden front door, and it was inside those doors that I greeted my guests.

The view of the vineyards, and the water off in the distance, was the first thing they saw as they entered the lobby. I was incredibly proud of the design.

As they arrived, I personally greeted them, offering a glass of champagne, and reminding them that the resort opening dinner and party would start at 6:00 p.m. They were welcome to walk the grounds, have a swim, or sample our wines in the newly built tasting room. A private concierge took their luggage and, after I was finished welcoming them, directed them to our check-in office.

In addition to the full-house I had staying at the resort, I'd invited over a hundred local friends and islanders to celebrate with us. I expected they would arrive in a couple of hours.

When Dax and Wren arrived, I was down in the lower level restaurant, sitting at a window table with the head chef.

They descended the circular staircase, looking like royalty, and it was all I could do not to laugh. They made a very handsome couple, and the possessive hold Wren had on Dax's arm told me she intended to let him know, and soon. I'd made the right choice, and I hoped Dax had come to realize that too.

Standing to greet them, I took both of Dax's hands in mine and he kissed me on both cheeks.

"Julie, the building is gorgeous. We did good." His smile was only slightly strained, but I could tell he was trying.

"We did good, Dax. Thank you for believing in me." I turned to Wren and held out my hand to her. "Wren. It's so nice to see you again. Thank you for coming."

Her icy demeanor shifted, and I saw her shoulders visibly relax.

She was stunning – a city version of Evie, with sharp blue eyes. "It's nice to see you too." She raised her eyes to the tall ceiling above. "That chandelier is exquisite. I can't wait to see it this evening. It looks like the light will reach into every corner of the atrium."

"Thank you so much! Riley found it for me. I love it."

Her eyes twinkled a little and a pretty smile formed on her face. "I can see that you do."

In that moment, I knew we would be friends. I felt my eyes start to water and I cleared my throat. "Well, should we get you two settled? Let me walk you to your rooms."

Reaching the top of the stairs, I watched as Riley came through the front door, still in his work clothes, dirty from finishing some last-minute planting with the gardeners.

Wren laughed at him. "You never did have the good sense to dress for a party."

He hugged her with onc arm, trying not to get her dirty, and planted a brotherly kiss on her cheek. "Glad you could make it, Wren. You look delightful."

"Don't try and kiss up to me," she teased him.

Riley chuckled, turned, and extended his hand to Dax. "Dax."

"Riley." An uncomfortable moment settled between the four of us before Dax continued. "You did a great job, Riley. Everything was on time and on budget, not to mention, a great design. Thank you for that."

I think it was the closest Dax could get to an apology, and Riley nodded curtly, doing his best to accept it. "You're welcome."

Turning to me, Riley reached for my fingers and held them loosely. "You ready to go? You need to start getting ready for the party tonight."

"Yes, just give me one minute." I called over a concierge and asked him to help Dax and Wren. "Mr. Bentley is our investor, so please take very good care of them."

"Yes, Ma'am. Mr. and Mrs. Bentley, if you'll follow me, please."

I pulled in my lips, trying not to laugh. Riley had turned towards the balcony, hiding his smile; Wren was speechless, and only Dax corrected him. "Actually, this is Ms. Johnson. If you could kindly show her where her room is? I'd like to take a look around first."

"Yes, sir, my apologies. Ms. Johnson, if you'll follow me."

Wren left us, and Dax said to me, "Do you mind if I check on things? Check the rooms and the kitchen? Make sure they are ready for tonight?"

"Not at all. It's yours to check." I reached for Riley beside me, holding his hand in mine, assuring him that I was his. "I'll be back around 5:30. Call me if you need anything."

Nodding once to me and then to Riley, he headed back down the stairs and towards the kitchen.

Riley and I stared at each other, wide-eyed. "That was interesting."

He pulled me close, kissed me quick, and led me out the front door. "C'mon, beautiful, let's get you ready."

I spent the rest of the afternoon alone. I took my time getting ready, meditating and responding to a number of texts from Evie and Shaye.

We're running late, Ellie's having a meltdown.

What color is your dress?

I'm so proud of you.

Did Dax arrive yet?

Nick said you better have Balvenie Scotch

Did you invite Amy?

I responded to as many as I could, and then gave up, preferring to spend my time getting ready and calming my nerves.

By the time Riley arrived to pick me up, I was sufficiently relaxed and ready to go.

I waited for him in the bay window of my apartment, and stood when I heard him coming up the steps. He knocked once and then opened the door.

We both took each other in, admiring each other. He took my breath away. He was so handsome in his suit.

"You wore that suit to Evie's wedding," I commented.

He looked down at himself, brushing imaginary lint from his arm and straightening the jacket. "I did? I guess I need to get another one. Maybe I should have worn my tux."

I laughed softly as I walked towards him. Adjusting his tie, I ran my hands over his shoulders and then rested them on his chest. "As much as I loved your tux, it would be a little over the top tonight."

Gently cupping my face in his hands, he whispered roughly, "God, you're beautiful! Let's not go to the party, I need to kiss you."

"Later. And you look very handsome yourself." I stepped back from him and grabbed my wrap from the back of my vanity table chair.

"I'm serious, Julie. Do you have any idea how much I love you? I want to just pull you in, keep you close, and never let go."

His words were achingly beautiful. He looked almost pained, and I responded softly, "I feel the same."

"I'm never leaving you. You know that, right?"

"I do."

He took my hands in his and gave me a sweet kiss on the cheek, careful not to mess my makeup. "That has a nice ring to it. Should we get married here?"

I pulled back. "Are you asking me to marry you?"

"Nope. I'm asking you where we're getting married."

"Presumptive of you." I laughed and headed for the door.

"Confident."

"I'll think about it."

"About marrying me?"

"About where," I tossed over my shoulder, as I went down the stairs.

Riley dropped me off at the front door of the resort. "I'll be there in a few minutes. You got this."

I stepped from the truck, straightening my dress, and confidently went through the front doors.

Many of the paying guests were already mingling on the mezzanine, looking out towards the vineyards. Others were on the large outside deck, casually relaxing around gas fire pits and cocktail tables that had been brought in for tonight.

The staff smiled brightly at me as I arrived.

Dax and Wren were admiring some glasswork I had sitting on a pedestal in the lobby, and I made my way towards them.

"Isn't that beautiful? It was made by a local artist. Dax, I hope you don't mind that I took some liberties with the art. I really wanted to showcase the work of some of our local artists."

"Not at all. I'm embarrassed I didn't think of it."

Wren jumped in. "It's stunning. All the different blue colors, and the white splash. It really looks like an ocean wave. I might need to have this."

"You are certainly welcome to purchase it. I will make sure you get the artist's number. Dax, can I borrow you for a few minutes? Guests for the dinner and party are going to start arriving, and I thought it would be nice if we were both there to meet them."

"Of course. Wren, you'll be okay?"

She nodded and told us she would make her way downstairs and catch up with us at dinner.

When we were alone, I took that moment to apologize to him.

"Thank you for not backing out of the project, Dax. I couldn't have done this without you."

Both of us were looking towards the front door. The undercurrents of awkwardness ran between us, obvious to no one.

"I'll admit I was a little surprised. But, first and foremost, I'm a businessman, Julie, and from the very start, your vision and your dream captured my heart. That doesn't happen often."

He nodded at a couple coming through the door, and I greeted them, welcoming them and directing them downstairs for dinner. When they were out of earshot, he continued. "When Nick called me that Monday morning, I did consider backing out. But then I realized I had been looking at the girl and the resort as one, and when the girl was removed, the resort was still a good business decision." He glanced quickly at me, and then back at the front door. "Don't confuse my acquiescence with forgiveness, Julie. You hurt me. And surprised me."

"I'm sorry, Dax." My heart hurt a little at what I'd done. Still, even given this new information, I loved Riley and I wouldn't change a thing.

He simply gave me a nod, put on a smile, and continued greeting our guests.

I was overwhelmed with hugs and praise from the people on the island, all of them wishing me well and commenting how proud they were of me.

The owner of the local bookstore commented, "I hope you don't stop doing orphan Thanksgiving and the Halloween party every year. You know we all look forward to those parties."

"No, ma'am. I would never. I love my community, and I'm happy to continue that tradition." I smiled broadly at her.

She patted me on the cheek. "That's a good girl. I always knew you were a good one."

When she walked off, Dax turned to me and laughed, shaking his head. "Is it always like that?"

I rolled my eyes. "Uhm, lately, yes. But not always."

Nick and Shaye, and Evie and Ethan all arrived together and I greeted them with enthusiasm. "I'm so happy to see you guys. Thank you for coming."

"It's perfect, Julie, just perfect," Evie said as she pulled back from me.

Nick shook hands with Dax. "You two did a great job. I'm impressed."

I couldn't stop smiling. "Thanks, Nick."

Shaye was gob smacked, taking it all in. "Julie. It's magnificent! That chandelier. It's just…I have nothing, it's just…" And she put her arms out to her side. "And you…you look like a movie star. I'm so proud of you."

"Thank you so much. I'm so glad you like it."

Ethan hugged me next. "Well done, Julie."

"Thank you, Ethan. Why don't you all head downstairs for dinner, and Dax and I will be down in a few minutes."

They took their time on the stairway, admiring the building, and making their way to the dining room, and bar, below.

Riley came to my side a few minutes later and asked if I was ready to head downstairs.

The three of us went down, joining Wren and others at a table. I was too keyed up to eat, so I wandered the dining room, and made sure everyone was enjoying themselves.

When the dinner plates were cleared, the guests were steered out onto the deck for dessert, and dancing – but first, there was a champagne toast. Riley led me and Dax to the edge of the deck, where he'd placed an elevated stage and podium.

The conversation in the group hushed, and I removed the microphone to speak.

"Good evening everyone, thank you so much for coming." Many responded, and I continued. "Building this resort has been a dream of mine for a very long time – since I was a young girl, really – and I am amazed and almost shocked that I'm standing here, in front of you, welcoming you to my home."

I paused to allow a few claps, and whistles, and to gather my emotions. "I would like to thank my friends Nick Reid and Ethan Archer, for helping me find just the right investor to help make this dream a reality. Please help me show my gratitude." I clapped along with everyone else and waited until it died down to go on.

"To Dax Bentley, our esteemed investor and partner." More clapping.

"I would also like to thank Riley Johnson, for designing and building this incredible vision: for taking my words and my ideas, and transforming them from pen, to paper, to reality."

Everyone clapped again, and I waited until it was almost completely silent before continuing. "Most importantly, my dearest friends, Evie Reid and Shaye Richards-Reid. Nothing is more valuable than friendship, and you have been with me, through happy and sad times, holding me and cheering me on. I cherish you, and love you, and thank you for your unwavering belief in me, even when I drove you absolutely crazy. I love you." More clapping, and some visible tears.

I raised my glass and took the scissors Riley handed me. "Please raise your glasses and toast with me the opening of Hunter's Moon Resort and Vineyards." I clipped the red ribbon that was hung across the podium. "Please enjoy your evening, and your stay!"

Shaye and Evie met me and squeezed me into a hug. Shaye was wiping her eyes and gushing about the speech.

"Oh, Shaye, stop. You are never this emotional."

"I know, but that was just such a lovely speech."

"Go enjoy yourself. I have to mingle." I swatted her away, not wanting them to see me cry.

"That was really well said, Julie," Evie added before they walked away.

I spent the next few hours talking with all the guests, moving from table to table, inside and outside, and making sure everyone was having a nice evening. Riley frequently brought me water, held my hand, and finally told me I'd done enough, and it was time to relax.

He led me outside onto the deck to one of the three gas fire-pits we'd installed. This one was farthest away from the crowd and had the best view of the vines. It was dark now, the full moon high in the sky, casting light down onto the vineyards. The earth appeared to be coated in silver.

Evie and Ethan were sitting side by side in plush outdoor chairs, their hands linked across the gap between the seats.

Nick and Shaye were snuggled up in a gliding love-seat. Shaye's feet were tucked up underneath her, and her head rested on Nick's shoulder.

Riley sat down in an oversized chair and patted his lap, holding his arms out for me. "Sit."

I did as he said and curled up in his lap, head on his shoulder. "What a night."

"It was beautiful, Julie. Magical."

I looked at Evie and saw her smiling – her sweet, loving, accepting smile.

"Thank you."

Nick added, "So what's next?"

Shaye raised her head, smacked him lightly on the chest, and looked at him bemusedly. "Are you serious?"

"What? This can't be it. Riley needs something to do. What about communal housing? Or a senior living facility. You need something to build."

Riley was rubbing my back, and I felt his chest shake with a laugh. "One project at a time. Let's talk next week. Tonight, let Julie bask in her success."

Shaye said, "Actually, Nick and I do have some news."

I said, "Let me guess..." Then Evie and I said together, "You're pregnant."

Shaye pouted, "That wasn't very fun."

I looked up at Riley. "She's always pregnant."

He put his hand on my head and I settled back down, breathing in sync with him, relaxing.

The sounds of the party, laughter, and music trickled out from the bar and we all sat in silence – in peace.

Evie broke the silence saying, "What a beautiful full moon."

"It's a Hunter's Moon," I told her.

She chuckled in surprise. "Aren't you a clever girl? Opening your resort tonight."

"Full moons are a symbol of completion. A Hunter's Moon is a time to prepare for change," I said almost quietly, and let the words settle around us.

Shaye spoke, entranced by the flames of the fire, "Out of the barren ground she comes. Astonishing is her loveliness, perfected is her power. She rises and walks among us as we bow, obedient, peaceful, and so in love."

Her words pierced my heart. "That was beautiful. Where did you hear that?"

"It's from a poem. Promise of a Hunter's Moon, or something like that. I can't remember the rest, but that part always stuck with me."

Evie let go of Ethan's hand and reached for her wine glass on the porcelain table. "I'd like to make another toast."

I scooted over on Riley's lap, reaching for my wine on the side table.

Evie said, "To friends."

"To friends," I echoed, and took a sip of my wine.

Shaye added as she looked at Nick, "To lovers."

Nick kissed her. We all hooted, and Ethan whistled.

When the laughter had died down, I turned to Riley, speaking directly to him. "To friends and lovers, past and present. To stories told, and those not written. To houses built, and homes that are made."

He leaned down and whispered, "I love you."

Then I raised my face, smiling at the circle of friends around me. "But most importantly, to Hunter's Moon."

We all raised our glasses, laughed, and said together, "To Hunter's Moon."

THE END

About the Author

Rie Anders was raised in the Pacific Northwest and has led a very colorful life, paralleling a previously successful career in the country's aerospace program and corporate America. Leaving behind the nine-to-five, she has woven her knowledge of aviation, Pacific Northwest culture, commercial fishing in Alaska, and the rugged landscapes of the west, into beautifully crafted, happy ever after, contemporary romantic fiction novels.

Rie lives in Texas with her husband and competitive figure skating daughter. She is sure there is a story in there as well, and enlists her daughters input on the daily drives to, and from, the ice rink. Topics range from character development to who will play the hero on the big screen, and what new song fits a scene to perfection.

If you want to know more about Rie, when her next book will be released, and where you can find her, please visit her website at www.rieanders.com and follow her at https://www.bookbub.com/profile/rie-anders https://twitter.com/RieAnders.

Where To Connect With Rie

Bookbub
Goodreads
Facebook
Twitter
Instagram
Amazon Author Page
And don't forget to join my Romance Newsletter on the homepage at www.RieAnders.com!

Please also enjoy an excerpt from the first in the Crown Family Series, CHRYSALIS (coming April 2021)

Charlotte "Charlie" Chase appears to have everything: a lucrative marketing career, a handsome fiancé, a mansion in Houston. But a chance encounter with the mysterious, and alluring, Paxton Crown (owner of L.O.V.E. enterprises) at a pole dancing studio, is forcing her to admit that she's disillusioned with her stellar-but-soulless job and frigid fiancé. The world of pole dancing pulls Charlie in, and the passionate, sultry environment has her questioning her life's direction. Taking a leave from her executive position, Charlie becomes immersed in a world of independence, unbending friendships, and sensual power. The studio and the thrilling knowledge of an upcoming competition become the only bright spots in her conventionally basic life.

Paxton is crass and unapproachable, and despite the delicious way her body responds to his presence, Paxton has made it clear he's not interested in an emotional attachment. As Charlie and Paxton work more closely together, Charlie finds herself caught between his vulgarity and his warmth. Wanting desperately to discover what has caused him to close himself off from falling in love, she pushes him to open up. As layers of a dark past are revealed, Paxton closes himself off further from Charlotte, preventing him from seeing how sensuous, courageous, and strong Charlie really is… And how this could be the love they both need, in order to live a life of not so basic things.

Please enjoy this excerpt from CHRYSALIS

1

"Charlotte! Charlotte, are you even paying attention?"

I turned to face the entourage of people around the large cherrywood conference table. They all looked confused, a bit concerned, and slightly embarrassed for me.

My mind had definitely been wandering. What had I been thinking about?

The eighth-floor executive conference room, with its plush carpet, cream colored walls, and elegantly displayed contemporary art, looked out towards the Buffalo Bayou; the dandelion sculptured fountain, water sparkling in the unusually perfect Houston spring day, had entranced me, taking me out of the moment.

Rapidly tapping the top of my pen against the soft laptop mat in front of me, I dug deep (and dug fast) for remnants of the conversation that had been taking place before I zoned out. The quick staccato of the clicking brought me back to the present, and I responded confidently.

"I'm sorry, Richard. Yes, I agree with the target demographic, and I feel confident that the campaign will bring in the sales numbers we're looking for."

His response was a slow drawl, and his look was still doubtful. "Okay then." He stood, grabbed his laptop and phone, and headed out of the conference room, saying over his shoulder as he left, "Charlotte, can I see you in my office?" Disappointment oozed from his tone.

Some of my colleagues turned and looked at me, shrinking down a little in their chairs. Some of them actually avoided eye contact. I could feel them thinking, *She's in way over her head.*

Gathering my belongings, I stood, adjusted my periwinkle blue skirt and buttoned the matching suit jacket. My expensive high heels dug into the carpet as I left the conference room and followed, embarrassed, dutifully behind my boss.

His gait was fast. I had to intentionally slow my walk so I could prepare myself for this conversation.

"Shut the door behind you, Charlotte." He said gruffly. He sat down behind his desk, leaned back in his chair, rested his clasped hands across his belly, and waited until I was situated directly in front of him.

"What's going on, Charlotte? Are you ok?" His concern was expectedly genuine. He had mentored me up through this company, which offered financial services, specifically retirement planning, for the past few years and I was ashamed that he thought I was distracted.

My career with the company had started almost right out of college. I'd been promoted steadily, and predictably, over the years. Most recently, I had been promoted to Vice President of Sales, and subsequently, became increasingly disillusioned with my life path.

Apparently, if this little chat was any indication, Richard had begun to sense my restlessness. The fact that I was daydreaming during our Monday morning executive briefing might have also given it away. Either way, he was about to call me out on it.

"I'm fine, Richard. I'm a little out of sorts today, but I'm totally on point. I promise."

"You do know that your promotion was well deserved. You earned this position." His eyes were kind, his tone gentle, and I knew that his gruffness in the conference room had been just for show.

I felt my shoulders start to sag, and I forced myself to sit up a little straighter. Don't show weakness, I thought to myself. Even if I didn't really understand what was happening to me, I didn't want Richard to have any doubts.

"I know, Richard, and you picked the right person." Fake it 'til you make it, I guess.

After a thoughtful pause, apparently satisfied that I was all-right, he changed topics on me, moving into the personal. "Are you looking forward to your party Saturday night?"

My fiancé Mark was hosting a *very large* engagement party Saturday night, to celebrate my promotion… and, to show off our beautiful new home just off Kirby Avenue. The house had a pool and a perfect yard for a party tent.

We had recently purchased an eight thousand square foot classic Georgian home, and oddly, the size actually made me feel suffocated. Mark had pressured me into buying it even though I had insisted I wanted to wait until we were married. But it was what he wanted for our future and so, I went along with his plan. Mark was a stockbroker, and good impressions meant everything to him. Mercedes. Check. Large impressive home. Check. Beautiful wife. Check, check, check.

Pasting an engaging mile on my face, I made sure it reached my eyes and responded, "Oh yes! Mark has found the most amazing caterer, and a lovely string quartet to play. It will be absolutely lovely. You are coming, aren't you?"

"Wouldn't miss it!" He leaned back again in his chair, seemingly satisfied that I was going to be back to normal…soon.

"If there's nothing else," I started to stand. "I want to make sure I get my forecasts in for the next quarter completed before the end of the day. You know how the Accounting department can be."

My attempt at levity was well received.

"I'm here for you if you need me, Charlotte. I hope you know that."

Nodding at him, I turned and left, shutting his door quietly behind me.

I went back to my corner office, removed my jacket, and draped it on the hanger on the back of my door.

Shutting the door behind me, I slipped off my shoes and went to stand at the window. My polished appearance reflected in the glass, and I grimaced at the image I saw staring back. The outward shell *looked* pretty, but inside I felt empty. My dark brown hair fell to my shoulders in an asymmetrical cut, meticulously flat-ironed straight. My eyebrows were dark and groomed, framing my dark blue eyes.

I stared vacantly out the window, past my reflection, and longed to just rip off this constricting suit, and burn it in the nearest trash can. The chains of corporate America were smothering me and I wasn't sure how much longer I could do this. This being my job. I wish I could say for certain the exact time I became so disillusioned, but I can't; it kind of just crept up on me, until one day, most likely the day I was promoted, I just stopped being happy.

Out the window and across the street, in a strip mall of shops, was the dance studio I had been going to. A pole dancing studio. I looked down at the sign and a brief flicker of excitement washed over me. I wondered what time classes were today.

Earlier this year, while working late on the mundane task of annual budget activities, Richard had sent me across the street to a local Irish bar to pick up dinner. The pole dancing studio was just around the corner, and the neon red letters, and heart on the marquis, had caught my attention.

A few days after that meeting, I stopped in on my way home and was instantly fascinated with the studio. The lobby was small, with thick white plush carpet, white leather couches and a mirrored wall. A rack of short, *short* shorts, and a variety of tanks and sleeveless T-shirts stood up against a wall and below that, a shelf of high-heeled platform shoes for sale. The shoes were hot pink, and glittered gold, red vinyl and clear plastic. I touched them gingerly, and with utter fascination, as I waited patiently to be helped.

The dark-haired receptionist addressed me, jolting me from my daydreams.

"Hi, can I help you?" She was placing the phone back on the receiver as she stood to greet me. I watched her unfold herself from the chair and continue to rise. She was *so tall.*

"Uhm, yes, maybe, I don't know." I laughed self-consciously at myself and bit the corner of my bottom lip. This was not a world I was familiar with, but it called to me, and I hoped she could ease me into it.

"First time?"

I smiled sheepishly at her. "Obvious, is it?"

Her eyes roved down my pantsuit and then back up. She shrugged and then giggled, crinkling up her nose. "Kind of."

Her youthful laugh put me at ease, and I felt my shoulders relax.

"Are you interested in classes?"

"I don't know. Maybe?"

She reached for a tri-fold brochure and slid it across the desk. Unfolding it, and pointing to a schedule, she walked me through the types of classes, and cost. I surreptitiously glanced at her figure, and her lack of clothing, as she talked, and found myself sucking in my abs a bit.

"You can sign up for ten classes, or fifty, or you can get a membership and come as often as you want to."

"Maybe I'll just start with ten."

Her face broke out in a huge grin. "Great! Do you want to see the studio?"

"Sure!"

She stepped out from behind the desk, and I glanced down at her feet, noticing that she wore six-inch platforms, leg warmers and a pair of shorts like the ones on the rack. I tried not to gawk, but her body was incredible, and while I wasn't on the heavy side, I had gone a little soft in the past few years. My size twelve suits had gotten a little snug.

"Now, you have to take off your shoes when you go in the studio. Only bare feet are allowed." She lifted one foot, took off her shoe, and did the same on the other.

I slipped off my pumps, placed them on a silver shoe rack, and waited for her to open the door. Smiling at me patiently, she raised her eyebrows, and asked as if she was unveiling the most delicious secret in the world. "Ready?"

Nodding at her, I followed behind as she opened the door to what appeared to be a ballet studio. But it wasn't. Gleaming gold poles stood floor to ceiling, shiny and polished. The polished wood floors shined up at me, and the red walls at either end gave the room a sultry vibe.

She flipped a light switch, and a soft glow shone from the canister lights recessed into the ceiling. One wall was floor-to-ceiling mirrors and the other a room separator, which could be open to the second studio if needed.

The room captivated me. I was enchanted by the secrets I thought it held. It was quiet and empty, but I felt the pull to touch one of the poles. Reaching out, I touched it gently, and then gripped it with my hand.

Looking over my shoulder at the girl, I said, "What's your name?"

She was smiling at me, like she knew I had been bitten by the pole goddesses. "I'm Erin."

"Hi, Erin, I'm Charlotte. You can call me Charlie."

"Hi Charlotte. That's a pretty name, I think I'll call you that. Should I sign you up for classes?" She had a cheeky grin on her face.

That had been months ago. I'd gotten stronger and leaner since then. My abs were now tighter, my thighs stronger, and my once size-twelve skirts had been replaced with tens.

I looked at the pink bag under my desk, sat down, and pulled up the studio website on my phone.

I saw there were two classes tonight at five p.m. and six p.m. I usually went on Tuesday and Thursday nights, but tonight, I felt like I needed it.

I looked at the clock on the wall of my office; not even lunch time. Sighing heavily, I glanced back at the site…a noon class. Could I make a noon class? Adrenaline rushed through my body at the thought of dancing off the mornings stressful meeting.

Renewed enthusiasm for the day sparked inside me. I hurriedly slipped my shoes back on, grabbed the bag from under my desk and my purse from the drawer.

Hitching my purse over my shoulder, I quickly left my office. My assistant was typing and I spoke in a clipped tone on my way out.

"Peggy, I need to run an errand. I should be back by two."

Peggy looked like a Peggy, and she had been with me for years. She stopped typing, glanced dubiously at my bag, and then back at me. "And what should I tell finance?"

Stopping in my tracks, I paused long enough to pull myself back into the moment. I looked directly at her. Her eyes were knowing, and I felt myself slipping farther from my position. "Tell them I had to taste cake, and I'll have the numbers uploaded by close of business."

"Should I update them for you?" She smiled kindly at me.

"I can do it Peggy. It won't take me long."

We continued to look at each other a beat longer, a stand-off of wills, until I smiled back at her. "I have to go."

I saw her shake her head, and then she went back to typing. "Be careful"

I left the plush office hallway, and went towards the elevator, waggling my fingers at her. The glass office doors shut behind me, and I stepped into the elevator, my smile growing the closer I got to the exit.

Made in the USA
Middletown, DE
20 January 2021

31823480R00172